# THE MYSTERIES OF WOODLAND ACADEMY

K.D. WILLIAMS

*The Mysteries Woodland Academy*




**Publisher:** Absolute Author Publishing House
**Hardback ISBN**: 978-1-64953-208-4
**Paperback ISBN:** 978-1-64953-204-6
**eBook ISBN:** 978-1-64953-214-5

# DEDICATION

I dedicate *The Mysteries of Woodland Academy* to Tyler and Nicole, my children; when all else fails, look to God, acknowledge Him in all your ways, and He will direct your path. Also, to my mother and father, who have supported me my whole life. I love you. I am blessed to have parents who encouraged me and loved me unconditionally.

To my mother, you have been my guidepost, and I have always looked up to you. I could not have asked for a better mother, and I can't see my life without you. You have always been my advocate.

To my father, you have always tried to give me the best advice possible. I will always cherish your words. Finally, to family and close friends.

And to Queda Denley, a great mentor who believed in me before I picked up a pen to write.

Also, to Jessica Cook and Andrea Bessick, who genuinely asked about the book until its publication date, you ladies were my biggest cheerleaders.

Aliyah, Maliyah, and Saint, you guys are my rock.

“Blessed are the pure in heart, for they shall see God.”
Matthew 5:8

# TABLE OF CONTENTS

# Chapter One

## A Day At The Mall

*Thank goodness it's Saturday,* thought Natalie, as she yawned, wiping her sleepy eyes as her angry alarm clock sounded at eight o'clock. The sun peeked from the sky as the room filled with natural light. It was time for her to rise and shine as she happily watched the sun's rays dance between the blinds. When her parents purchased their home, Natalie chose a bedroom with lots of windows and a walk-in closet with plenty of shelves for her shoes and handbags. Natalie quickly threw off her pink comforter, covering her high four-post canopy bed, showered, brushed her teeth, got dressed, and started styling her thick, heart-shaped curls with no time to waste. She looked at her hair in the mirror and thought, *My curls are popping,* which was how she liked it.

Feeling satisfied, she put away the Shea Moisture styling products and hair pick. Then, Natalie sprayed Happy onto her neck and wrists and meticulously placed it back on the vanity with the other fragrances. She looked one last time in the oval floor-length white mirror at her outfit. Natalie looked put together in her black Adidas jacket, skirt set, and a white T-shirt. To finish the look, she donned a pair of white ankle socks and K-Swiss from the walk-in closet. *Um, something seemed to be missing. Accessories.* She thought and opened her jewelry box and chose a pair of diamond stud earrings and a tennis bracelet she got last Christmas. Her honey-brown skin looked soft and dewy thanks to the Neutrogena skincare line she'd been using for a month. Pleased with her look, she grabbed her purse and backpack and headed downstairs to eat breakfast with Lucy in the kitchen.

Natalie expected a fun-filled day with her friends at the mall. She was thankful that most of her friends' summer family vacations had ended. Now, they were free to catch up, hang out, watch movies, shop, and discuss their plans for the upcoming school year. While eating a bowl of cereal with Lucy, their housekeeper, the house phone rang. She jumped straight up. "I got it, Lucy!" She bolted to the phone and quickly answered. "The Evergreens residence."

"Hi! Nat."

"Hello, Sam."

"Are we still on for the mall today?"

"We sure are… I can't wait," said Natalie.

"Me too. However, my folks can't drive me to the mall today as planned."

"Why?" Sam began pacing the floor in her bedroom while crunching a piece of bacon into the receiver.

Annoyed, Natalie removed the phone a few inches away from her ear and continued to listen on the other end. "They had to leave early for work." Pausing, she asked. "Can you pick me up?"

"Not a problem, *Chica.*"

"Cool," said Sam.

"I will ask Roberto, our driver, to pick you up, and we're off to the mall. Hey! Will the rest of the crew be there?"

"For sure! Denise and Tiffany said they'd wait for us in front of the carousel."

"Awesome! Roberto and I will be at your house at a quarter to one."

"Alright, see you then," Sam said and hung up the phone.

Natalie finished her breakfast when Roberto walked into the kitchen with a newspaper in one hand, ready to pour himself a cup of coffee. "*¡Bueno, Díaz,* Natalie!"

"*Bueno, Diaz! ¡Señor Roberto*!" Natalie smiled at him, handed him his favorite mug from the cup holders. "I have a favor to ask of you, *por favor*."

"¡Sí, *señorita*!"

"Will you drive Sam and me to the mall?"

Roberto answered, "*Qué hora*?" and gave a friendly wink at Lucy.

Lucy smiled and continued putting the dirty dishes into the dishwasher.

Natalie replied, "Half-past twelve."

Roberto agreed and finished drinking his coffee at the small round avocado table. She thanked Roberto and retrieved her backpack. Pleased as punch, she kissed Lucy on the cheek, excused herself, and walked out the kitchen's French doors onto the gazebo. She followed a stone path to a white-painted gazebo with lovely, colored flowers planted around its base. Inside the horseshoe seating gazebo were six large, cozy, flowered print pillows. There in the gazebo was her favorite place to write when she was home. She sat and opened her journal to "June 13" and began journaling.

Hours passed. Suddenly, she heard, "*Señorita*, sorry to disturb you." Glancing down at his watch, he said, "It's time to go."

"It's fine, Roberto. I lost track of time; thanks for reminding me."

Natalie placed her pen and diary inside her brown leather, gold hardware backpack.

Roberto, a middle-aged man, had been with the Evergreens for seven years. He moved from California to Memphis to avoid earthquakes and wildfires. He stood in front of the gazebo wearing a black chauffeur hat, a black jacket, black slacks, and well-polished black shoes.

Natalie went back inside the house to inform Lucy that she and Roberto were about to leave. In her pressed black and white maid uniform, Lucy was busy vacuuming the living room carpet.

"Lucy! I'm leaving for the mall, and I will be back at four-thirty."

"Okay! Honey, be careful and have a good time," she bellowed as Natalie was leaving out the front door.

Roberto waited out in front of the car. Natalie stepped out the door, and Roberto held the car door open. He closed the door behind her, got into the driver's seat, and drove the black Mercedes out of the driveway to Sam's house. Although Memphis's traffic was extremely heavy, Roberto arrived at Sam's house at precisely 12:45 p.m. Roberto pulled into the long driveway and drove up to the estate. The lawn was well-cared for and freshly cut. Natalie pressed the lightly tinted window button down to smell the fresh green grass, which smelled of green onions, as they got closer to the house. She admired the large Grecian water fountain in the center of the yard. Sam's house was overflowing with tons of southern charm; it was gorgeous. They pulled up to the front door. Roberto opened the door for her, and she slowly exited.

She rang the doorbell.

"I'm coming! I'm coming!" shouted Sam as she approached the door. Sam, wearing a light print sunny dress and leather flip-flops, opened the tall wooden glass door.

Beaming from ear to ear, the girls did their secret seven-year-old handshake. "Thank goodness you're here."

"What? Your lil' brotha' driving you nuts, again?"

"Ugh, yeah. He's always pestering me and touching my stuff in my room. And he always gets away with murder. Yesterday, at dinner, he threw a carrot across the table and hit me smack in the face when mom and dad weren't looking. I threw a piece of broccoli from my salad plate at him to get even, but I missed. But guess who got caught throwing food?"

"Who?"

"Me, I tried to explain. Jayden started it. Instead, I got lectured and a month of washing dishes.

"You're kidding, right?"

"Nah, I'm not kidding."

"Boy, I am glad Grandma picked him up. He just left a few seconds before you got here."

Sam's face turned red as a tomato. Sam hated how her little brother always got the best of her. Natalie tried to hide her laughter without making Sam angrier while entering the back seat of the car. "Look, sis. You and ya lil brotha are going to be all right."

"The little runt gets on my nerves. You're so lucky you're the only child."

"You know, Sam, being the only child isn't all it's cracked up to be. It's lonely being the only child. It's cool having someone to talk, play, and hassle with."

"If you asked me, I would say you're the lucky one."

"You know, you're right, Natalie. I'm sorry, and I didn't know you felt that way. Thanks for being such a good friend."

"No biggie, that's what friends are for? Now, how bout we listen to some jam up in here?"

Roberto, hearing the girls talking, turned the radio dial to HOT 1071 KXHT-FM. The car filled with the sounds of Khalid's "Talk," and the girls began singing along with the artist as they continued down the highway to the mall.

Roberto dropped the girls off in front of the Wolfchase Mall entrance. "I will be back to pick you up at four," Roberto said before he drove away.

Natalie's cell rang; it was Denise and Tiffany on the other end. Natalie pressed the speaker so Sam could hear.

"Where are you guys?" asked Denise.

"We just arrived; stay put; we are on our way," said Natalie.

"Okay, bye," said Denise.

The girls met, shopped, and had a blast trying on different outfits and sunglasses. Denise Evans, with jet-black hair, olive skin, and a nose ring to match, was a hoot who played double Dutch, "Miss Mary Mack," and hopscotch with kids who moved into the neighborhood, and she took nothing from anyone. The gang called her "Mouth" because she spoke the first thing on her mind. Her parents were politicians.

Tiffany West had a passion for dancing and photography. Tiffany's hair was long and natural, and she wore it in a sleek press daily. The girls met in school and remained amigos until the present day. Each of them made the principal's list every nine weeks. They took learning seriously, but don't be fooled; these young ladies were not mere nerds but had a passion for fashion, and they were the hottest dancers at school. Known for their sense of style and popularity, everybody wanted to dress like them, be like them, and hang out with them.

Stopping for a bite to eat at the food courts, the girls ordered, got their meals, and sat at their special table and ate. Suddenly, Tiff noticed some boys from her school's football team were about to order food; she uttered, "Guys! Don't look now, but look who's headed our direction?"

They cried in one voice, "Who?"

"It's Trever McCall and Damon Yates!" said Sam.

Without a moment to lose, the girls asked each other, "How's my hair?"

"Your hair? How's my make-up?" asked Sam nervously.

The boys were only a few steps away from the girls' table; Sam mumbled under her breath, "Guys, we look great. O. M. G., they're coming over right now!" Sam said, "Happy as a kid in a candy store.

Damon spotted the girls and nudged Trever to look in their direction while the rest of their friends in blue jeans and t-shirts were waiting in line for their food at Checkers. Trever McCall was the most popular boy in school, and the best quarterback Germantown Middle School had seen in years. Damon Yates, Trever's best friend, played wide receiver. Leaving their friends in line, they walked over to the girls' table.

"Hi, ladies!" said Damon.

"What's going on, fellas?" said Mouth in her black-and-white striped shirt, black cargo overalls, and long crystal-studded cross necklace that dangled in front of her overalls when she stood up to greet them. Covering the crown of her head was a black hip-hop beanie with the word "CUTIE" stitched in big white letters in front of the cotton-skull cap. To give her style a bit of street flavor, she added a pair of large black combat boots and white socks.

"Nothing much. Funny, we should meet here today," said Damon.

"Yeah! What a coincidence," replied Tiffany.

Trever remained quiet while Damon did all the talking.

"My birthday is a few days away, and I am having a birthday party; you guys should come."

"Maybe we will text the address to my cell. "It's nine, zero, one, six, seven, eight, four, five, one, one," said Sam.

Saving Sam's information on his phone, he smiled and said, "Hope you guys come and the theme's Hollywood. It's going to be the dopiest party of the summer," said Damon.

"Outstanding!" said Natalie.

Trever smiled at Natalie before he and Damon left to join their friends at their table, and she discreetly smiled back at him.

"I saw that," Sam said.

"What?" said Natalie.

"That smile," replied Sam.

"Aw!!!" the girls sighed sweetly.

"I think Trever is into you, Nat."

"I don't think so, Sam," Natalie said bashfully.

"I think Trever is sweet on you, too, Natty. I saw the way he looked at you," Mouth wittily implied.

"He's super cute," said Tiff, who was dressed nicely in a blue jean skirt and blue jean top. Her belt buckle read Diva right above her belly button. Instead of tennis shoes, she chose an open-toe flat brown sandal to show off her red polish pedicure nails.

Changing the subject, Natalie asked, "So, are we going to Damon's birthday party or not?" She tried hard not to reveal to the gang how much she wanted to see Trever again without them knowing how she felt.

"Yes, we are. Everyone from school will be there, and it's the last summer party before school starts. Girls, we must look super chic; you know the Satin Dollz will be there." Said Sam.

Tiff rolled her eyes at the name of Satin Dollz being mentioned in her presence.

"We must dress to impress," said Mouth, standing to her feet.

The rest of the girls stood up with Mouth as she issued a challenge, "The last one to H&M is a rotten egg."

"You're on!" the girls screamed, rushing to the store.

The girls purchased the perfect ensembles for Damon's party. Leaving the store, they heard a loud commotion coming from the floor below. Music was playing in the background, and crowds of people were standing around a platform stage. The girls took the escalator down to see who was performing, and there they saw their archrivals, the Satin Dollz, who were known for their cool jackets and dance routines at school. Their manager, Jerry Weinberger, had booked their performance for the store's entertainment. Jackie Smith, Tina Fagin, Sandy Moore, Melody Farmer, Jade Bossler, and Pippa Westbrook were the Satin Dollz. Satin Dollz were talented dancers; however, they were snobs. There they were, performing death drops and tumbling routines on the stage. Satin Dollz performed wearing red, silver tassels, and battle uniforms. They performed two routines, and the crowd applauded loudly for the girls who had once come close to battling the Dancing Dolls on the Lifetime hit TV show *Bring It*. They were popular in Memphis. After their performance, the girls took pictures with fans and signed autographs.

Natalie and her friends looked on as the Satin Dollz signed autographs. Two of the Dollz walked over to Natalie and her friends and sarcastically said. "Well, well, look what we have here," said Tina to Pippa, who was standing beside her. "If it isn't the tacky Fashionistas," said Pippa.

The Satin Dollz didn't care for Natalie and her friends very much because they often competed against them in school.

"That's rich coming from you Satin Devils; oh, my bad, I meant Satin Dollz," said Mouth, as Natalie, Tiff, and Sam laughed them to scorn.

"Did you catch the show? We schooled y'all once again on the floor," said Pippa. "I know you didn't go there. Y'all been biting our style for what, how long now?" Asked Natalie, cutting her eye at Mouth, who held up two fingers indicating two years, and said, "As I recall, the last time we battled, we beat you."

"Y'all got lucky, that's all, but we will battle again, and you know we want the smoke," said Pippa. "We'll just see about that," said Tiff as her crew snapped their fingers, whipped their hair, and left.

"This isn't over, not by a long shot," Tina said as they walked away steaming.

Returning home from the mall, Natalie hung her things in her closet and spent the rest of the day with Lucy.

Natalie and her parents lived in Germantown, Tennessee. Natalie's family was well off with good jobs. Dr. Melissa Evergreen is a neurosurgeon who works for Le Bonheur Children's Hospital. Dr. Lloyd Evergreen, her father, was a biochemist. They often featured her parents in *Ebony* and *Time* for their tireless, groundbreaking stem cell and cancer research work.

The Evergreens worked long hours but found time to spend with Natalie as often as they could. Lucy, their sixty-year-old maid from El Salvador, was Natalie's second mother. Lucy took excellent care of Natalie when she was a baby. She looked after her whenever her parents were away at work or on several business trips. Lucy knew how much Natalie missed her parents whenever they were away. Often, she would say, "Your mommy and daddy love you; they work hard because they want the best for you."

"I know, and I understand, but as long as I have you, I am not so lonely," Natalie would reply. Lucy smiled, embraced Natalie, and said, "Little Nina, you are wise to be nearly thirteen years old. You have an old spirit. You're incredibly special, and I love you."

"I love you too, Lucy," Natalie whispered.

Natalie was not a spoiled brat, even though she had wealthy parents. Although she had every right to be, Natalie's parents gave their daughter everything she wanted and didn't ask for. There wasn't anything she couldn't ask for and didn't get; whether it be a Wii game, a pair of Jordans, the latest iPhone watch, or an Apple phone, you name it; she had it. Natalie loved sports, and she was happy when she was cheering and dancing with her squad. Natalie was five feet tall with dark, naturally curly hair, like her mother. The boys back at school thought Natalie was beautiful, but she never gave it much thought. Her parents taught her from an early age that genuine beauty comes from within. She cared for those who had less, so Natalie donated her clothes to Goodwill every Christmas and her old toys to Toys for Tots this Christmas. *It felt good to give back*; Natalie would always think to herself. Later that evening, Natalie's parents returned home from work, ate dinner, and watched *Frozen 2* with Natalie in the family room. They sat comfortably on the sectional couch, eating popcorn, and she thought today was a good day.

# Chapter Two

# Sam's Big News

The Harpers were a devout family who taught their children to help others. Samantha Cortez Harper was the couple's third child, whom they called Sam, with Jayden being their youngest. Her mother, Emily Garcia Cortez, worked as an architect. Years later, Emily married Nathan Harper after the passing of her first husband, Ian Cortez, who died from pneumonia. Ian and Emily shared two daughters, Lydia and Harmony. Lydia and Harmony were adopted by Nathan, and he worked as a software developer in Memphis. Emily was a great mother, and she planned the best slumber parties for Sam. Natalie often stayed overnight to attend Sam's slumber parties. During the sleepover, the girls would stay up late, braiding each other's hair while painting their nails and toes. Afterward, they pulled names to sing along with the karaoke machine. Mrs. Harper served delicious fruit trays, veggie trays, chips, candy, and pizza. They talked about boys and fashion until everyone was fast asleep in the night. Sam's two elder sisters had gone into the Peace Corps. Lydia chose to work with the youth sector, while Harmony served in Agriculture. Sam and Natalie shared the same values; they both wanted to change the world someday, just as their families were.

The next day, Sam phoned Natalie. She knew this day was going to change their friendship forever. Natalie's cell rang three times before she picked up. "Hello!"

"Hey, Natalie! How's it going?"

"Swell, and your day?"

"There is something I need to tell you. Do you mind if I come over?"

Hoping nothing was wrong with Sam, she replied, "Tell me now."

"I'd rather not discuss it over the phone. I should come over and talk face-to-face." Sam replied in her most grown-up voice.

Natalie did not want to accept no for an answer; so, she kept trying to get Sam to give her a hint, but she wasn't budging. Natalie reluctantly had no choice but to wait until Sam came over.

"It's fine; come on over. What time will you be here?"

"How's eleven sound?"

"Eleven sounds fine."

"Great! See you then."

Natalie's mind was racing, wondering what Sam had to talk to her about. *Never has Sam called with urgent news she couldn't discuss over the phone. This was a first even for Sam*, thought Natalie.

Ding-dong! Ding-dong echoed through the house. Hearing the doorbell, Natalie yelled, "I got it, Lucy!" Before exiting the car, Sam told Emily to wait because she was not going to be inside long. When Natalie opened the door, Sam was standing no taller than her with light green eyes, deep brown hair with honey blonde streaks running through her hair. She stood on the welcome mat, wearing a pink shirt, jacket, dark blue jeans, and brown furry ankle boots.

"Hey, girl! Come in."

"Hey, Nat," said Sam.

Natalie had pulled her hair back in a bun, wearing blue jeans and a captioned yellow shirt that read "POP PRINCESS" in black letters. Sam came inside, and Natalie asked, "Would you like something to drink from the kitchen before we head up to my room?"

"No, thanks."

At the top of the stairs to the left was Natalie's bedroom. Sam glimpsed the pink-flowered mural painted on her wall before she plopped down on Natalie's bed. "Natalie, you have a beautiful room."

"Thank you! But I know you did not come here to tell me how pretty my bedroom is, now spill it."

"Nat, you know how much I love pink."

"Yeah, yeah, what is it you couldn't tell me over the phone?"

She paused, took a deep breath, and said, "I got in. My letter of acceptance came today."

"You mean that school you kept raving about last year?"

"Yes, the very one."

"Oh! Wow, congratulations, Sam."

"Thanks, Natalie."

While celebrating, Natalie realized she would leave soon to start school in the fall. Turning misty eyes, she said, "So this is goodbye."

"I am afraid it is," Sam whispered.

Sam was her best friend. Where in the world was she going to find another friend like her? They had been best friends since grade school, but now they were about to be separated for the first time. The thought of it gave her a stomachache. “Sam, I am happy for you, but it’s also bittersweet.” “I know.” Replied Sam. *This can’t be happening right now. Something has to be done. I can’t lose Sam,* thought Natalie.

Natalie knew how much Sam loved this school, and talking her into staying was out of the question, because too many times, Sam had said, *‘Millions of students would give their left arm to go to Woodland Academy.’* Back from her thoughts, Natalie sneered. “What’s so special about that drafty old school anyway? If you’ve gone to one school, you’ve been to them all.”

Sam looked at her with a twinkle in her eyes and said, “This school is different. It’s special.”

“Don’t dramatize it, Sam, for Pete’s sakes.”

“Woodland Academy offers special perks and privileges for its private students that no other school does.”

“Like what?”

“For starters, Woodland offers special interest classes; my sisters, Lydia and Harmony, went to Woodland. They told me Woodland Academy was a place of adventure and wonder. The classes are small, and once you graduate from Woodland Academy, you can attend any college of your choice.”

“Okay, now you're speaking my language,” said Natalie. “How do you get in? Do they have a good cheer squad? Where is it located?”

“Apply, yes, and Virginia,” Sam said as she got quiet, looked into Natalie’s eyes, and yelled, “Wait a minute! I have a crazy idea. Why should our friendship have to end because I am transferring to a new school?”

Natalie wasn't sure what she was getting at as Sam leaped off the bed, screaming, “Come with me!”

“Come where?”

“To Woodland Academy!”

“Oh, Sam! That's a brilliant idea.”

"Do you think your parents will let you go?"

"I mean, sure, I must convince them some, but it's an easy sell. I know my parents will let me go; it's a good preparatory school, right?"

"Yes, it is," said Sam. "My parents will not say no to any college of my choice after graduating from Woodland Academy on the table; I mean, it's a simple decision."

"Trust me, Sam," with a sly grin on her face, "I got this. But I'm gonna need your help."

Feeling intrigued and more determined than ever to save their friendship, Sam replies, "What do you need me to do?"

"It is quite simple; all you need to do is bring over some brochures of the school and its curriculum, and leave the rest up to me. Once my parents see how great the school and campus are…"

"And they will," Sam said before she could finish.

"And how much it means to me. I am positive my parents will say yes, and I will be enrolled before you know it."

"That's good because Woodland Academy will start soon, and under no circumstances will you get in if you miss the deadline. They are strict!" cried Sam.

Natalie could hear the warning in Sam's voice to be quick, or else their plans to attend Woodland together would go up in smoke. "I will, Sam, I will."

Looking at her watch, "I have to get home and start packing." Natalie walked Sam out the door and waved goodbye. Natalie put her plan into action. Summer was ending fast, and they still had Damon's party to attend. With less than a couple of days to go until Damon's party.

Sam texted Natalie, "Thursday, June 15, 2023."

**Sam**: "Just heard from Damon; the party will be at 1611 Fairfield Lane, Friday at 2 pm. Do you want to meet up there?"

**Natalie**: "No, tell the gang to meet at my house at 1:30 pm, and Roberto will drop us off at the party. We will walk in, making a memorable cameo."

**Sam:** "Okay, I'll text them now. I'll holler."

**Natalie**: "Oh! Yes, my parents had to leave on a business trip. They will return on Monday. Bring over the school's brochures then."

Natalie's mother called from New York to check in with Lucy to see how things were going back home. After Lucy assured her, all was well, Melissa asked to speak to Natalie. Lucy called Natalie from the foyer to pick up the line.

"I got it, Lucy!" she shouted from the library next to the foyer.

"Okay, honey!" and continued cleaning.

"Hello, Mom! How are you and Dad?"

"We're both fine, baby! We are sorry we had to leave on such short notice. Do you need anything?"

"No. But there's this birthday party."

"Let me guess; you want to go."

"All my friends are going."

"When is it?"

"Friday at two."

"Whose birthday is it?"

"Damon Yates, a boy from my school."

"First, let me ask your father, and if he says yes, then you can go. Hold on a second."

Natalie waited with her fingers crossed.

"Looks like you're all set. Your father said you could go, but you must be back within an hour, and you must complete all your chores. Lucy tells you if not, the party is off."

"Mom, I am not a baby. One hour isn't long enough. Can I at least stay for two hours?"

"No."

"How about an hour and thirty minutes?"

"One hour, take it or leave it."

"I'll take it." Natalie said in a severe tone, "Mom, when you and Dad return, I have something I want to discuss with you."

"Is there something wrong?" Her mother asked frantically.

"No, there isn't anything wrong."

"Then what is it, dear?"

"I don't want to discuss it over the phone. It can wait until you come home."

"Alright, sweetheart. We will be back first thing Monday morning."

"I love you, Mom, and kiss Dad for me."

"I will, and we will see you soon."

Later that day, Natalie told Lucy her parents had given her permission to attend the party. Lucy didn't worry because Natalie always did as she was told.

# Chapter Three

# The Invitation

Roberto and the girls arrived at Damon's house. The Italian villa was 12,000 square feet with a tennis court and additional lots. A five-foot hill, "HOLLYWOOD" in large printed white letters, showed at the gate with two to four feet Hollywood spotlights positioned in front of the sign caught his company's eyes as they arrived. Valet men in red jackets, black slacks, and white gloves opened car doors as the motorcade pulled to the house's front entrance. Upon opening the doors, a valet took the girls by the hand and helped them out of the car to walk the extended red carpet of thirty-seven and a half-inch rope railing aisle divider that led alongside the house to the pool area. The red carpet was bright red, with large golden stars woven into the fabric. Fifty gold Oscar statues with black and gold balloons stood behind the dividers as guests walked the red carpet to the celebration. The DJ spun tunes on the turntable as everyone danced to the music. Natalie felt this was the closest thing to Tinsel Town she was going to get. While taking in the Hollywood props from Damon's personalized birthday clapboard to the Hollywood camera lights, Sam said to Natalie, "Wow, this party is amazing; I feel like Elizabeth Taylor right now."

"This party is off the charts," said Natalie as they continued the tour.

The backyard was bigger than Sea World, with an in-ground and spa luxury pool with water flowing over a bed of rocks into the pool. There were boxes of popcorn and plastic movie reels on the party tables. There was a VIP photo setting, perfect for taking star-quality memories. They filled the food table with Skittles, movie theme cupcakes, hot wings, and everything a teenager loves to eat. Sixty invitations had gone out, and there were over a hundred people who attended, including adults. Some of Damon's friends' mothers and fathers helped chaperone. Many of GM's kids were having a good time at the party. Damon was the perfect host.

Guests arrived as their favorite movie characters, Spiderman, Wonder Woman, and some from *Star Wars*, as Princess Leia, Han Solo, and Darth Vader, as well as characters from *The Wizard of Oz*, Dorothy, the Scarecrow, and the Wicked Witch of the West. Others came as Marilyn Monroe, Scarlet O'Hara, Charlie Chaplin, and Whoopi Goldberg.

Natalie and her friends wore "Roaring Twenties" costumes from *The Great Gatsby*. They became the center of attention; everyone admired their outfits except the Satin Dollz, who appeared as themselves in matching jackets. When the Fashionistas passed by, they sneered at them. However, the Fashionistas stole their spotlight, and the Dollz continued to enjoy the party.

Damon dressed as James Bond, and Trever and the football team were dressed as *Men in Black*. Right before Damon blew out the candles, Trever and the boys performed the routine *Men in Black* on the dance floor. Their show was phenomenal; the Dollz and the Fashionistas loved their act and congratulated them when it was over. The music changed to a crowd favorite, and everyone took to the dance floor and enjoyed the party.

A short, statuesque blonde-haired woman in a black jumpsuit, red pumps, and a shiny herringbone necklace interrupted the party by tapping her champagne glass. "Gather around, everyone. It's time! Let's join in and sing 'Happy Birthday' to my one and only son, Damon Yates!" announced Eleanor Yates, as the guests watched the servers roll out Damon's three-layered cake on a covered white linen cart. The cake was red with white frosting. After the song was over.

He took a deep breath, blew out twelve candles, and made a wish. He looked up at the crowd and said, "I thank everyone for coming and for my gifts. I want to thank my mother for planning this awesome party and my father, who couldn't, unfortunately, be here today. And to my brothers on the team and everyone else, enjoy the party." After speaking, he noticed Sam standing by the punch bowl with her friends, and he walked over to her. "Sam, I am so glad you came. Are you enjoying the party?"

"Yes, I am, and happy birthday."

His knees were shaking as he continued, "You look very nice today."

"Thanks, you look cool too."

"Are you ready to return to school?" he asked.

"I won't be returning in the fall. I am transferring to Woodland Academy." Sam smiled.

"That's great; however, I'm going to miss seeing you at school."

"What? I didn't think you noticed me at –"

"Sam, you're hard to miss."

Sam's face turned red. "Can I write to you?"

"I'd like that."

Approaching from behind, Natalie softly touched Sam on the back and said, "It's time to leave. Roberto is here."

Trever stopped Natalie before leaving and asked her out. Natalie couldn't believe Trever asked her out; butterflies fluttered inside her stomach.

"Sure, I'd like to go out with you, but can't."

"Why not?"

"I'll be too busy with Woodland Academy's application and admission video."

Intrigued, he asked, "What school are you going to?"

"Woodland Academy."

"I've never heard of that school."

"It's a private school in Virginia, but if I don't get in, I'd be delighted to go out with you."

Then, a mysterious man caught her eye, watching everyone at the party from far off. Natalie was sure he had just arrived because she hadn't seen him earlier during the party. His body language and grim face implied he was up to something. Natalie got an eerie feeling about him, and then Roberto showed up and motioned to his watch three times. Nodding to him, she said to Trever, "I have to go."

The mysterious man was gone as she looked back at him. Before departing, she waved goodbye to Trever as he watched her leave the party.

Natalie's parents arrived early Monday morning, and Natalie explained that Sam was leaving to attend a Virginia school. "Mom, Dad, may I enroll in Woodland? If Sam's going, I want to go with her."

"Let your mother and me talk about it, and we will let you know as soon as we can," Lloyd Evergreen said.

"Dad, I know this is a big decision, but I promise, if you let me go, I will maintain my grades." With Woodland's brochure behind her back, she gave it to her parents. "I'd like you to view the campus and its curriculum," said Natalie. Often, Natalie could tell if her parents were on board with her whenever she asked for something; however, their poker faces gave nothing away.

"We'll read it and let you know, sweetheart," he said, kissing her on the forehead before leaving the living room.

The next day, Natalie's parents thought it over and let Natalie attend Woodland Academy. A week had passed since Damon's party and since she had applied to Woodland. Time was of the essence. The academy will start classes in the middle of September. Days turned into weeks, and now August, and she couldn't count the countless times she had gotten up early to open the mailbox to find no letter from Woodland Academy. She had been dying to get in more than ever now that Sam had been accepted. It was the third week of June when she applied; no word came from the school. Natalie's parents thought it would be good for Natalie to get away for a while to take her mind off things. They told Natalie they were going on a family trip. This makes Natalie happy because she loves traveling and spending time with her parents, which she seldom gets to do.

The Evergreens booked a trip to Hawaii for two days and Florida for four days. The trip proved to be what Natalie needed most; she didn't think about Woodland once because she was having a great time swimming, walking on the beach, collecting seashells, and camping around the fire while watching the sunset on the beach with her parents. Natalie thought it was their best summer vacation yet as a family.

During July, Lloyd decided to take Natalie and his wife to spend some time with Melissa's parents in Denton, Texas. There they stayed and celebrated Natalie's 13th birthday afterwards, and they returned with less than a few weeks to go before the fall quarters started. Natalie continued to check the mailbox every day, hoping it would be the day she would receive her letter. Natalie remained hopeful and continued with her day as usual.

The weekend had arrived. Natalie arose from her bed in her PJs, put on her housecoat, opened her bedroom door, and went downstairs to check the mail. The carrier ran early on the weekends, and Natalie was eager to check the mail. The aroma of brewed coffee, bacon, and eggs was coming from the kitchen. Walking into the kitchen, she heard Lucy singing a song in Spanish. Not only did Lucy speak Spanish fluently, but she also spoke English. Lucy was busy preparing breakfast. *"Bueno dais!* Natalie."

"*Bueno dais*, Lucy," she replied.

Lucy was teaching Natalie Spanish in her spare time. Tending to the bacon in the frying pan, Lucy asked, "*Bien, ¿quieres huevos o panqueques con tu tocino*?" In English, she was asking if Natalie wanted eggs or pancakes with her bacon.

Straightway! She said cleverly, "*Huevos, por favor, señorita* Lucy." "Scrambled eggs, coming right up." Said Lucy. "How's my Spanish coming, Lucy?"

"Ah! It's *excelente,* Little Nina."

*Lucy is the best cook in the world*, Natalie thought, as she headed out the front door to check the mailbox. She knew Woodland Academy would start soon, and there was no letter of acceptance, and the clock was ticking. She opened the painted flower mailbox, and again it was empty. "Oh, well! What's another day?" she said tonelessly. Dragging her heels, she closed the mailbox and returned inside.

Monday came, and no letter, Tuesday, no letter, and this continued to Friday. It's Saturday, and as she did every Saturday in her PJs, she went outside to check the mailbox. There was no word from Woodland Academy during the week, but Sam assured her she would hear from Woodland with a letter of acceptance or rejection, and to be patient. *Gosh, it would be awful getting rejected this close to the deadline.* The thought of that made her head hurt. With a deep breath, she swallowed her hard-faced fears once again and opened the box to retrieve a stack of mail. Closing the mailbox firmly, she held the mail in her hands and began slowly thumbing through the pile. Suddenly, she noticed a crème square envelope with a lovely green ribbon tied around it, addressed to Natalie Evergreen.

Natalie's eyes widened, thinking, could it be the letter she had been waiting for all summer? Anticipation erupted as she turned the letter over and saw a beautiful golden seal sticker with the Woodland Academy crest embossed in the gold seal. After waiting for what felt like a decade, she couldn't believe she was holding either her acceptance or rejection letter in her hands; either way, she knew her life was about to change. Natalie raced inside the house. "It came! It came!" she shouted, going into the house.

Natalie's mother, hearing the excitement, came down the foyer's stairs to see what the commotion was about. "What came?"

"My letter from Woodland Academy!" she screamed.

With exceeding joy, she smiled and said, "Well, don't just stand there, open it!"

Natalie's curiosity had gotten the best of her; she couldn't bear it any longer. The suspense had mounted to its boiling point. She removed the ribbon and carefully ripped the golden seal apart, and read the letter aloud.

*August 24, 2023*

*Natalie Evergreen*
*1745 Central Ave*
*Memphis, TN 38109*

*Dear Miss Evergreen,*

*Congratulations! The board has reviewed your application, and we have selected you to attend Woodland Academy: A School of Premier Excellency and Learning. Woodland Academy received over 15,000 applications this year, and your academic accomplishments, extracurricular achievements, and personal qualities stood out among the strong pool. We were impressed with your admission video and all your hard work.*

*Thank you for applying.*

*We look forward to you continuing your education with us in the Fall.*

*If you attend Woodland Academy, please be advised that supplies and books can be purchased at the campus bookstore. Classes begin September 20th, and orientation begins September 17th-19th. Woodland Academy is pleased to offer dorm rooms to its students who take up residency. Purchase all books and supplies before starting classes. Expect to receive your schedule and supply list in three days following this letter.*

*Once again, congratulations and welcome to Woodland Academy: A School of Premier Excellency and Learning!*

*Sincerely,*

*Headmistress & Dean of Admission Lois Stein Howell*

"Good for you, sweetheart," said her mother.

"Dad, come quick! Dad, Dad!"

Her father, leaving the kitchen, said, "What's all the fuss about?"

"Dad, I got in; Woodland Academy accepted me into their school!"

"Well done, pumpkin-nose."

Her parents looked suspiciously at each other and retorted, "Honey, we knew."

"You knew what?"

"That you got accepted a month ago."

"What? I can't believe you guys knew." Natalie's face expressed, "You knew, and you didn't tell me!"

"Natalie, we hated not telling you. We wanted to tell you, but we wanted it to be a surprise. The school contacted us a month ago and told us you had been accepted," said Melissa. "Your father and I have purchased a home in Norton. Your father has accepted his new job as the Lead Research Microbiologist at the Centers for Disease Control and Prevention, and you're looking at the newest head neurosurgeon at UVM Children's Hospital."

"Really?"

"Yes!" said her parents, who were happy to deliver the news that all arrangements were taken care of.

"The movers will be here next week," said Melissa.

"Mom, is Lucy coming with us?"

"Sí," said Lucy, walking into the room. "You don't think I'm going to let you have all the fun with those preppie kids up there, do ya?"

"No way," she said, laughing. "I feel a group hug coming on," said Natalie, and they hugged. "I promise you guys I'll get good grades."

"You better," her mother said with a serious face before smiling.

"You're the best family a girl could ever have."

Lucy took an eggshell hankie and dabbed away the tears rolling down her cheeks.

Natalie, misty-eyed, said, "Mom, I know this move or decision couldn't have been easy for you two."

"Natalie, you mean the world to us, and we knew how much this meant to you, and we are so proud that they accepted you into this wonderful school, and now you and Sam can be together."

Natalie cupped her hands to her face like Macaulay Culkin did in *Home Alone* and then kissed her parents on the cheek and said, "I'll never forget the sacrifices you made. I love you guys so much."

"And we love you too, buttercup."

Then she excitedly ran off to her room to let Sam know the good news.

# Chapter Four

# Woodland Academy

*School's back in session*, thought Natalie, as she sat in the front seat of her mother's car. She couldn't believe how quickly summer had ended; it seemed only yesterday they were having fun vacationing in Florida, and now it was over. Natalie turned her attention to the window and gazed at the leaves on the trees. Like a tossed salad, the leaves—red, brown, and orange—blended into the autumn foliage as Melissa drove her daughter to attend her first day at Woodland Academy. Breaking the silence, Melissa said,

"Sweetheart, are you excited about your first day?"

"A little," she mumbled as they neared the school. "During all the planning to come to Woodland, I forgot I'd have to go to bed early now that school is back in session." Looking at her backpack by her feet, she agonized over going to bed early instead of staying up late talking with her friends on the phone. "Honey, I thought you were excited about starting Woodland Academy."

"I am." "Are you having second thoughts?"

"No. It's just that our summer vacation was so great, and I didn't want it to end."

"I know, sweetie! Look on the bright side; at least you and Sam are together. Plus, we have all fall to plan our next vacation." They chuckled a little, and Natalie said, with wide eyes, "You're on." Feeling relieved, she was ready for the new school year. Her mom always knew what to say to make Natalie feel better. "Thanks, Mom, you're the best." They arrived at Woodland, and Dr. Evergreen drove to the drop-off zone, parking next to the curb. "Are you all set?"

"Yes! I think so." Natalie said with her purse and backpack in her lap; she reached for the door handle to get out. Her mother leaned over and kissed her daughter's forehead before letting her out. Natalie got out of the car. "Are you sure you're going to be alright?" As the window rolled halfway, Natalie said, "Yeah, no prob-blem-o." Natalie backed away from the car. "I love you, Du-boot, and say hello to Sam for me."

"I will, and I love you too." Said Natalie as her mother drove away. She quickly began walking up the pavement, taking a deep breath, thinking goodbye to summer and hello to a *new year*. She was starting seventh grade with her best friend. Where? Of all places, Woodland Academy, the most popular private school in Virginia, according to Sam.

Getting into Woodland was not a simple process. Once enrollment was over, no students could register for the school year. Parents failing to enroll their child on time were placed on a one-year waiting list. Students who scored high on the school's administrators' assessments were most sought after. Carefully selected pupils, gifted, talented, and well-rounded, received an invitation from around the world to attend Woodland. Also, legendary students whose parents had attended Woodland before received invitations to the school. Woodland Academy was a prestigious, strict school holding its character and bylaws in the highest regard. Woodland differed from any other school Natalie had attended before. *The school was magnificent to look upon; the pictures in the brochures didn't do the school justice,* thought Natalie. Woodland Academy was an excellent institute that looked like an enormous castle from a fairy tale. It was grand in all its splendor. Woodland Academy offered the best classes and clubs for special interest groups, and then there were the Elder's Chosen Vessels.

The chosen students who have proven themselves worthy in Woodland's annual games are selected to attend restricted classes set apart from the student body. She didn't know what her peers would be like or what to expect, but she and Sam were together, and that's all that mattered. Natalie gazed at the property before entering the building. A huge banner hung in front of the school's building, welcoming students to Woodland. She noticed five flags of the school's crest centered in the middle of the flag, swaying in the wind on top of the school. The crest was a shield with four sections of four distinct Heraldic designs. A royal crown rested above the shield. On the left side, at the top, was a white dove with an olive branch nestled in its mouth, with a striped background. Underneath it was a knight's head in silver armor, and in the center of the shield was a sword with a capital Old English W. At the top right corner was a small graduation cap, a football field goal, a torch of fire between it, and a tag field. Below it was an open book, its leaves exposed, with bright rays illuminating behind the book and a quill. The crest featured a curved olive branch reaching the top of the shield, and below it was a scroll with the Woodland Academy School of Excellence written on it.

Woodland Academy was four stories tall with clean halls, a gym, and a pool. The floors shone like diamonds throughout the school, and the ground was a green carpet.

The football fields were green with white numbers painted on the field, and the track field was smooth and new. An oval stadium easily seated faculty, students, and visitors. East of the campus was a beautiful Weeping Willow, with several of the loveliest monochromatic eating tables outside the lunchroom. West of the campus was the tennis court and field house. Finally, the girls' softball fields were at the school's front entrance; the boys' softball field was in the school's back.

The cafeteria was the largest room in the school. Sixth-grade tables were oblong and long. Round tables seated seventh graders, and eighth graders sat at tall tables with highchairs to match. The ninth-grade through twelfth-grade students sat at long rectangular tables in the room. Students referred to the lunchroom as the canteen because one could eat from several food courts. It was like eating at a miniature mall. Not only could you order those foods, but also order delicious lunchroom meals.

In the hall, students could buy candy from the school's store. The shop sold fizzy drinks and many flavored beverages. After consumption, it made them belch their favorite tunes. Gum turned to chocolate and melted marshmallows when chewed. These puffy, soft delights are a sweet treat that Woodland students enjoyed. When students threw them into the air, before chewing, they magically turned to snow, tasting of sweet wafers on the tongue, melting before touching the floor. The swirly lollypops and red hots were sweet to the palate. Gray steam whistled like a hot kettle on a stove, as gray mist emerged from their ears, after tasting them.

Then there were the fun gadgets to buy, the Tacky Tacks, a popular gag gift amongst Woodland's students, because they sounded like popped bubble plastic wrapping exploding like firecrackers on the surface. The label attached said USE OUTDOORS. But the students paid the warning no mind, which is why they loved them so much. Once the popping stopped, each tack disappeared into the air. The store kept stocked shelves of small velvety pouches tied with yellow strings that cost three golden tokens. They contained an element of surprise. The pouch was empty. But when students reached inside the pouch, they pulled out a tiny wonder of the world, like an erupting volcano from the Jurassic period, and sometimes, the past and present events of Woodland Academy; each wonder was meant to be cherished in the palms of their hands. The students loved all the magic the school offered and kept the wonders and secrets within its borders.

The campus was crowded with Woodland students wearing navy blue, white, and hunter-green colored uniforms. Girls wore vests, white-collar button-down shirts, sweaters, and jackets, along with pleated skirts featuring Woodland's crest sewn onto each regalia. The girls could wear socks with loafers. Only boys could wear black slacks with sweaters, white shirts, ties, and jackets. Students were laughing and mingling with returning students as they headed inside the building.

Natalie walked to the front entrance when she heard, "Natalie, Natalie!"

Natalie knew whose voice it was. She turned around and said, "Hey Sam! How are you?"

The girls hugged, for it was the first time they had seen each other since Damon's party.

"Fine, and you?" Natalie replied,

"Super good," with a smile.

"Can you believe it? We are here!" said Sam.

Both girls screamed, "Ah!" at the same time.

"Well, who do you have first period?"

"Miss Sherman… Mr. Griffith, second period. Here is my schedule. Do you want to see it?"

"Yes!" Sam scans it carefully. "Guess what? I have all your teachers except for math."

"So cool, we have almost identical schedules."

The girls entered the building. A voice over the intercom spoke, “Everyone, report to the Commons Area promptly.”

Natalie and Sam followed the crowd as they were being redirected from the Commons Area into a room a few feet away. Everyone went through the double doors, and above the doors read Gathering Hall. The room was long, and students took their seats at long, oblong harvest-decorated tables. Beautiful long burlap table runners ran down the center of the table with various fall pumpkins serving as the centerpieces; fall leaves, flowers, and orange-brown plaid ribbons finish the table setting. There, students sat quietly while they waited for their professors to be seated.

The faculty table was shaped like an upside-down U. In the center was a glass podium. Their table of harvest décor, gold crystal water goblets fit for royalty, on a stage. There were four long steps in front of their table, and behind them was a large floor-to-ceiling window. The glass was stained with images and the names of the twelve disciples of Jesus Christ. Above their table was a crystal chandelier with large candles.

On the walls hung large hurricane candle sconces perpendicular across from each other. Soon, every faculty member had taken their respective places. The light flickered, and there appeared two men dressed in long white robes appeared. On their chest, a breastplate hung front and back with twelve precious gemstones. In their hands were shofars, and on top of their heads a white turban. The two men looked as if they were in their mid-sixties with short snow-white hair. They blew the shofars three times. A distinguished woman appeared.

The men had disappeared, and the next voice students would hear would come from the mysterious woman standing before them. She was six feet tall, excluding her heels, which made her look like a giant; her brown skin had a caramel glow, and her locks a long bob of golden bronze. She stood in a long black dress robe. The buttons on her dress sparkled in the light, and her heels were black with glitter. She stood behind the podium with her hands stretched apart between her colleagues. Etched in front of the podium was the school's crest, and on top of the podium was a lamp and a flexible microphone stand. With its microphone in position, she approached the podium with enthusiasm and said,

"Welcome, welcome to Woodland Academy. A school of premier excellence and learning! I am your Headmistress, Lois Stein Howell, and we have selected you to attend Woodland Academy from a pool of candidates from around the world. Here we are, an extended family, and we will help you reach your full potential. You will study music, fine arts, literature, historical events, and sacred text. Woodland is a school of diversity, and no matter where you are from, you are most welcome. Every year, your classes will become more rigorous than the last until you have completed your education. However, some of you will be chosen by the Elders of the school to attend special classes. The Elders will lottery each grade level to determine which will take part in our school's highest honor, a tradition that has gone on since the school's opening. Then, students will be required to participate in these classes by participating of their own free will in the Woodland Annual Games. Taking part is not for the faint of heart. If you enter the games, I advise you to take it seriously because it will require genuine commitment, endurance, and faith. If chosen, you will go where no other students have gone before, except for students before you. We will tell you more about the restricted classes later, but for now, know Woodland Academy is a place of wonder and learning. Please maintain your grades and follow the rules. Read your manuals and syllabus thoroughly. Any rule-breaking will adhere to serious consequences such as detention, letters, a phone call home, probation, and expulsion. If each grade level does well, each grade will be generously rewarded. Each grade level must strive for excellence. This is what we expect from our students at Woodland Academy. Now, I will introduce some of your professors. The rest of the professors you'll meet once you enter homeroom. First, Miss Sherman, Language Arts, Mr. Blackmon, Arithmetic, Miss Peterson, Creative Writing, Coach Adams, Physical Education, Miss Headley, Cheerleader Coach, and Mr. Griffith teach history. Last but not least, Ms. Bee, Sacred Text."

As the Dean called each instructor's name, each one nodded. Each instructor wore distinguished, aged black graduate caps and gowns. The instructors were ready to work with the first-year and returning students. Headmistress Howell dismissed the teachers and students to their study room while calling for Professor Townsend to give the orders.

Just then, a little man came forward in front of the student body and said, "Let the school's prefects come forward."

Six of Woodland's returning students came and stood in front of the Woodland student body. Then Thomas Freelon, with olive skin and red hair, oversaw the six-graders to their quarters and study hall. Abaeze Lawal guided the seventh graders. Calian Holt showed the freshmen to their domains. Melody Greenhouse led the sophomores, Walter Simmons led the juniors, and Amy Yang guided the seniors.

Thomas Freelon walked to the front entrance of the door and announced, "All sixth graders, rise and follow me."

When it was Sam and Natalie's grade, they rose and followed their guide to their quarters. They gave each grade level into the hands of their guides until they cleared the Gathering Hall.

Natalie called home later that evening and told her mother about her first day. "I love Woodland Mom, and Miss Sherman is my favorite teacher. They will hold cheerleader tryouts next week, and I am going to try out."

"Natalie, the coach would be crazy not to choose you." Her mother searched the back of the fridge for strawberries while holding her cellphone to her ear. "You dance like an angel, and I know you will make the squad."

"Woodland has a magnificent coach, Ms. Headley. She graduated from NYU and was a former Dallas Cowboy cheerleader." Natalie said, lying on her bed in her private room. Her cell phone was on speaker as Natalie continued telling her mother about Coach Headley. "She is tall, thin, with light blonde hair and green eyes. Sadly, her cheerleading career ended early because of an unfortunate, horrible accident."

"What kind of accident?" asked her mother.

"No one knows. Despite her injury, Coach Headley worked hard, got in shape, and began teaching others how to dance and cheer," said Natalie.

"She sounds like an amazing woman."

"I'm sure I will learn a great deal from her if I make the team."

Natalie tried out and made the team. Coach Headley choreographed routines, and she was tough on the squad; her cheerleaders had to be in the best shape to cheer. Their uniforms had to be sparkling white, and missing practice or being tardy was unacceptable. Ms. Headley worked hard to make the squad champions.

The squad made Natalie the head cheerleader in one month because she was the team's best dancer. Coach Headley collaborated with Natalie to create fresh hip hop, stand, and cheerful routines.

Natalie was a fast learner and a patient teacher who helped the girls on the squad learn their routines in record time. Her squad loved her, as did Coach Headley.

# Chapter Five

# The Assignment

In Miss Sherman's class, during the first period, the class was eager to learn about the secret reading assignment Miss Sherman had kept under wraps until today. She told her class she wanted it to be a surprise. Miss Sherman was the coolest teacher at Woodland Academy and was favored among faculty because she made learning fun and exciting, surprising students with new concepts. She loved challenging students to engage in higher-order thinking skills, which she executed perfectly in her classroom. No one seemed to mind that she'd ever missed a day of school or did not recall a day she'd been out sick. No, not one.

Miss Sherman's class is well-structured and well-run, with minor discipline problems. No one ever misbehaved in Miss Sherman's class, not after she caught Danny and Jeffery wasting time playing in class.

One Thursday morning, Miss Sherman was writing notes on the board, and Danny Singleton was, as usual, trying to get Jeffery Newsome's attention to impress him with his silly paper airplane. While Miss Sherman was busy writing, Danny had gotten Jeffery's attention to see his in-action flying airplane. Immediately, Miss Sherman sternly said, "Danny, see me after class!" and continued to write as if nothing had happened. It seemed she had eyes in the back of her head, knowing the culprit was misbehaving without turning her head.

Miss Sherman was five feet and eight inches tall with fair skin and long, flowing brown hair cascading like a waterfall down her back. She had clear baby blue eyes and a petite figure. She was only twenty-five years of age; the aroma of sweet strawberries and cherries lingered when she walked up and down the rows in the room. Miss Sherman was fair, polite, and her smile was as bright as the sun.

In Miss Sherman's class, Natalie was waiting for the instruction bell to ring and began thinking of new cheers she would present to the squad during practice after school. She hardly paid attention to what was on Miss Sherman's desk before taking her seat.

The instructional bell sounded, and Miss Sherman said, "Please, everyone, settle down." Waving her hand slowly over the case, she continued, "I know each of you is wondering what's hidden under this black satin scarf in the locked glass case on top of my desk."

The class was intrigued. Not a sound was heard as they listened intently to Miss Sherman as she spoke.

"It's your reading assignment I've selected for the class to read." Turning away from her desk, Miss Sherman walked to the center of the room, while applause followed afterward.

There was the mystery book that Miss Sherman's class had been waiting for since the beginning of school. Speculation of the covered book in the glass case piqued the class's curiosity. "Ooh, ooh, I wonder what kind of book is under there?" cried Shelly Longstreet.

"It's a horror book!" exclaimed David Cohen.

"No, it's not David," shouted John Melton.

"I know it's a comedy book," roared Eddie Piper.

"You'd think that since you're the class clown," replied Charlotte Simpson.

"Charlotte, that's not nice," cried Miss Sherman, but the class had a merry laugh about it.

Eddie gave Charlotte a mean look afterward.

Charlotte, the cleverest girl in the class, didn't like Eddie so much because he took everything as a joke.

The children's constant chatter filled the room, ranging from science fiction, fantasy, myths, and historical to mystery.

"You've made wonderful guesses, but the only way to know if you're right for me is to reveal it right before your eyes right now!" said Miss Sherman excitedly as she returned to the concealed case on her desk.

The children were on the edge of their seats, waiting anxiously to see Miss Sherman open the case. She stood behind the case in her dark blue A-lined shirt collar pocket dress. A thin belt, the same color as her dress, fastens in front with a tiny gold buckle that fits snugly through the belt's loops around her waist. Next, she took out a small silver key from her pocket, opened the case from behind, and prepared to remove the scarf. Her students didn't know what kind of book they would read, but hoped it would be something they could sink their teeth into.

*Perhaps a good meaty book selected from Coretta Scott King's awarded books or the Newbery & Caldecott listing,* they thought before Miss Sherman removed the scarf.

While Natalie prepared for the big reveal, Sam whispered to her, "Natalie, Natalie, what do you think we will read about?"

Natalie turned to her and shrugged her shoulders. With blank stares on the class's face, Natalie did not understand or know what she'd be asked to read, which would count as one-half of her grade.

"On the count of three!" said Miss Sherman.

"One, two, three, echoed the class."

On three, she shouted, "Ta-dah!"

"Is God Real?" read the class aloud.

"We're going to read about God and Heaven," said Sam, who lit up like a Christmas tree.

"Yes, we are, Sam. I know this is not what MOST of you were expecting," said Miss Sherman.

*I'll say*, thought Natalie.

"I'd hope you will keep an open mind when you read the book." Miss Sherman held up the book in her hands, where everyone could see. The cover showed a heavenly staircase and a blue sky with puffy white clouds, and a star illuminating the sun's rays behind the clouds, and in bold letters written across the picture was the title of the book. While Miss Sherman explained the book, she mentioned that the author of the book remained anonymous.

Natalie thought to herself, *Why would the author not want anyone to know he had written the book?* Intrigued by the title, Natalie wanted to read the book.

Miss Sherman said, "I want all of you to think about the book. Write what you think about the book based on your prior knowledge. I'd like you to jot down a few questions you would like answered. Finally, write a prediction of how you think the book ends. You will have ten minutes to write your thoughts. We will also go to the library on Friday; Mrs. Finely has the class set waiting for us to check out." Miss Sherman took a paper from her desk and held it up in front of the class. "Before I set the timer, have your parents sign this permission letter stating whether you can take part in the reading assignment. You must have your letter signed and returned no later than Thursday. You can pick up your permission forms after you turn in your classwork during dismissal." She flipped the timer and set it next to the stack of permission forms on her desk. "Please begin writing in your Response Journal."

The class had many questions about God and Heaven. It was clear that everyone wanted to read the book. When Natalie read the book's title, she wanted to know more about God. She wanted to learn more about this invincible God and this magical place where God supposedly lived. Is God real or is God a figment of someone's imagination were two of her questions she had written in her journal. Natalie wanted to know more about this God business. She couldn't explain why, but she had an overwhelming feeling to read the book, for her parents never talked about God or anything religious. The more she thought about God, the more questions she wanted to be answered. *Who is God, and why is He so mysterious, and what is this enigma concerning what happens after death? Don't people die? Or is there something more after we die? Maybe Heaven is real. Besides, they say all dogs go to Heaven! If this is true, then all pets are in Heaven. How can I go to Heaven, assuming Heaven is real?*

The Evergreens reared their daughter not to believe in myths or fairy tales. They once said to her, "God is like the Easter bunny and the Tooth Fairy, and like them, he is not real." But here, she's asked to read a book about God and Heaven. She realized it was time she learned the truth and read the book to discover if God and Heaven are real or false. Getting the answer to those burning questions would not be a walk in the park. How was she ever going to convince her parents to let her read the book? Suddenly, a thick black cloud assembled over her head. Natalie, without a doubt, knew her parents would never allow her to read the book. Her parents were not religious, and they didn't believe in God. Therefore, reading the book would be out of the question if they had anything to do with it or say about it. Natalie finished journaling as the timer went off.

Miss Sherman told everyone to put away their journals, take out their textbooks, and turn to the previous story they were reading. She began lecturing on context clues; afterward, her students worked independently on context clues. They worked on the assignment; the bell rang, and it was time to dismiss. Students retrieved their permission letters and submitted their classwork to Miss Sherman as they walked out the door.

Natalie and Sam left Miss Sherman's room and were off to history class.

Sam began spewing about the book assignment. "I can't wait to get my letter signed and start reading the book. Oh! Nat. It's going to be interesting discussing key points about the book in class," said Sam.

"Yes! It's going to be out of sight." Natalie said with a bit of hesitation.

"We'll talk more about it after class," said Sam, beaming. Natalie agreed.

There was no question that Sam's parents would sign her permission letter because they were Christians. She once playfully said to Sam, "That's all your family does is stay in church." Natalie recalled the time Sam shared with her, wittily, one night her family went to service and came out the next day. Sam said, "It was the longest shut-in of her life." They both laughed about it afterward.

Natalie just couldn't bear to tell Sam there was no chance in a million years her parents would consent to her reading the book for a grade or not. Natalie never told Sam how her parents felt about religion, the one thing she kept from her best friend. Although Sam's family loved God, the Evergreens told Natalie she could be friends with her if she remained faithful to their beliefs. Natalie pondered this later as she walked to math class.

Three o'clock came swiftly, and she dreaded having to tell her parents about the book, especially the part of asking them to sign her permission slip. The thought sent chills down her spine. She could imagine the look on their faces once she told them, a look of disgust merely mentioning God's name, followed by a long lecture. God isn't real, which would last half an hour.

Natalie detested the idea of telling her parents about the reading assignment. School ended for the day, and Natalie focused on cheerleading practice. She taught the squad new cheers and formations. The squad loved everything she taught them … and were excited about doing the routine at their next football game. She wished telling her parents about the reading assignment would be half as easy as cheering. She encouraged the squad to keep practicing for tomorrow's practice.

Thursday came, and Natalie did not turn in her permission slip. She couldn't check out her book until her parents signed the slip. That weekend, Natalie was going home and would get her parents to sign her permission slip. Natalie's mother had phoned and said she would pick her up from school on Friday instead of Roberto. At the end of the week, Dr. Evergreen arrived in her Mercedes. Natalie got in the car.

"So, how is school going?" asked her mother.

"Fine," said Natalie.

"Are you ready to go?"

"Yes, I am."

"Okay, buckle up," her mother said as they drove away. "Natalie, your father will be home early tonight. He phoned five minutes ago and told me the good news. It's been quite some time since you have been home, so your father got someone to cover his shift, so he'll be home when you get there. We'll have takeout. What do you prefer to eat tonight, pizza or Chinese?"

Natalie thought and said, "Most definitely pizza."

“Pizza it is,” said Melissa as Bruno Mars' “24 Karats” played on the radio as they went home.

# Chapter Six

# The Signature

The Evergreen's Virginia home was magnificent. Seven tall white columns were the focal point of the front porch. The lawn was neatly mowed with the best landscaping money could buy. Voted the Best Yard of the Month twice by the Chamber of Commerce, made the Evergreens proud to be a part of the Virginia family community.

"Anything exciting happening at school?" asked her mother as she unlocked the front door and entered the parlor.

"No. Why do you ask?"

"Honey, what kind of mother would I be if I didn't ask how your social life is going? I mean, how many daughters do you think I have here?"

"I'm sorry, Mom. I have a lot on my mind with school and all. My social life is about the same, but I have met someone."

"That's wonderful, sweetheart!" Natalie sighed. "There's just one thing. He's back home, and I am here."

"Maybe you might meet someone else at Woodland."

"Maybe?" she said slowly. "Mother, may I be excused? I'm beat."

"Why don't you relax a bit, and I will call you down when your father gets home. Then we can go out for pizza."

Natalie went to her room, closed the door behind her, and removed her permission letter from her backpack at her study desk.

The phone rang, and it was Sam on the other end. "Did you get it signed yet?"

"No, not yet."

"Well, don't take too long. It must be in as soon as possible."

"Yeah, tell me something I don't know. I will call you back once it's done."

"Cool, I have to go anyway; I have a history paper to write, and it's due next week for Mr. Griffith."

"I know…he told us to write about a significant event that took place in US History." Said Natalie. "Which of these topics sounds good to you, The Great Depression or the Titanic?"

"Gee, Sam, those events are super sad. Why not write about a famous inventor like Thomas Edison or George Washington Carver? I mean, where would we be without our iPod if Thomas Edison hadn't discovered the record player?"

"You know, I didn't think about famous inventors."

"So, Pearl Harbor is out? Just kidding, I will have to think about it more. I want to impress my history teacher."

"Don't worry; your essay will be outstanding. Let me know what you decide upon, Einstein."

"Will do, bestie," said Sam, and she hung the phone up.

Natalie glanced back at her permission letter. She wanted to read the book, but knew keeping the permission slip a secret for a week from her parents was wrong. Determined more than ever, they wouldn't understand. She hid the letter in one of her books on her bookshelf and took a nap until it was time to go to dinner with her parents.

The weekend ended, and Natalie was back in class early Monday morning. Miss Sherman asked, "Who here has his or her forms signed and ready to turn in today?"

Everyone in the class turned their letters in except Eddie Piper, John Melton, and Natalie.

Miss Sherman smiled and said, "You have three days left. If not, I will have to reach out to your parents by phone."

The color left Natalie's face when she heard what Miss Sherman said. She couldn't risk her parents finding out about the book or the consent form; she had to do something fast.

Miss Sherman continued with the class, teaching fundamental ideas and supporting details. She placed her pupils into cooperative learning groups. Miss Sherman reviewed text structures and assigned each group to write a brief story using a text structure of their choice, and then swapped those stories with a different group. They aimed to tell and explain the story's text structure using a graphic organizer to justify their answers. The last task was to write about what would happen next in the story.

Miss Sherman set the timer to facilitate each group. The first timer went off, and each group discussed its text structure.

The second timer sounded, and it was time for the students to play a game with the main ideas.

"We will use the round robin," laughed Miss Sherman.

"Yeah," cried the students in one voice.

"Let's start with Group A."

If one group provided the main idea, then another group had to give the supporting detail. Alternatively, groups could challenge each other by providing both the main idea and supporting details. If a group failed to complete the challenge when called upon, it would lose points. However, if a group could find the hidden inference in a story without help from Miss Sherman, they scored extra points. The game was designed for groups to earn several points: five points for identifying text features, ten points for explaining a context clue, three points for pointing out the author's purpose, and so on.

Miss Sherman intervened to keep the game flowing smoothly, ensuring students did not break the game's rules. Also, she helped guide their thinking without giving away the answers using hints and clues. If students could not figure out the answers, Miss Sherman would go back over it after the game was over. Also, she reviewed and retaught skills with them at her reading table. At the end of the month, the group with the most points would win the "Miss Sherman's Extraordinary Readers" award. Miss Sherman called the game the Battle of the Readers.

The bell rang, and the class cried, "Aw, is it time to go already?"

Miss Sherman said, "Yes, it is. Continue studying your notes from unit one of your textbooks. You will have a unit test coming up soon."

Natalie couldn't bring herself to show her parents her consent form. So she signed it that Sunday night in her bedroom. Natalie knew it was wrong to forge their signatures. Natalie felt terrible about what she was doing to her parents and teacher. The next day, after class, Natalie gave the permission slip to Miss Sherman.

While Miss Sherman was holding Natalie's permission slip, Natalie looked flushed. Concerned, she asked, "Are you alright, my dear?"

"Yes, Miss Sherman." Natalie felt as if she knew what she had done.

"Did your mother or father sign this letter, Natalie?"

"Yes, ma'am, they did."

"Very well." Miss Sherman handed her a copy of the book from her desk. Natalie stared long and hard at the book. Miss Sherman asked, "Is there anything else? "No, there's nothing else," Natalie said. "Then off you go, then." Natalie took the book and headed to her next class. Miss Sherman filed her permission slip into a blue folder inside her desk.

Mrs. Finley, the school's librarian, a week ago, had checked out a class set of the chosen book, Miss Sherman had selected for the class book report. When they returned to the room, Miss Sherman issued each student's books to those who turned in their signed permission slips, all except Natalie, for she had not turned in her permission slip. Miss Sherman told them to read the book every day and to take good care of their books because it was their responsibility for the next nine months. At the end of the term, they would do a presentation on the book using any primary source of their choice to back their thesis and defend their position on whether God is real or not in front of the class.

Friday, the school buzzed because it was their first pep rally for the Woodland Warriors at 1:00 p.m. that afternoon. Natalie's squad cheered and performed, inspiring their team. The crowd was insane, stomping and echoing the cheers from the bleachers. Cheerleaders cheered while they danced to the beat of the squad's dance routines. They turned the lights off in the gym, and the disco ball lights reflected around the gym. The spotlight centered on the squad on the floor as they built a difficult pyramid, using signs as they cheered. Once they broke formation, they followed up with somersaults, half-twists, backflips, and splits.

The spirit stick went to the eighth graders because they were the most spirited class in the gym. For a moment, she had forgotten she had forged her parents' signatures on the permission letter. After the pep rally, they dismissed students to their quarters.

Later that evening, Sam told Natalie she had gotten her consent form signed and her copy to read as they walked to the football game. She asked Sam how far she had read, and she told her to the second chapter. Natalie told her she hadn't started but planned to catch up over the weekend.

Sam said, "The book is truly life-changing."

"How so?"

She looked at her and said, "You will have to find out for yourself."

"Oh, come on, Sam, can't you give me a hint of what you mean by that?"

"Nope, I will not spoil it for you; my lips are sealed."

"Great, have it your way."

"I wouldn't have it any other way."

"So, what did you write about for your history paper?"

"The heroes of 9/11."

"See, I knew you would figure it out. You aced it, sis."

"Yeah! I did," exclaimed Samantha.

"But why didn't you tell me you got your consent form signed this week? And you didn't submit it to Miss Sherman until Tuesday."

"So?" asked Natalie. "So, today is Friday. I thought we were best friends; I thought we told each other everything, some friends."

Sam walked ahead of her to the game.

"Sam, wait!" but she kept walking with Natalie following behind her. They arrived at the game; the Woodland Warriors were going to war with the Magnolia Academy's Raptors. The Raptors played an excellent game, but the Warriors scored three touchdowns, beating the Raptors ten to seven.

Between the football games, cheerleading, and her classes, Natalie stayed afloat with a 4.0 GPA. One student famous on the hardwood field was Caleb Grey. Caleb was athletic and particularly good at sports; he would be an All-American one day. He played offense on the team, and he noticed Natalie at the game. Outgoing, friendly, and talented, Caleb was a bright star athlete who came from a family of three. His twin baby sisters, who were only eight years of age, Tia and Mia, were back home in Chicago. His parents were not well off, but they saved their hard-earned money to send their son to Woodland, where he would get an excellent education and be away from Chicago's violent streets. His father, Stephen, was the police department captain, and his mother, Vivian, taught high school English. Caleb didn't want to leave home, but he did as his parents asked him and made the most of attending Woodland Academy.

# Chapter Seven

# The Election

Headmistress Howell announced over the intercom in the middle of Miss Sherman's lecturing on the point of view. "Attention, attention, teachers, and students report to the Gathering Hall."

"Everyone, please place your pencils down. Boys and girls line up to walk quietly to the Gathering Hall. The last person in line closes the door behind you," said Miss Sherman.

The Gathering Hall was noisy, with students flooding into the room as they took their seats. Huge Olympic bowls on stilts were a blaze of fire, with greenery wrapped around the stilts like a candy cane. Teachers' seats were arranged in a triangular position next to the glass podium. A hush came over the room. Everyone wanted to hear the announcements.

Suddenly, the fires flickered, and the room faded to darkness for a second and lit again. Headmistress Howell appeared at the podium. Lightning and thunder followed her presence as a massive deluge poured from the sky. Outside the window, the wind howled, and the beads of water ran down the stained glass as she stood with her hands stretched apart behind the podium. She wore a long black hooded cloak with a red oval medallion surrounded by brilliant diamond crystals that fastened at the neckline. Her gown was silk, an A-line silhouette. She said, "The time has come for Woodland's annual games. Woodland has taken part in these games since the school was built. We honor this tradition every year as new students arrive at Woodland Academy. The first games will be in a special arena designed to test the mind, your courage, and your heart. The Elders of the school will pull grades to see who will take part in the games. A boy or a girl chosen from specific grades can only enter the games by self-nomination or class nomination. Here at Woodland, we look for the brightest and bravest to represent the school for ages to come. A word of caution: do not enter the games without giving them careful thought. The games are challenging, but if you stay the course, you will be in the running to become a member of Woodland's special elite group. If entered, you cannot withdraw from the competition; you must finish the games or disqualify your grade from the games this year and the next. Woodland never had students who failed to complete his or her game obligations; therefore, I must emphasize choosing your candidates wisely, and if you nominate yourself, make sure you're up for the task. Now, I shall tell you the grades chosen by the Elders, and they are six through nine."

Each grade level chosen was applauded happily.

"You can select ten candidates from each hall. Only eight of your favorite candidates from each hall can compete in the games. Teachers, you must turn in those ten names by the end of the day today. Afterward, there will be a second election; the student body will vote for the final eight to enter the games. I will announce the winners next Friday after the homecoming game is over. If I call your name, you will be a tribute in the games. Now I shall briefly explain the rules of the games. Only students from chosen grade levels can help with tributes in the games. Students in tenth through twelfth grades may not help with tributes during the games, no exceptions. Anyone breaking the rules will be disqualified and placed on a month's probation; a letter will notify your parents. In the first games, each grade level will compete for first place. Whoever comes in second place will face off with the first-place winners, and third place will face off with fourth-place winners. Those tributes will move on to the last tournament, Tag-O-Lit. Whoever wins Tag-O-Lit will be the winners of the Games and win one hundred points along with bragging rights throughout the ages to come. Winners of the tournament will receive a trophy with their grade level, names, and the tournament's date engraved on the trophy. We will place the trophy in the center of the school's atrium's special case on the first floor. We will take the winners to the school's private area as victors and the school's Elders' special choice. There, we will enlighten you with the school's wisdom and knowledge; you will learn how to change the world. The elite classes are the highest honor students can achieve here at Woodland Academy. You will continue with your regular courses and elite classes until graduation. The games will air the acts of bravery, talent, and sacrifice, moments of triumph and achievement throughout the school's halls, reminding us that genuine victory doesn't come by accident but by firm conviction and compassion. Before the games begin, we will have a Christmas Ball to honor the tributes of the games."

Hearing this, applause followed.

"When we return from Christmas break, tributes, we will escort you to a part of the academy where only tributes can prepare for the games. Finally, students caught by school officials who are training privately will have points deducted from their hall. Teachers and students, when you return to your classes and regular schedules, let the nominations begin!"

Students were elated and eager to start the voting process. As soon as the Headmistress finished speaking, a strange gust of wind blew in, lights flickered, and the students sighed.

Natalie nudged Sam. “Whoa, where did these guys come from?” Sam whispered, “I don't know.”

The men appeared again dressed as Levites' Priests of Israel and blew into their shofars. The floor torches lit up when they blew their horns. A pin dropped could be heard when students saw what happened next. The Headmistress's clothes had changed to a dazzling white hooded cloak with a sapphire brooch enclosed around it. Her gown, a white, silky, satin floor-length A-line dress, and upon her head, a star-studded crown, shimmered as did her cloak in the light. The faculty in black clothing rose, and right before the student body's eyes, their garments were white. The Headmistress dismissed her students from the room. Men on the platform blew their horns to start the games. As they blew into the horn, the floor-length lamps were a bright blue, glowing fire.

When Natalie saw this, she thought, *What kind of school is this*? Leaning closer to Sam, she whispered, “Sam, your sisters were right about what they said. There is something mystical and mysterious about this school. This school differs from any school I have ever attended.”

“I'll say the food is better.” Natalie smiled at her friend, but she couldn't shake the feeling that something strange was going on there. “I'm going to find out what kind of school Woodland Academy is. I believe there is more to this school than meets the eye. Are you with me, Sam?”

“I am,” said Sam.

# Chapter Eight

## Breaking the Rules

Today was Tuesday, a week before homecoming. Natalie noticed the lawns changed daily as she and Sam walked to lunch. “Sam, this school is amazing. Just yesterday, the grass was striped. Today it's checkered. How does the groundskeeper tend hundreds of acres of land every day? When did they do it, and when did they cut it? What makes the grass grow so quickly? Sam, there is something unusual about this school.”

“Do you not like it?”

“I do, Sam. It's not like any school I've been to before.”

“Natalie, this is Woodland Academy School of Wonders.”

“No school compares to the unexplained things I witnessed here. I do not know what kind of magic tricks they used in the Gathering Hall when the faculty clothing changed right before our eyes last week," said Natalie.

"Aren't you curious about the strange occurrences that go on around here?"

"I agree there's more to Woodland than we know, Nat."

"I am going to get to the bottom of it."

"How?"

"The library. If we are going to get any answers, we need to research the history of the school."

"The library is a great place to start," said Sam. "But Natalie, *The History of Woodland Academy* is in the restricted area, forbidden to students. Only top school officials enter that part of the library, and it's virtually impossible to get in there during school hours," said Sam.

"I thought about it. We're going to sneak in after-hours and get the book."

"Sneak in! Are you out of your mind? Tell me you're joking," cried Sam. "If we're caught, we could get into big trouble for breaking the rules."

"We won't get caught; I promise."

"Students are not to leave their quarters after dark, not to mention stealing. Plus, school officials will lock and guard the library," said Sam.

"We will not steal it but borrow it, and when no one is looking during regular hours, I will return it."

"How are we going to get in?" asked Sam with a bewildered face.

"I will catch up with you later; I have to take care of something."

"Like what?"

"I can't explain now, but I'll fill you in later on," said Natalie as she left the table, leaving Sam to finish her lunch alone.

In the middle of lunch hour, Natalie went to the school's basement, where no students ever set foot. She knew where the groundskeeper worked and entered their domain following a flight of stairs that led to double doors. Her legs were spaghetti strings, and her heart raced every second at the thought of being caught beyond student borders. Nothing could stop Natalie from achieving her goals once she had made up her mind. Above the double doors was a posted sign, “Grounds Keeper Room.” The door was half-open, and Natalie went inside. No one was there; she was alone.

The room smelled of chemicals and pine, and the shelves were neatly stocked with cleaning supplies, tools, and lawn equipment. Several tall red lockers numbered one to thirty were against the wall. Natalie tiptoed, being extra careful not to make a sound. She made it to the end of the lockers, and she turned to the right and noticed on the wall several brass keys hanging on small hooks in front of her. *But which key unlocks the library door?* Natalie thought to herself. She went to the keyboard and started at the bottom, looking for the key to unlock the library. With no luck, she turned her attention to the top row of keys. She combed the top row carefully. In the middle of her search for the library key, she heard the door slam and then footsteps.

Someone was coming. Natalie had to make a run for it; she hid quickly.

A short, stocky man in a light-green Woodland Academy uniform walked into the chambers, sensing someone was there; he asked, of curled lips. “Is there someone here?”

Natalie recognized the groundskeeper after seeing him tending to the flowers the first day she came to Woodland. He ambled around the room, dragging his right leg. *Maybe he got hurt on the job*, thought Natalie.

Seeing no one, he shrugged his shoulders, thinking it was a draft of wind. He placed his hand on his growling stomach, realizing he had forgotten the lunch his wife packed for him. He could hardly wait to taste the delicious roast beef sandwich, potato salad, and pecan pie.

Natalie's heart skipped two beats; the rotund, clean-shaven groundskeeper was walking to the locker she hid inside.

Nearing the locker, she saw J. Buford written on his shirt through the slits of the locker. Seconds from reaching the locker, he opened it and retrieved his lunch from locker thirty.

Natalie was relieved that she hid in locker twenty-nine.

Buford removed his lunch from his locker and left the room.

Natalie exhaled, stepped out of the locker, and continued to search for the library key. Every key looked the same, but as she looked closer, she recognized one key with small images of books etched into the bottom of the key handle that stood out among the rest. *This is the one I found it.* She tucked it inside her sweater pocket and returned to class.

Natalie hurried to find Sam in the hallway among the students going to class. She pulled Sam to the side away from the crowd and said, "Sam, meet me in front of the library tomorrow at 8 p.m."

"Alright, but how are we going to get past the school's prefect?"

"We will create a diversion."

"But how are we going to get into the library? I am not breaking in."

"We won't have to because I have the key."

"Solid!" said Sam.

***

Eight o'clock had arrived. Natalie grabbed her lantern and was off to the library as planned. She took the secret winding staircase in her hall away from her quarters, which led her to the bottom of an open arch. There Sam was, waiting for her with her lantern at the bottom of the stairs. They recognized the school entrance's lobby, and across the hall was the Headmistress's office, and two doors down, the library and Chase Sullivan.

"Oh, great, a welcoming committee!" said Sam.

Natalie reached into her pocket, threw a pebble while his back was turned down the hall. Hearing the noise, he left his post to investigate.

"Come on; we have little time until he comes back," whispered Natalie.

The girls raced to the door. Natalie reached inside her sweater pocket and pulled out the key to unlock the door. The key fit perfectly inside the keyhole; with a quick snap of the wrist, she turned the key to the right, and it popped. She unlocked the door swiftly and hurried inside.

Soft lamps were burning in small corners of the library. They blocked the restricted entrance with a black chain hooked from one floor pole to the other, like a museum exhibit closed to the public. A sign attached to the chain's center read in black letters and Latin, "Restricted Section."

"We made it. Let's go," whispered Sam.

They went under the chain with their lanterns. The moon was bright in the sky, casting light into the library. The girls found the W section for Woodland's History on the top middle shelf. Natalie retrieved the ten-inch thick, weighty book with over two hundred parchment pages written in black quill ink in old English. The book cover was bound in brown leather, with the school image imprinted into the leather. They took the book and cracked open the entrance door to see if the coast was clear. The prefect hadn't returned; locking the door behind them, they dashed up the stairs and returned to their quarters.

"Natalie, I am going to bed. It's been a long night. If you find anything in there, let me know."

"I will."

"Goodnight, Nat."

"Goodnight, Sam. Get some rest, and I'll see you in the morning."

***

Natalie didn't sleep a wink. The next day, during study hall, Sam asked Natalie quietly, "Well, what did you find out?"

"Nothing explains the strange phenomena of the school. I covered the book from front to back; however, I discovered that no teachers or headmasters were photographed, only the students, since the 1800s. Strangely, professors' names were recorded with no dates or years."

"Odd, why do you think that is?"

"I don't know."

Headmistress said, "The Elders of the school will choose victors, and those victors chosen will attend the secret elite classes and learn the secrets and mysteries of the school," said Sam.

"It is clear what we have to do; we have to enter the games."

"And what do we do until that time?" Sam asked.

"We wait," said Natalie.

Miss Sherman finished voting in her room last week. Natalie, Sam, Lyle, Eddie, Dave, and Charlotte were nominated from their classroom to enter the games. Natalie and Sam were surprised and happy to be chosen to enter the games. Soon, all elected officials were turned into the office. They gave students ballots to vote for the final eight of their halls. Natalie and Sam's names were on the final ballot. Students finished during the sixth period. Votes were tallied and submitted to the office. The school was abuzz, waiting to hear if they had chosen their favorite tribute to enter the games.

School had ended for Monday, and Natalie paced back and forth in her room, wondering if she and Sam would make the cut. The wait was driving her insane; she made a call. "Dial home," she commanded her phone.

Her mother answered, "The Evergreen residence."

"Hi, Mom!"

"Hello, sweetheart. How are you doing?"

"I am doing great."

"I'm so glad to hear from you, sweetie. How are your classes coming?"

"Just fine! I have important news to share with you and Dad. Is Dad there?"

"Sorry, Natalie, your father isn't here; he is at the lab."

"Please share your news with me. I'll tell your father as soon as he comes home."

"Woodland has their annual games, and my peers chose me and Sam to compete in the games, but it's not official until the Headmistress announces at the homecoming game."

"Natalie, that's wonderful!"

"They're going to announce the tribute names after the game is over."

"I would love it if you and Dad could come to the homecoming game and cheer me on."

"Sweetheart, you're a cheerleader, taking on a full load with your classes. Are you sure the games will not interfere with your studies? Nat, I don't want you taking on more than you can handle."

"If I fall behind, I promise I will stop cheering, but I don't have long to cheer. Football season is ending soon. I should be fine."

"Well, if the games mean that much to you, compete."

"But Mom, I haven't got in yet."

"You will. Besides, sports are in your blood. Your father and I played sports in high school. Your father played football, and I played basketball. We are so proud of you, and we will be there to cheer you on. The game is coming at a good time; your father and I have some time off this weekend."

"What time should we be there?"

"Seven o'clock this Friday."

"Alright, we will see you then, and I love you, sweetheart."

"Love ya, give Dad and Lucy my love."

"I will, and we will see you soon. Bye-bye."

Natalie placed her cell phone on her desk and began working on her math homework. Calling her mother made her feel better, but she was homesick.

# Chapter Nine

# New Friend

A week passed, the voting process ended, and homecoming was today. Miss Headley, Natalie's coach, practiced the squad and dance team hard by throwing in some unwanted extra practices during the week. She wanted both squads to put on a high-impact, show-stopping routine for Woodland's homecoming pep rally that afternoon. The Woodland Warriors will face the Shiloh Giants tonight. Woodland's homecoming week was fun because students could dress according to the school's theme events each day. Also, students decorated their hall during homecoming week. They imported tasty striped lollipops that swirled in front of you and gummy bears that tasted like warm homemade chocolate chip and peanut butter cookies. Custom mouthwatering candies change to animal shapes once sucked and were shipped in from Scotland for students and faculty to buy during homecoming week.

The Headmistress and two school board members were the hall judges. The judges looked for creativity, originality, and school spirit as they judged the hall and classroom doors. Every hall took part, hoping their door and hall would win the homecoming celebration. The Headmistress told the student body and faculty during the morning announcements, the halls would be judged during the day's pep rally, and at the end of the game, she would announce who won the hall and door challenge. The school was filled with excitement because Woodland's homecoming week was the week to have fun, make friends, and create memories of a lifetime.

Participants in the pep rally were summoned ten minutes earlier from class to go to the gym. Next, students heard over the intercom, "Everyone report to the gym for the pep rally," said Miss Sugarman, the school's secretary, and everyone went to the gym. Inside the gym, the bleachers wrapped around the room in an oval shape, and there in the center of the shiny hardwood was Woodland's crest. At the end of each court, painted in bold letters, was "Woodland Warriors." An image of the head of a warrior was painted on four corners of the court, and several championship banners hung above the stands.

The gym filled quickly with Woodland's students and teachers as they sat together according to their grade levels. When everyone had taken their seats, the pep rally began. Coach Sax, head coach of German descent, stood six and a half feet tall and bald as a baby's bottom, walked onto the hardwood floor. His clean three-button white collar shirt was pressed nicely. Around his neck was a black necklace with a whistle dangling in the middle of his shirt. His pants were black windbreakers, and, on his feet, he wore Puma tennis shoes. Coach Sax reached for the hand-held microphone and said, "Good afternoon, boys and girls. We are here to cheer for our Woodland Warriors and let them know they can win and beat the Giants tonight. Let's show the Giants who's boss, shall we? Boys and girls, rise to your feet, make some noise for Woodland Warriors. Let's go, let's get it!" Just then, the lights shut off, and Coach Sax's voice rose once again. "OHHHH Woodland Academy, give it up for the conquering Woodland Warriors," in his Dick Vitale voice.

The roars thundered as the team formed two lines. A bright spotlight was cast on the roster's offense and defense players as Coach Sax stated their positions and first names. The spotlight moved over the crowd like white orbs of light dancing under a microscope slide.

Beaming with excitement, Woodland students cheered and whistled. After roll call, music blasted through the speakers, and students danced in the bleachers as the team danced in a huddle on the floor.

"Y'all Ready for This?" thundered through the speakers, and the cheerleaders took to the floor, tumbling and backflipping as they danced to the music. The cheerleaders' silver, black, green, and navy-blue uniforms looked terrific on the floor with the letters "W-A-S" stitched across in white letters on top of their uniforms. Silver and green metallic letters glimmered and sparkled as the lights reflected off them. The music switched to "Welcome to My House." The team and cheerleaders danced in sync as the music played.

When the song ended, Coach Headley, on the sideline, asked with the mic in her hand, "Are you ready, Woodland cheerleaders? Get your yell on!"

Natalie and her squad gathered in the middle of the floor and yelled, "Ready, okay! Offense here to give you more… In the end zone, watch them score. Score, score, score! Woodland Warriors have just begun… their defense is number one!"

Everyone cheered afterward.

The cheerleaders said, "Warriors turn up the heat."

"Why?" Students shouted, and the squad and student body responded, "We're too deep!"

"Go, Woodland Warriors, go!"

"Come on! Let's Go! DJ, kick that funky beat," cried the cheerleaders. "Soulja Boy" billowed through the speakers as ten football players moved in between the cheerleaders and transitioned into a cool swagger "Soulja Boy" dance while everyone in the stands rocked side to side. The crowd waved their school-colored towels in the air.

The song changed to "Watch Me (Whip/Nae Nae)," then the school's mascot broke through the ranks with flips and backflips in the air as the squad and guys continued to dance. When "Watch Me" ended, the cheerleaders lined up with letter cards in their hands as a domino effect flipped their cards over, spelling "BEAT THE GIANTS" to the crowd, and they followed up with pyramids, stunts, flips, half twists, and backflips on the court.

After the squad finished, a few football members performed a small skit to "One Moment in Time," moving in slow motion. They moved slowly, portraying a touchdown in the end zone, with flashes of fluorescent camera lights creating a slow-motion effect in the semi-dark gymnasium, creating a "moment-in-time" scene. Before the pep rally ended, the dance team danced to "Teach Me How to Dougie" mixed in with "P.Y.T." The school went wild as the dance team knocked the school on its knees with their routine.

The pep rally was a success, and now it was time to determine which class had the most school spirit. Coach Sax asked, "Who has the most school spirit?"

Natalie took the spirit stick to each grade level section, and whichever grade yelled and screamed the loudest won the spirit stick. Each class roared as Natalie stood in front of each grade. After hearing every grade, the judges talked it over and wrote the winning class down on paper. Coach Sax retrieved the card and said, "The judges have made their final decision, and the spirit stick goes to," pausing for a brief second to build anticipation, he said, "The seniors!"

Every senior rose and exclaimed, "Y'ALL KNOW!"

Miss Headley walked back onto the court and asked the student body, "Who's the best?"

"Woodland Warriors!"

"Who's going to show the Giants the king of the gridiron?"

"The Warriors!"

"Who?"

"The Warriors!"

"That's what I thought you said!" She handed the microphone back to Coach Sax for his last remarks.

He turned, faced his team, and said, "Warriors tonight, go out there and bring this home. You're ready! Stay confident, play with heart, and leave everything on the field. They have asked me to remind you of tonight's events. After the game is over, Headmistress Howell will proclaim who will compete in the upcoming Elite games and who won the homecoming hall and door contest. Come back tonight and hear the conclusion of homecoming week. If you have not purchased your homecoming tickets, you may purchase them at the gate. The game starts at 7:00 p.m. sharp. This brings our pep rally to an end; see you guys tonight. Now, sixth through eighth grade are dismissed from the left side of the gym, and ninth through twelfth are dismissed from the right side of the gym in a single file line."

Caleb was a member of the football team. When he saw Natalie, he asked one of his team members her name.

Charlie, who played wide receiver, replied, "Oh, that's Natalie Evergreen. This is her first year here. She transferred here from Memphis. She is in seventh grade."

Caleb thanked the platinum blonde-haired team member. "How do you know so much about her?"

"When it comes to the prettiest girls in the school, I do my homework."

Caleb shook his head at Charlie because he was known on campus for being a ladies' man.

"Are you thinking about asking her out?"

Caleb didn't answer.

"Go ahead; I hear she's nice."

With that, he went and huddled with the rest of the team. The truth is, Caleb liked Natalie the moment he laid eyes on her and wanted to ask her out, but he was shy. Since it was homecoming week, he thought, what better time to introduce himself and ask her out? He wasn't completely sold on approaching her because he was nervous.

Natalie walked away from her squad to retrieve her water bottle from her black tote bag. She opened the top of the bottle and took a big swig of it. Her throat was screaming for more; she was thirsty from performing on the floor.

Caleb thought to himself, *It's now or never*. He walked over to her while everyone was leaving the gym, and she was alone getting water. He swallowed his pride and said, "Hi! I'm Caleb."

Natalie looked at him from head to toe and thought this brown-haired boy with brown eyes was athletic and cute. He was her height and age.

"Hello, it's Natalie, isn't it?" Caleb wanted to run away because that wasn't the coolest thing to start with. Wanting to kick himself, he panicked, for he didn't know what to say. No running away; he had to go along and pray he didn't blow it with her.

"Yes, and you are the quarterback on the team, right?"

"How did you know that?"

"Coach Sax said it when he called your name during the rally."

"Aw, yeah, he did, didn't he?" He wasn't sure if she thought he was a dork, forgetting that everyone at the rally heard his position. "I thought you were incredible today."

"Thank you."

"I was wondering if...," interrupted Miss Headley.

"Natalie, Natalie! Come over here, please. I need to discuss tonight's routine with you and the squad one last time."

Natalie gazed at him and said, "I'm sorry, I have to go; maybe I'll see you around sometime."

"Yeah, see you around," replied Caleb.

She grabbed her bag and put it over her shoulders, and then turned to him before leaving and said, "Good luck tonight!"

He smiled and joined his teammates.

Later, back at their dormitory, Natalie told Sam about her encounter with Caleb.

Sam asked, "Is he cute?"

"He's alright; I think he's nice." Changing the subject, Natalie told her she had spoken to her parents, and they were coming to tonight's game to cheer them on.

"All we have to do is make the cut, and we'll be one step closer to finding out the secrets of the academy," said Sam.

"You're right; everything is riding on tonight's results," said Natalie.

# Chapter Ten

# The Homecoming Game

The Evergreens and the Harpers took their seats in Section F. They wore the school's jerseys, jeans, and beanie caps. The field was lush green, with the head of a warrior painted in the center of the field. Woodland was written on the left, and Academy was written at the right end of the field. They painted both field goals white.

The track field was hunter-green with white lines around it. The game started promptly at 7:00 p.m. Winning the coin toss, the Giants were first to kick things off.

Natalie was busy on the sidelines, cheering for her team; she searched the stands, hoping to see Sam and her parents. She noticed a white poster with bold black and gold letters with silver and green pom-poms that read, "Good Luck Natalie and Sam Tonight!" It was her mother, holding the sign high at the top of the stands.

Her mother and father were glowing from ear to ear. It was a chilly night, but seeing her parents made her feel warm on the inside. She blew her parents' air kisses from the sidelines, waved to her parents, Sam, and the Harpers.

The Giants' game got underway. The Warriors and the Giants played man-to-man football and continued to halftime. At halftime, the Giants were winning as the red and blue teams went into the locker rooms.

The Warrior and Giant cheerleaders cheered for their teams. Caleb and the others didn't say a word. You could hear a pin drop in the room, for the boys were losing, and they knew Coach was about to come down hard on them. Coach Sax entered the room, and he looked at each one in the eye and said, “Guys, anyone can see you are playing with a lot of heart tonight. But here's what we're going to do. We are going to step up the defense, and we are going to stop their running game. If we do that, we can win. Guys, we are still in this football game. Now. Who's with me?”

Motivated by their coach's speech, the boys were ready to play the second half. “Everybody ready? Defense on three one, two —”

“Defense,” shouted the team.

“Let's go, Warriors,” said Coach Sax as they left the locker room to return to the field. Half-time was up.

The Warriors got the ball back in the second half of the game. The scoreboard was 14 to 18, and the game continued to the fourth quarter. The Warriors were down by four points with 23 seconds left on the clock with one timeout remaining. The Warriors were down on the ten-yard line with 18 seconds left on the clock. Coach Sax called a timeout; Caleb received the play, and the Warriors took to the field to run the last play. The Warriors came out of the huddle, hiked the ball. Then Caleb scrambled until he found Charlie Gibson open in the end zone. He threw the ball into the wind and scored a touchdown. The Warriors won the game 20 to 18. Coach Sax, leaping and jumping on the sidelines, was submerged in yellow Gatorade. Navy, dark green, silver, and black confetti rained on the players as the

Warriors made confetti angels on the field. Afterward, the coaches and teams shook hands, congratulating each other on a wonderful game.

The Headmistress walked onto the field and then stood on a four-step platform with the microphone in her hands and said, "Warriors, outstanding job. Well done, Coach Sax. I tip my hat off to the Giants. You guys played an impeccable game tonight. You didn't make it easy for us. Warriors, you make us proud. Outstanding game. Without further delay, it's time to announce the winning tributes who will compete in the annual Elite Games. But before I do, the winner of the homecoming hall is … and this was a hard decision, but with much deliberation, the hall the judges felt stood out the most, drum roll please… freshman hall. The winner of the door challenge is Miss. Peterson from sixth grade, earning fifty points. Take a bow, Miss. Peterson, well done to you and your classroom." Miss. Peterson stood, waved, and bowed gracefully to the crowd and took her seat.

Ninth-grade students cheered immensely.

"Excellent work, freshman. Your class is awarded one hundred points. Finally, I will announce the tributes who will participate in the games according to grade. Ninth grade, your tributes are Shannon Fleming, Seth Misters, Kevin Strong, Shane Miller, Thomas Lynch, Brock Myers, Mike Simmons, and Randy Styles. Eighth grade: Simone Redd, Richard Cole, James Gaudy, Tim Meeks, Sarah McPherson, Connie Edmunds, Marlene Travis, and Derrick Kingsley. Congratulations, eighth graders. Seventh grade: Dexter Greene, Charlotte Simpson, Samantha Cortez Harper, Eddie Piper, Dave Kissinger, Mary Tolls, Lyle Boggs, and Natalie Evergreen. Finally, the sixth-grade tributes are Dale Lester, Jack Rhodes, Nandi Harris, Commodore Stevens, Carrie Hemphill, Matt Foster, Glen Johnson, and Shelton Summers. The games will begin after the Christmas holidays. Thanks for coming out to tonight's game, and I bid you all good night."

Leaving the field, Natalie rushed to her parents' arms. When Natalie and Sam's parents heard their girls make the team, they congratulated them and took them out to eat dinner to celebrate. Natalie told her parents how much she loved Woodland, but she never shared the school's strange, unexplained occurrences. Natalie thought it would be best to keep it to herself until she knew more about the school. For now, she was glad to be with her family once again.

Caleb and the team were still celebrating, but he stopped celebrating long enough to watch Natalie. He saw her leave the field with her parents after the game was over. *Another failed attempt,* he thought. It dawned on him that asking Natalie out would not be easy because she had become a tribute, but he was determined more than ever to ask her out, and nothing was going to stand in his way. NOT EVEN the games! He knew in his heart he would do anything for her.

Caleb left the field and celebrated with his team because his parents could not attend the games. They couldn't afford to travel the long distance since they had sent Caleb to Woodland. Like Natalie, he missed his parents, but he wrote to them every chance he got.

Natalie and Sam returned to Woodland after the homecoming weekend was over. Classes continued as usual, and the Thanksgiving holidays were near. Natalie was looking forward to going home for the holidays. The pressure was escalating; the more she delayed telling her parents about the reading assignment, Miss Sherman assigned, the more she felt guilty about keeping this God thing a secret from her parents.

She was glad football season had ended, and now she could focus on finishing the book. During the break, she promised herself she would start reading it. In the meantime, she would have to keep the book hidden from her parents, and she had to be smart not to let them see her reading *Is God Real* until she completed her book report. At the end of the reading, she convinced herself she would come to the same conclusion as her parents, who ALWAYS said, "THERE IS NO GOD; JUST PEOPLE." End of story.

Natalie studied hard and maintained an A-plus average, just as she promised her parents she would do. Progress reports were going to be mailed the week of Thanksgiving break. Natalie relished the thought of how pleased her parents would be to see her good grades when she returned home.

# Chapter Eleven

# Family Dinner

It was the Thanksgiving holiday, and Woodland dismissed its students for a week. Natalie, Sam, and Caleb went home for the break. Sam and Natalie kept in touch every day, whereas Caleb wanted to ask Natalie out but couldn't because each time he tried, it was never the right time. Against his wishes, he had to wait until Thanksgiving was over to make his move.

Natalie and Sam's new home was as spacious as their last abode. Natalie's bedroom had fewer windows, but a closet fit for a princess. She looked at the top row of books above her head in her room, sitting at her white study desk; instead of reading the book Miss Sherman assigned, she reached for her diary and began journaling.

***

*November 22, 2023*

*Dear Diary,*

*Today was great; my parents and I had a fantastic day together. Mom and Dad took me bowling, and then we went out to eat. I am thankful to spend Thanksgiving with my family and Lucy. Mom and Lucy have been cooking all morning long, preparing tonight's dinner and Thanksgiving dinner. Every year, our house is busy with relatives flying in from all over to dine with us. It's always the same repetitive questions from my aunties. "Nat, how old are you now? What grade are you in? Do you have any boyfriends?" Blah, Blah, Blah, thank goodness it's only for a day. I tell myself to deal with my aunt's boring questions, and one afternoon, of pinched cheeks. On a lighter note, I have splendid news. Sam and I were chosen to take part in Woodland's annual games. If we win, we will become a part of the elite class of the school. Woodland is a school of mystery. There is much about the school I can't explain logically. But I'm dying to discover. But once I win the tournament, I will discover the school's hidden mysteries and why unexplained magical events seem to happen more and more at Woodland. As far as the games, the headmistress said, 'The games will challenge each tribute mentally and physically.' I pray I survive the games. While on break, I plan to catch up on reading the book Miss Sherman assigned. On top of this, no one has asked me to the ball, and I haven't decided what dress to wear yet. I pray I find a magnificent dress. Wish me luck.*

*Natalie*

***

In the dining room, Melissa said to Lucy, "Thanksgiving is going to be great!" as they decorated the family's table with fall décor. Lucy smiled and nodded in agreement.

Melissa placed a special place setting for each relative on the table. Cornucopia leaves, assorted orange pumpkins, and candles were in the center of the table. Water, wine goblets, polished silver, and fine China lay on top of the beige tablecloth, arranged with care. A burlap table runner of country chic farmhouse served as the theme of the design. A crystal candle chandelier hung above the table, adding an extra touch of class. Melissa's table setting looked like a White House Head of State dinner.

Melissa's Thanksgiving dinner consisted of her marvelous mustard greens, chicken dressing, green beans, turkey, brown gravy, potato salad, mashed potatoes, pea salad, and desserts consisting of caramel and German chocolate cake and sweet potato pies. The smell of greens, dressing, cakes, pies, and turkey lingered in the house.

Natalie entered the back-kitchen stairwell into a well-designed kitchen. A large kitchen island with white marble countertops sat in the middle of the kitchen floor with stainless steel sink faucets. The backsplash behind the stove was the perfect geometry, light beige, and cream tiles pattern. The cabinets were white with silver stainless-steel handles, and inside the largest cabinet, concealed in a sizeable wooden compartment. The Evergreens loved their home and all its hardwood flooring throughout the house. It had heated floors and tall windows, displaying snowcapped mountains and spacious grounds. A red-carpet rug flowed down the wooden steps of the grand stairs. You could look down from the top of the grand staircase and see a round circular etch design in its entirety on the floor.

Back in the kitchen, Lucy opened the oven range and gently basted the turkey as Melissa stirred the gravy. "Natalie, are you excited about the games?"

"Yes, Mom, the sooner I win, the sooner I know what Woodland's hiding?"

Both women eyed each other and continued cooking. Natalie walked over to the cookie jar with her back turned to her mother, expressing an OH NO look on her face. She realized she said too much and had to think of something quick to throw her off what she said.

"Um, what do you think the school is hiding, Natalie?" asked her mother.

Looking at the ceiling, she turned to her mother with a chocolate chip cookie in her hand and said, "I can't wait until Dad gets home. He promised to teach me how to drive. Mama, when's dinner? I'm starving?"

"Dinner will be ready in five minutes."

"Great, I could eat a whale right now!" she said while biting into her cookie.

"Not too many of those, Nat, I don't want you to ruin your appetite for dinner."

"Yes, Mama! Okay, I'll be in my room; call me when dinner is ready."

"Hold on, young lady, not so fast. What did you mean the school is hiding something?" she asked calmly.

"I said Sam is hiding something."

"I thought I heard you say Woodland was hiding something."

"The ball is approaching, and Sam hasn't said a word about the dress her mother picked out for her."

"Sam, secretive? You guys tell each other everything."

"I know, right! I can't believe how Sam is keeping this one under wraps."

"I am sure she will tell you about it eventually. Are you sure there is nothing else you want to tell me?"

"No, Mom!" Before leaving the kitchen, she turned to her mother and said, "Sam has her dress, and I don't have a clue what kind of dress to wear. Would you help me pick a dress?"

"Sweetie, I will be delighted to help. Why don't we go during Black Friday to Carol's Boutique?"

"I'd love it; I can hardly wait."

"It's settled; we're off tomorrow to get the perfect dress for you."

Relieved her mother had bought it, she felt terrible about not telling her mother the truth, but couldn't risk her finding out, not when she was so close to her goal. She left the kitchen to go to her room when the front door opened, and Natalie's father walked in.

"Hi, Daddy!"

"Hello, pumpkin pie; I'm happy you're here for the holidays."

"It's wonderful to be home. Happy Thanksgiving, Daddy." Natalie hugged her father. "Mom said dinner is almost ready."

"Well, let's not keep your mother waiting."

"I'm heading upstairs to wash, and I will be down in a second," said Natalie.

He took his white coat off and hung it in the closet behind the front door, and walked into the kitchen. "Hello, beautiful," giving his wife a warm hug and soft kiss.

"¡*Hola*, Lucy!"

"*Bueno, Tarde, Señor* Evergreen."

"What's for dinner tonight, ladies?"

"Meatloaf, mashed potatoes, broccoli, chef salad, rolls, and for dessert, peach cobbler," said Lucy.

"Yum, Yum!" He looked at his hands, and with that, he departed to wash. He returned to eat dinner with his family.

The food was delicious. Natalie cleaned her plate.

"Dinner was splendid, Mom. You and Lucy have outdone yourselves. May I please be excused?"

"You may be excused."

Natalie left the table, went to her room, showered, and got ready for bed. Before falling to sleep, she took the book from its place and began reading several chapters.

Thanksgiving Day arrived, and the family began pouring in for dinner. Everyone took their seats around the table. The Evergreens hired more servers to help serve dinner. Servers in black and white uniforms served the food. One server placed the turkey on the table.

Natalie's father carved and sliced the turkey for the dinner party. Everyone at the table expressed what they were most thankful for and ate. Natalie's relatives stuffed themselves and retired to the parlor room. Aunt Millie took to the Baldwin and began tickling the ivory. Everyone gathered around and started singing, "We are Family" with raised ginger ale glasses and sparkling cider. The Evergreens had a wonderful time together; even Natalie admitted she was enjoying her family. The hour drew late, and everyone returned to their hotels for the night.

The next day, Natalie and her mother went shopping for her dress. They took the Jaguar into town and headed to Carol's Fashion Boutique. Carol had the trendiest dresses and gowns to choose from for any occasion. With its large bay windows, the store displayed the most stylish dresses and gowns. The store carried all sizes on its racks. On the walls hung elegant dresses around the store. The dressing room had many stalls for changing and trying on clothes. Outside the dressing room was a couch, two wing-back chairs, and a small table for shoppers accompanied by friends and family. A woman with a full bob, black suit, and red heels met Natalie and her mother at the door. Inside, customers were standing on a four-inch platform with 3-D mirrors, admiring the garment's fit on their bodies from every angle. The lights above the platform capture the essence of the fabric.

"Welcome to Carol's Fashions. I am Carol, and how can I help you today?"

"We are here for her junior formal."

"May I ask what kind of formal it is?"

"It's a ball," said Melissa.

"A ball, how exciting! You have come to the right place, and I have the perfect dress for you. Now, if you would follow me." Carol took them to her private collection in an enormous room in the basement filled with thousands of dresses in plastic bags. She pulled a light powder blue princess dress. It was a stunning version of the gown Cinderella wore to the ball. The dress was elegant and modest.

Natalie knew it was the one for her.

"What do you think of this one?" asked Carol.

"I love it!"

"Let's go upstairs and have you try it on."

"Sounds good," said Natalie.

Melissa sat on the couch and waited for Natalie to come out of the fitting room. While Natalie was trying on the dress, a sales associate offered her mother espresso, sparkling water, and ginger ale. Melissa respectively declined the beverages and waited anxiously for Natalie to come out of the fitting room. Natalie took to the platform; she looked like an angel in the floor-length princess flower dress. The dress had ruffles, shoulder straps, shiny beads across the bust, and a small brooch at the waist. Around the hip was textured with ruching, and the rest of the dress was rayon. The fabric shimmers like silk at the base of the dress.

Natalie's mother bought clear two-inch heels to complement the look. Natalie took the dress off and told her mother to purchase it. After shopping, Natalie and her mother grabbed lunch at a retro diner. The barstools at the counter were red, and on the countertop was a blackboard with the day's special written on it. Natalie and her mother took a seat at one of the red booths by the window.

The server's uniform reflected the diner's design. The server's shirt was red with a checkered print stitched to the collar and sleeves, and an apron sewn onto her red skirt. Checkered black and white tiles covered the floors. "Good afternoon. Welcome to Roscoe's Diner. My name is Halley, and I will be your server today." She placed their menus down along with their straws on the table. Ready to take their orders, she removed a pen from behind her ear and the checks from her apron pocket and asked, "What would you like to drink?"

"I would like a Coke," said Natalie.

"I will have a small cup of coffee and a glass of water with lemon," said her mother.

"Great, I'll be back with your drinks," replied the server.

Natalie and her mother looked at the menu as the waitress approached with their drinks. "Are you ready to order?" she asked.

"I will have a medium-well ribeye steak with A-1 sauce and a chef salad with light Ranch dressing," said Natalie's mother.

Halley wrote her order onto her ticket, turned to Natalie, and asked, "And what will you have?"

"I would like a cheeseburger and Cajun fries."

She smiled, took their menus, and walked away.

"Who is the lucky young man who is escorting you to the ball?"

"Unfortunately, no one has asked me yet. There is one I would like to go with, but he's back in Memphis."

"Really? Tell me more about him."

"He loves sports like me, and he plays football at Germantown Middle School. Trever McCall is the best football player GMS has seen in years. Trever is very considerate. His eyes are amber, and he has the cutest freckles here." She pointed with two right fingers down the bridge of her nose, under her eyes, and her cheeks slowly. Melissa chuckled and said. "Trever is a nice name. I like him already. Does he know how you feel about him?"

Natalie's cheeks were apples, said, "No. He's in Memphis, and I am here. I don't think I will ever see him again."

Their server returned and refilled their drinks. Melissa, understanding how her daughter felt, said, "Honey, I am sure someone from school will ask you to the ball soon." "The ball is days away… and there's still time for someone to ask me to go."

Within ten minutes, Halley had returned with their order. "Ah, the food is here," said Natalie.

"Is there anything else I can get for you?" asked their server.

Natalie's mother replied, "No, we're fine."

"Enjoy, and I will be back to check on you in a sec."

Hungry customers began pouring into the diner during rush hour. Natalie picked up her cheeseburger and took a bite of it, and squirted ketchup on her fries. After the meal, Natalie's mother paid the check, left a tip, and returned home.

Natalie hung her dress and placed her glass slippers on one of her closet's shelves. She took the book from its respected place, locked her door, lay on the bed with her back against plush pillows, and began reading. After reading for three hours, the book had inspired thought-provoking questions. She learned God lived in Heaven and was self-existent. She had many questions about the Creator alone, whom the book said was eternal, and the Watchers. The spirit world fascinated Natalie. The more information she learned, the more she wanted to finish the book.

# Chapter Twelve

# Mystery Dates

The air was frigid, for seven inches of Virginia snow blanketed the town, and Natalie loved every moment. She couldn't wait to go outside and build a snowman. Although it snowed in Memphis, it rarely snowed in November. To her, Virginia was a winter wonderland fit for sledding downhill and snowball fighting with her friends and family. The thought of Mouth and Tiffany playing in the snow made her miss them more as she looked outside her bedroom window. She walked over to her closet and looked at her dress. It hung neatly with the rest of her things. She thought about Sam and what she had chosen to wear to the ball. With that, she left the closet, reached for her cellphone off the nightstand, and made a call. "Hello."

"What's going on, Sam?"

"Nothing much, Bestie!"

"How was your Thanksgiving?"

"Believe it or not, it was wonderful, and yours?"

"Oh, it was great. Have you been reading the book?" asked Sam.

"I have."

"And?"

"The chapter about The Watchers was pretty far-fetched. I mean, it sounded like something out of the *Twilight Zone,"* said Natalie as she laughed. There was silence on the other end of the receiver.

"Oh, come on, Sam, that's hilarious! But you're not laughing."

"No, I am not. Natalie, it's not a Sci-Fi movie or make-believe; it's real."

"Sam, don't tell me you believe The Watchers were the Watchmen who were angels in charge of watching over the Earth and humans. Many of them began corrupting themselves with women on Earth, for they were fair to look upon. As a result, their offspring were not born human but a Nephilim, part angel and human. Their offspring appeared normal, but as they grew, they became giants in the land. They killed, stole, and murdered for pleasure. They were an abomination that did terrible things to animals. The Earth was filled with violence; every thought man thought of was evil. It grieved God; He had made mankind, and you're telling me you believe that?"

"Yes, Nat, I do."

"And what you said was correct. God was furious with the sons of God. He assigned them to keep watch over humanity and see that things were well on Earth. They stopped doing what God had commanded and started corrupting themselves and humanity. These fallen angels embodied evil, teaching men sorcery and witchcraft. Then there was Azazel, an entity who was the Watchers' leader, who taught men how to make swords out of metals before corrupting and leading them astray. He taught them about war. God never intended for men to make war with each other, but to live in peace and harmony with one another.

God spoke to Noah and told him he was going to destroy the Earth with a great flood. Noah was commanded to build an ark, and all not found inside would die. When the flood came, some of the fallen angels who morphed themselves into humans gave up their human bodies to return to Heaven, but could not enter Heaven again. God punished the sons of God because they had corrupted themselves and God's creation. Finally, God told archangel Raphael to bind Azazel's hand and foot to a pit of darkness forever on the Earth. He was never to be let out except on the Great Day of Judgment, where he will be cast into the lake of fire along with the rest of the fallen angels whose bodies died in the Flood, but their perceived souls survived, and they became demons. As for everyone else, who was not in the ark, they died. When the waters receded from the Earth, Noah and his family came out of the ark, and God promised not to flood the Earth again. Then, He blessed them and told them to be fruitful and multiply on the earth."

Natalie listened and asked, "What happened next?" Sam continued.

"Later on, God spoke to Abram, who was from Noah's bloodline, and God changed his name from Abram to Abraham, and God made a blood covenant with him, and Abraham became the father of many nations, and his wife, Sarah, became the mother of nations. God numbered His descendants beyond man's count, and the Hebrews became God's people. Isaac, Jacob, and later Moses, who received the Law in the wilderness, and Joshua became the Hebrews' new leader after Moses's death. Joshua led the Israelites into the promised land, and throughout Hebrew history, the holy text was written, and later, King James translated their history into the Bible. The Bible is not just a bunch of stories. They are true events that happened in actual time. Historians and true witnesses who lived during those eras wrote every word in the text. There are sixty-six canonized books in the Holy Bible."

"What does canonize mean?" asked Natalie.

"It means those books met God's rule of being the inspired Word of God. God told Eve in the Garden of Eden, 'One would come and crush Satan's head, and Satan would bruise his heel.' God spoke of the Messiah, His only begotten Son, who will save His people from their sins. The theme of the Bible is Jesus Christ. Whom you will read about in Chapter Fifteen," said Sam.

"You believe one man can save the world from their sins? How can that be?" Natalie asked.

"Natalie, my mother has kept me in Sunday School and Bible class since I could walk. I accepted Christ as my Savior when I was ten years old. When I heard the good news, Christ died for my sins, I gladly received him in my heart. I am hoping one day you will believe in Him, and everything will become clear to you. You asked me if I believe it; I do because He, the Witness, testified to the truth that God is real."

"Who is the Witness?" asked Natalie. "Keep reading, and you will find out in Chapter Sixteen. What chapter are you reading now?"

"I am on Chapter Fourteen. The first five chapters were about the creation, God, angels, demons, and the infamous Watchers."

"When you finish Chapter Fifteen, let me know, and we can discuss the crucifixion and compare notes."

Sam was glad to share her faith with Natalie; it was the first time they had talked about God in-depth since they became friends.

Natalie heard the sincerity in Sam's voice when she spoke of God on the phone. She loved God very much and defended His existence to her with passion. Natalie thought it was time she shared her secret. She said to her, "My parents never taught me these things, but the more I read about God, the more I want to believe. My heart says one thing, but the things in my head they taught me don't add up."

"Natalie, go with your heart and ask God to reveal Himself to you."

"Do you think He will listen to me? I am not a believer like you, Sam," she said without a hint of hesitation.

"That doesn't matter, Nat."

"Why, Sam?"

"Because He is real, whether you believe or not, He for sure knows you."

"He has plans for you, Natalie; I know in my heart He does," said Sam.

"Anyway, have you found a dress?"

"Yes, I did. My mom took me shopping the moment she learned about the ball."

"What color is your dress?"

"It's light-pink salmon, and I hate it. My parents wanted my dress to be modest. The dress is plain and boring, and there are only two things I like about it. One is pink. Two, it's paid for." Natalie chuckled. "I mean, it's a nice dress, but I would never have chosen it for myself."

"My dress is light blue, and my mom helped me find it at Carol's Boutique."

"Sam, we have the gowns, but no one has asked us to the ball."

"We have dates."

"We do, who?"

"Damon Yates and Trever McCall, of course. That day at the mall, I saw how he looked at you. He couldn't take his eyes off you, and I know you like him."

"Alright, maybe I do a little."

"You light up like a firefly when he's around you, and you can't stop smiling when you talk about him."

"Fine, how are they going to escort us to the ball when Memphis is over a thousand miles away?"

"I called Damon and told him everything. He was super stoked and suggested we go together," said Sam. "So, what did you tell him?"

"I said, yes."

"I'm so happy I know how much you guys like each other!"

"You know what's even cooler?"

"No, what?"

"Trever will escort you to the ball."

As soon as Natalie heard Trever was coming, she felt her heart flutter. "Sam, you're kidding."

"Girl, you know I got your back," said Sam.

"Tell me more about the arrangement."

"Well, Damon has family here, and Trever is coming up with him."

"I am curious, though. How did you convince Trever to come?"

"Damon and I thought we should double date."

The last thing she wanted was for Trever to think she was desperate. "Sam, I could murder you."

"Come on, Nat, Trever likes you. As soon as Damon told him about the dance, he was definitely on board."

"Sam, you're nuts."

"I know! Now, grab something to write on and write Trever's number down."

"Okay, hold on a second." She opened her nightstand drawer and grabbed a stack of heart-shaped pink Post-its and a black pen. Ready to write. Natalie said, "Ok. I'm back. What is it?"

"It's nine zero one, four three eight, seven five eight six. Trever's expecting your call. Also, tell him the color of your dress. Call him ASAP, Natalie."

"I have, too, don't I. Otherwise, I'd look pretty ridiculous walking into the ball dateless?"

"I'm shocked, Sam. You would do this, but I'm glad you did. Good looking out! You think of everything."

"That's what friends are for. I gotta go, but I will talk to you tomorrow. Keep me posted, ciao."

The girls hung up, and Natalie thought to herself, *"It's better if I get it over with right now.* She built up her courage and dialed Trever.

Immediately, he picked up. "Hello, Trever, it's Natalie."

"Hi, Natalie, I was waiting for your call. Did Sam explain everything?"

"She did, and thanks for rescuing me."

"No problem. I am glad I could help."

"Do you think your parents will let you come to Virginia?"

"My parents are cool with me coming to Virginia. Damon's parents and my parents are close friends, and Damon and I have been best friends for a long time. They completely trust me in their care. Damon's parents are paying for our flights, and once we land, we will stay with Damon's uncle."

Natalie was glad he and Damon were coming to Virginia. She started daydreaming about what it would be like to gaze into his amber eyes again, and how his lips would feel next to hers during her very first genuine kiss.

"Natalie, Natalie, are you still there?"

Back from her daydream, she replied, "Yes, I'm here. My phone was on mute." That was not true, but she kept talking,

"So, do you like your new school?"

"I do. It's not like any school I ever attended."

"Everyone back at school misses you, including the Satin Dollz."

They both laughed.

"Natalie, there's something I have wanted to tell you since Damon's party."

"Yeah, what is it?"

"Look, I know we haven't known each other for a long time, but I like you, and I never stop thinking of you. When Damon told me about the ball, I had to see you again."

"So, you know you have been all I have thought of since I moved to Virginia." She didn't understand why he was the only boy who made her feel the way he made her feel. Natalie knew she never wanted to stop talking to him. But Miss Sherman's reading assignment could not be ignored. Reluctantly, she said, "I'm sorry, Trever, but I must go… I have a book to read for a book report." She asked him to call her back later.

Trever didn't want to hang up, but he didn't want Natalie to neglect her homework. He politely said he'd call back and for her to enjoy her reading.

Natalie ended the call and removed the book from its secret place on her shelf of books. Everything was going as planned, but falling for Trever wasn't part of the plan. Cupid had shot his arrow into her heart when she least expected it to happen. She had no time to be distracted. She was in the middle of solving a mystery concerning the school, and then there were the games to think about, and she was reading a book her parents would forbid her to read, let alone bring into their home. Even though she was smitten with Trever, she was unwilling to let him get close to her until some irons were taken out of the fire.

# Chapter Thirteen

# New Quarters

Miss Sherman faced the class. "Welcome back, boys and girls! Did everyone enjoy their Thanksgiving break?"

"Yes, Miss Sherman!" replied the class.

"I trust you've been reading the book because today, I would like to break you up into groups to discuss the questions written on the board." Dressed in a retro black gown, tied around her waist by a gold rope that she used for a belt. She donned a small, round cap on her head of sheer black fabric hanging from her head to her back. She looked like a medieval lady, and so did the faculty who had gone from wearing modern clothes to vintage wear. Woodland was over two hundred years old, and Natalie thought no teacher back at her old school would ever step out of their front door dressed like that. She loved it because it was something different, and their apparel coincided with the school's architectural structure. On the blackboard were questions written in white chalk.

1. Do you think God is pleased with the world? Why or why not?
2. If you could ask God one thing, what would it be?
3. Explain why the author wrote the book.
4. Tell why some believe God does not exist. Are they right or wrong?
5. Describe God. What do you think He looks like?

"I want you to discuss the questions for ten minutes. Then, write a summary about question four. You will have ten minutes to complete it. Group leaders will collect the papers and turn them in."

Students began working on their assignments while Miss Sherman circulated from group to group, keeping her students on task. She jotted anecdotal notes and key points she'd discussed with the entire group with a clipboard in her hand. Wasting no time, students completed their work, and Miss Sherman asked students to share what they learned from the assignment. Natalie raised her hand to ask a question.

"Yes, Natalie."

Before speaking, Natalie looked at her classmates and bravely spoke, "Miss Sherman, why did you choose this book for us to read?"

"A fair question to ask, indeed, Natalie, and perhaps you're not alone. I assume many of you are wondering why I chose this book." She found her sitting stool in front of the room and sat comfortably on the seat's cushion and replied.

"I thought this book would raise valid questions to pique your interest in inquiring about an unseen God. Learning if He is, why He is, and to answer questions like why terrible things happen in the world?" Staring her class in the eyes, she asked. "Why does God let bad things happen to good people if He's almighty?"

"Why do people get sick? Drive drunk, causing deadly accidents?" asked Charlotte, with a hint of sadness in her voice.

"Those are excellent questions, Charlotte, and can be answered with a parable. First, it is important to know that God is the self-existent One who had a plan for man. Before He made planets, God created persons like Himself."

"You mean the angels!" said Eddie. He eagerly interjected while she was speaking. He was curious about angels.

"Shh!" cried the class.

"Yes, Eddie," she said as she turned her gaze to Charlotte, who was hanging on to every word Miss Sherman uttered into her account. "To answer Charlotte's questions, we must start with the beginning of creation. In the beginning, God created the constellations and planets. He created a planet good for growing food and drinking water. That planet was Earth, and God created it for man to inhabit, for no other planet in the universe was suitable for living. Later, God created a garden of paradise, and He placed it somewhere in Ethiopia, Africa. It was the most vibrant garden in the entire world. There God made animals, male and female, but He saw something was missing. Do you know what it was?"

"People," said Sam.

"That's right, so God created Adam, the first man. From the dust of the ground, he formed him, and with His breath, He blew into his nostrils, and man became a living soul. Eden was Adam's home, and God gave Adam dominion over all animals. One by one, he named the animals in the garden. The Highest charged Adam to take care of the animals and keep the garden clean. Everything was perfect until God saw that every animal had a companion except for Adam. God said, 'It is not good for man to dwell alone.' He caused Adam to fall into a deep sleep, and from his rib, he took one and formed a woman. She was called a woman because she came from a man. Adam called her Eve, and she became his wife; they lived happily in the garden for a brief period until Lucifer, a cherub, rebelled against God in Heaven and His creation. Lucifer was the anointed covering of God's glory. He hovered over God's seat, casting and illuminating God's glory onto God. Lucifer was music, for he had musical instruments activated from him. Lucifer, who was striking, had become prideful in his heart and desired to be worshipped like God. He had abandoned his sacred duties of worshipping God and protecting the mercy seat. At that moment, sin filled his heart, consumed with pride, he said, 'I will be like God and exalt my throne over the Heavens and sit on the throne in the east.' God cast him out of Heaven, and he led a revolt against Heaven. Michael, the archangel, and his armies overthrew Satan and a third of the angels who joined his ranks."

A pin could be heard falling to the floor; everyone listened as Miss Sherman continued telling the tale. "Lucifer has many names, but is formally known as Satan, the Devil, and the Serpent. Satan is no friend to us but our greatest enemy; he is evil in every sense of the word. His primary goals are to kill, steal, and destroy. Satan will never stop trying to kill your joy and your faith. He likes nothing better than to rob you of God's gift of eternal life and destroy your souls, for he knows he has a short period of time before God banishes him and his demons forever ."

"Then why does God suffer him to continue to live, knowing he will continue to deceive the world?" asked Natalie, who couldn't understand what was going through God's mind, assuming that any of this was real.

"I'll explain in a moment, but for now, I will tell you what happened. In Satan's treachery, he led a revolt in Heaven. Michael, the archangel, and his army of angels overthrew him and cast him down from Heaven. Lucifer, the fallen angel, had fallen from grace. He works continuously to destroy God's creation and mankind through the flesh. Our flesh is not just the outer layer of our skin; it is the sinful part of man that seeks his own self-pleasures and self-will. It seeks to oppose the laws of God and His Spirit that He placed in our most inner hearts and minds. God promised He would put an end to Satan's wickedness one day. God has prepared for Satan and his demons to suffer an eternal torment in the lake of fire and brimstone, and it's also for anyone who worships Satan and partakes in lawlessness."

"But what does Lucifer have to do with Adam and Eve?" Eddie asked this time, raising his hand to speak.

No one shooed him because this was a question everyone wanted to know the answer to.

Miss Sherman took her seat behind her desk and continued. "Adam and Eve had everything they needed in the garden, including God's love, protection, and free will. God warned Adam and Eve never to eat from the Tree of Knowledge of Good and Evil, for if they did, they would surely die. The Tree of Knowledge of Good and Evil was God's tree. It was not to be touched. God did not put the tree in the garden to punish or trick Adam and Eve. God knew what sin would do, and he never wanted them to depend on their knowledge or wisdom, but on His wisdom. God wanted their love and obedience to be given to Him of their own free will. He didn't want to treat them as robots; therefore, he gave them free will. Lucifer wanted to disrupt God's plan for his creation, living in peace, wellness, and harmony. The enemy wanted to get revenge on God; Satan turned to God's creation to create havoc in God's plans, for he was no longer welcomed or needed in the Kingdom of God. The serpent entered the Garden of Eden and beguiled Eve into eating from God's sacred tree. Eve ate from the tree, and she gave Adam the forbidden fruit, and he ate. Realizing they sinned, they hid from God, for they were ashamed; their eyes were open because they knew they disobeyed God. After sin entered the garden, it brought forth death. Satan tricked man into giving up God's provision for wanting what was off-limits, and it was he… that made the serpent talk to Eve in the garden. Still, God loved Adam. He extended mercy by promising them they would one day return to their home someday when one of Eve's offspring would bring forth a Savior who would redeem man back to God. Satan told Eve she would not die, but she would be like God, knowing good and evil. Satan didn't tell Eve that if she ate the fruit, it would damage her relationship with God and cause her and her husband to lose their home in the Garden of Eden. They did not know the hardships they would face outside of Eden. Skilled at mixing lies with the truth, Satan succeeded at separating man from God, so he thought. God had a plan, but for now, Adam and Eve sinned, and they could no longer eat from the Tree of Life, for if they had… the punishment of sin would not have been paid in full. To be clear, it wasn't the tree that led to man's fall from grace, but man's choice. Because of that choice, God couldn't go back on His word. Adam and Eve were evicted from the Garden of Eden."

Miss Sherman paused before telling the worst part of the story. "It was not a clear win for Adam and Eve because their children were born and shaped into iniquity, giving sin a welcoming mat into humanity." Going back to her students' earlier questions, Miss Sherman began answering them to a silenced and enthralled class.

"Why do bad things happen to good people? Because of unbelief and where there is unbelief, there's sin, and its fruit produces violence, persecution, and wars. Satan's evil influences corrupt man's hearts. When bad things happen, it's easier to believe God doesn't exist, believing He could let such things happen. God hates sin, and it was never His plan for mankind to suffer. His plan from the beginning was for man to live forever in paradise, never to get sick and die. He wanted man to live in peace and harmony in his presence for all eternity. From the beginning, sin came into the world; its evil has not been removed from the Earth. But the little god of this world's reign of terror will be over when he is condemned to the lake of fire, no longer able to deceive the nations again. That time is soon to come; it is at the very doorstep. I wish men were immune to the evils and the bad things that happen when drunk drivers drive. Satan influences depression and causes dependency on drugs and alcohol. God wants man to turn to him for love and strength instead of worldly things that only promise empty pleasures, for they cannot heal the soul. But be of good cheer; there is hope. God will always be there to help his people overcome the evil of this world with good. God keeps his promises just as He did in the Garden of Eden. He will restore peace on Earth. God is raising an army that will submit to Him and resist the enemy. His elite will reign with Him always."

While Miss Sherman was finishing the story, the class attentively listened as she told the past events. "Finally, God's angels are always with us."

"I've never seen an angel in my life," said David.

"Miss Sherman, is it true angels walk among us daily?" asked Sam.

"Yes, they do. Most of the time, we are not aware of it; they look like we do. The Holy Bible calls them ministering spirits. They protect, guide, defend, warn of danger, bring joy, and send messages of peace to man. You must learn to call upon them for help. Never should you worship angels because they are servants like us. God releases them to work His purpose in our lives because He loves us."

Charlotte understood God's plan and reiterated, "Bad things happen because of Satan's evil influences on creation. God will punish Satan and his evil demons, and He will restore the world to good."

Miss Sherman was pleased with Charlotte's answer. "Satan's time is almost up; the clock started ticking when

Adam and Eve left the Garden of Eden. Later, God revealed to His prophet Daniel His prophetic time clock, also known as Daniel's prophecy. I will end here for now, but keep reading the book."

Natalie heard nothing about the Bible at home, but she found the stories intriguing and wanted to know more. She could not stop now. She vowed she would finish reading the book.

Changing instructions, Miss Sherman said, "Alright, everyone, let's talk briefly about your book report. I will send home what should be included in your report; you have the option to do a Reading Fair Board and enter it at this year's Reading Fair for extra points. Some of you can present your report in front of the class at the end of the assignment. Also, make sure you are reading daily. You will have a pop quiz soon, so prepare yourselves. Tributes, I was informed that you will receive your packets concerning the game events and the rules. You will be given special uniforms to be worn in the games. The Christmas Ball will be one week before Christmas. Tributes, you will be the first to start the dance. You will dance Woodland's annual dance, the waltz. Be sure to put your dancing feet forward. I trust everyone is familiar with the dance. If you are not, a dance instructor will teach you how to dance during your free period. We will hold the ball on Monday night, and the next day the games will begin at noon. The last tournament will take place on Thursday. We will crown the winners of the final tournament victors of Woodland Academy. Are there questions?"

No hands were raised.

"Very well, shall we continue class?" She passed out a long non-fiction passage with twelve comprehensive questions to answer. "Silently, read the passage and complete the questions at the end of the passage before the bell sounds. Please begin."

The tribute's schedules remained the same, but the tributes were moved to the school's private sector. Lois, the

Headmistress, announced over the PA, “Professors, dismiss tributes from class thirty minutes before class dismissal. They will be taken to their new housing quarters. Thank you, teachers, students, and staff.” Whenever she announced the news, a catchy jingle played over the intercom before she spoke and after she finished speaking.

Classes were over for the day, and Natalie found Sam sitting on a wooden bench with black iron designs, with the WA centered in the iron on both sides of the bench.

“Have you called him?” asked Sam.

“Yes, we talked, and it was great, and I can't wait until the dance.”

“How do you like our new quarters?”

“Honestly, Sam, it's spectacular. It's like staying at the Waldorf Astoria. It's magical here.”

“Especially the balcony overlooking the quiet river, lush trees, and snow-capped mountains.”

Upon their arrival, they brought their luggage to their rooms. Girls and the boys slept two to a room, separate from each other. Lying on the bed, a crème envelope waited for Natalie to read it. At the foot of the bed, there was an ancient vintage trunk with their names engraved outside the trunk, with a key left inside the keyhole. Sam and Natalie stood, wondering what the letter had to say.

“Well, you'd better open it, Natalie.” She opened it and read it aloud.

*Congratulations Tributes:*

*Welcome to your new houses. I'm delighted you made it this far. Your training will begin soon. You will find everything you need inside your trunks. You are expected to attend every training session. Study the handbook's games and rules. It can help you in the games. In the meantime, get settled, explore the castle until tomorrow.*

*Respectfully,*
*Headmistress Lois Stein Howell*

School continued as usual; the ball was a few days away. Sam and Natalie were nervous about the dance. They had gone through the long, tiresome, rigorous training sessions. Woodland offered training in hand-to-hand combat, survival skills, and physical training. The tributes learned from their handbook that they would have to survive the games quickly. Each group will be placed in a separate arena. Their goal will be to figure out the game's mysteries, using the game's clues to end the game. Extra lives will be rewarded to tributes who are lucky enough to find them in the games. However, tributes had to figure out the hidden mysteries within one hour to end the games.

Each group was competing for first and second place. The teams that place first will receive three times outs, and the second-place team will receive two times outs. Third and fourth place will receive one time out in the last tournament. First and second place winners will face off; third and fourth place winners will face off in the second half of the last tournament. Fifty points go to first-place game-winners and their winning grade level hall. Thirty points will go to second place and the hall winners. Ten points to third-place winners and fourth-place winners shall receive five points.

Natalie made it to Chapter Fifteen, where she learned about the Messiah, God's only son. She read about His life, burial, and resurrection. She wondered why Christ would leave his home to die for humanity. For the first time, Natalie wanted to know God and His Son because He loved man so much. He gave His only begotten Son to die for the world who knew him not. Christ's crucifixion touched her heart, where she couldn't shake it.

The next day, Miss Sherman walked into the garden and saw Natalie sitting with her head down. Miss Sherman asked if something was bothering her; she replied, "Miss Sherman, I have a problem."

"What is it, dear?"

"I've been reading the book you assigned, but in all my life, I have never been taught about God or Jesus at home. My parents are great, but they are not religious. They believe in science and scientific reasoning. They told me once, when I asked how the world was formed, that billions of years ago, there was a big bang in the universe. It created the stars, the moon, galaxies, and life began from the Big Bang, but their theory contradicts what I read in the book and what you discussed in class about creation. I have been reading the Holy Bible that Sam let me borrow. I came to believe God is real," said Natalie.

"I am happy you heard His voice and accepted the truth. Only those who hear His voice accept the truth."

"Why did I not hear his voice before?"

"You had never heard the gospel until now."

"You can accept the truth because you have accepted Him by faith. God gave us His Spirit and created us in His image. We have an inner conviction that death is not the end of life, and Heaven exists. Many people deny the truth or ignore it, but our conscience speaks. A still small voice tells us it is true. Natalie, you don't have to ignore His voice anymore; you must trust what He is saying to you in your heart and His Word."

"Sam told me God would make Himself clear to me, and she was right."

"Natalie, many are called, but few are chosen, and you are a chosen vessel. You have faith now and do not lose it. Natalie, you believe without seeing Him face to face."

"You told me you had a dilemma; what is it?"

"My parents will not understand my new faith."

"Are you telling me your parents are unbelievers?"

Natalie nodded her head.

"I don't understand. Your parents signed the permission slip agreeing you could read the book along with the class."

Natalie didn't want Miss Sherman to know her parents didn't sign her permission slip. She responded, "They signed for educational purposes."

"I see. Eventually, Natalie, you will have to tell your parents about your faith."

"I will; I am still working on how to do it."

"Natalie, God is with you, and He is going to help you trust Him." Miss Sherman replied.

"Thanks, Miss Sherman, for listening to me."

"I am always here for my students whenever they need to talk." She smiled and left her in the garden.

# Chapter Fourteen

# The Ball

Natalie's mother sent her dress by a carrier to her school. The dress was pressed and steamed inside the garment bag when it arrived. She held the dress in its plastic clear bag up to her body in the mirror. The ball couldn't come quickly enough, for she was eager to wear the dress to the ball.

Trever phoned and reminded her that he and Damon would wait for her and Sam in the corridor the night of the ball.

There in Huldah's Hall, Woodland began preparing for the most grandiose ball of the century. Huldah Hall was a marvelous room with a grand dance floor, and the professors spared no expense in decorating the hall. Floors, walls, and tables received the royal treatment using the finest décor Woodland Academy offered. An ice sculptor of the school's mascot dove was flown in from France, with an olive branch perched in its beak, and was placed on a base above the punch bowl. While the hall was being tended to, students were busy rounding up dates to the ball.

Eddie Piper passed Charlotte Simpson a letter in history class, asking if she would attend the ball with him. It surprised her. He asked, for they differed entirely from each other. She read the note and smiled and nodded.

Danny and Jeffery were finding it hard to find dates. Every time they asked a girl to the ball, they replied, “I've been asked, sorry.”

Danny and Jeffery thought they might never find a date to the ball and become the school's laughingstocks, but they agreed to keep trying.

John Melton, the boy's good friend, hung out with them often. They all stood in archery uniforms on green artificial turf with their bows and arrows in their hands, each shot their arrows, hitting their bullseye targets one by one.

“I hear you guys haven't found a date yet,” said John.

“It isn't as easy as it looks. Everyone we've asked was already asked to the ball,” replied Jeffery.

“What about Shelly Longstreet?”

Jeffery wasn't jumping for joy when John suggested Shelly because he thought she was a wallflower. “What about her?”

“I hear she hasn't been asked to the ball.”

“Shelly is a lovely girl, but she doesn't talk very much.”

“She is perfect for you because your mouth is a regular Seven Eleven.”

John and Danny chuckled hysterically while Jeffery mocked them with a pretend laugh expression. “Real funny guys, real funny.”

“Seriously!” said Danny. “You'd better get a move on it before she's taken.”

“Guess what, genius? You're still dateless too, Danny.”

"Not for long, my friend. I am asking Mary Tolls today."

"You know she is a tribute, and someone could have asked her before you," replied John.

"She's always in the garden in the afternoons. Why don't you ask her there?"

"That's brilliant! Thanks, John."

"Don't thank me yet; you still have to ask her out."

"I got this dude; it's in the bag. But just in case, wish me luck," Danny said as he shot his last arrow into the target range.

The ball was approaching quickly, and Jeffery knew time was running out, and he had to ask Shelly Longstreet to the ball before it was too late. He found her in the library, looking for a book to check out. He pretended to look for a book behind her, and when she turned and noticed him, he said, "Hi! Shelly."

"Hi! Jeffery. Do you need help to locate a book?"

"I am looking for *Lord of the Flies*."

"Oh, yes, that's written by William Golding, and it's a great read. I think you will enjoy it. The book is about a group of boys stranded on a tropical island without adult supervision. The boys elect a leader named Ralph, and things take a dark turn in the book."

They walked to the fiction section, and Shelly found the book on the middle shelf and handed it to Jeffery.

"Thank you."

"You're welcome. You will let me know what you thought of the book once you finish, won't you?"

Jeffery thought to himself that if he had been looking for a book to read, *Lord of the Flies* would have been it. Shelly had painted an intriguing summary of the book. "Sure, I will," he said cheerfully. Jeffery didn't realize how much Shelly loved to read. He came to appreciate her love of books. Jeffery did not understand books that could be fun to read. Although he got good grades, he came to Woodland because his parents made him. Jeffery was from a wealthy family, and he was quite good-looking, with blonde hair and a great sense of humor.

Shelly was impressed with Jeffery's choice to read *Lord of the Flies* and saw a different light in him. She thought to herself, maybe there was more to him than meets the surface. She could kick herself for misjudging him.

Jeffery knew if he was going to ask her to the ball, the time was now. His hands became sweaty, and his knees became weak. "You know the ball is a few days away, and I was wondering if you would like to go with me." He couldn't understand why he behaved in this manner. Never had he acted this way around her before.

Shelly had gray eyes, fair skin, and long, wavy, strawberry blonde hair, pulled back into a ponytail. Jeffery was tall, with light brown eyes, didn't know if she would say yes or no, but he hoped she had not been asked to the ball.

Shelly was relieved that he had asked her to the ball. The previous boy who asked her canceled because of a tragedy in his family. She thought before answering, "Why not? It could be fun."

Elated, he finally got a date. Now it was time to check on Danny.

Later that afternoon, Danny found Mary in the garden, but she was not alone; her friends surrounded her. Reluctantly, Danny didn't want to talk, not with her friends being there. He left the garden and found John and Jeffery back at the dormitory.

"Did you seal the deal?" asked Jeffery.

"No, too many of her friends were around."

"How did things go with you?"

"She said yes."

"Dude, that's outstanding!" said Danny.

"One down, one to go," said John.

"Dan, ask her today, but it looks like you are going to need reinforcements. John and I are going to help you. Now here's what we are going to do," Jeffery said.

The boys started plotting a divisive plan.

The boys found Mary and her friends sitting at the picnic tables outside the cafeteria. John and Jeffery walked over to the girls and put their plan into action.

"We have a message from the Headmistress. She summons you to meet her in the Gather Hall."

The girls stood to leave.

"Except for you, Mary!" Jeffery interjected.

Mary looked at her friends and said, "I'll catch up with you guys later," as she finished eating her grilled chicken salad. The boys followed behind the girls, passing Danny, standing nearby, and signaling the coast clear. Danny winked his right eye at his friends and walked over to Mary's table. He sat across from her and said, "Hello, Mary."

"Hi, Danny!" she said kindly and continued.

"Is there something you wanted?"

"I wanted to ask you… How's your day going?"

"Fine and yours?"

"I don't know yet; it's still early."

Mary couldn't help but laugh at his witty remark.

"How does it feel being a tribute?"

"Exhausting! The training sessions are brutal, but I'm prepared."

"Speaking of the games, would you like to go to the ball with me?"

"I have been asked several times, but I haven't decided who should take me."

"How about taking a swing here with the Gusto Kid?" He pointed to himself while doing the backhand bounce in front of her.

Mary laughed. "Gusto? Are you telling me you can dance?"

"Dance, what does this tell you?" He stepped on top of the table, clapped his hands, wiggled his hips, and did a backflip off the table, and then transitioned to a half split as he came up from the ground.

Students standing by clapped when they saw what Danny had done.

"Thank you! Thank you very much," he said in his best Elvis Presley impersonation voice. "Well, my lady?"

Wowed with his moves and playful wit, she said coolly, "I will let you know."

"When will you let me know?"

"Not when, but how. If you see a pink carnation pinned to the school's elm tree today at four o'clock, my answer is yes. If you see a violet floral, my answer is no."

"Four o'clock, eh? You're on."

She smiled at him and left the table.

Danny found his friends after his encounter with Mary in the courtyard. His wide grin screamed. He had a date for the ball.

"Did she say yes?" asked Jeffery.

"Not exactly."

"Then why are you smiling?"

"Because she is going to say yes."

"I have to go to the school's elm to find a pink carnation at four o'clock today."

"What's a flower got to do with the ball?" John asked.

"It means she will go to the ball with me."

"What time is it now?" asked John.

Jeffery looked at his watch and said, "12:30 p.m."

"Wonderful! Why do girls make you wait so long for an answer? Don't they know keeping us in suspense is torture on us?" John asked his friends as they laughed down the hall to class.

Danny couldn't concentrate in Professor Blackmon's math class; he couldn't possibly take being rejected again. Waiting for the day to end was driving him nuts.

Danny thought four o'clock would never come. When it did, he and his friends raced to check the elm with him. Placed at eye level, they saw a pink carnation pinned to the tree.

"Congrats. Hombre! You got a date?" said Jeffery.

"Not just a date, a tribute!"

"Thanks, guys, for all your help."

"We got you in the door; the rest was all you," John replied.

"That had to have been one surprising rap you laid on her," replied Jeffery.

"Fellas, when you got it. You got it," replied Danny.

***

Natalie thought to herself, *Tonight is the night* as she looked at herself in the mirror. She looked fetching in her dazzling blue gown. In twenty minutes, she'd walk out the door to the ball. Sam, Damon, and Trever were waiting for her in the corridor. The moment she walked in, Trever's heart skipped two beats when he saw her. Trever took her by the arm. "You look like an angel tonight, Nat."

"Thank you, and you look handsome."

The boys wore black tuxedos with bow ties matching their dates' dresses. Sam wore a long sweetheart mermaid dress and elbow-length white gloves. On her left wrist, she wore an exquisite heirloom bracelet that sparkled in the light. Sam's hair was styled curly, while Natalie's went with an updo French roll.

Damon and Trever were two Princes of Wales.

Coach Sax walked in and announced, "Tributes, it's time to march in; follow me." He led them down a long hall of large antique mirrors hanging on each side of the hall. Music on the other side of the wall thundered as they walked down the hall. Royal guards on both sides of the hall stood in a line from each end as they watched the couples escort their dates into the ball. Entering the ball, two Royal Guards stood on each side of the double doors. They blew their trumpets and entered. Everyone in the ball stopped to watch them enter at the top of the stairs.

A guard announced, "Please rise for this year's tributes of the Academy's games."

They remained standing as they made it to the dance floor. A guard dressed in maroon, gold, and white royal attire said, "Let the ball commence."

Applauding with cheer, the party got underway. Headmistress Lois took the stage and said, "Let the waltz begin."

The orchestra chose a famous Austrian waltz piece. Each tribute and their escorts took to the floor and danced the waltz, as did the rest of the party. Once it was time to slow dance, the ceiling became a starry sky with a large, round moon casting its moonlight onto the dance floor. Snow flurries fell as they danced under the stars.

Natalie fell in love with Woodland Academy and Trever at that moment. She was living a fairy tale, and she didn't want the night to end.

The faculty dressed in royal attire, and every girl wore elegant ball gowns of different colors and fabrics. Despite Sam's dislike for her dress, Natalie thought her dress was adorable. Sam admitted to Natalie that she had the bodice, and the bottom of the dress was reconstructed while their dates got them a punch. "That sweetheart top was a great design idea." Said Natalie. "I thought so too." Said Sam.

On the stage were two throne chairs, one for the Headmistress and the second reserved for Coach Sax. A crystal palace was the ball. Enchanting design features were etched into the floor, and the columns were decorated with white lights and exquisite fabrics wrapped around them. The stage was decorated with a royal canopy of royal fabric trimmed in gold designs at the fabric's border. They decorated the tables with beautiful crystal sculptures and flowers. A modern band played after the orchestra had left the ball.

John, Jeffery, and Danny had a blast laughing and dancing with Mary, Shelly, and Nina. They had a grand time together. The dance lasted until eleven o'clock. School chaperones kept a watchful eye on their students.

Trever and Natalie took a break from the dance floor. They sat down to talk and got to know each other better. Trever asked Natalie to go steady with him, and she accepted. Trever and Damon told Sam and Natalie how much they loved Woodland and wanted to attend the school. They danced until the ball ended.

Damon and Trever went back to Memphis, but each promised to write and call every chance they got.

Caleb watched Natalie when she entered the ball with Trever. Caleb didn't ask Natalie to the ball because he had promised one of his teammates he would escort his sister to the ball. Although Caleb was a perfect gentleman to his date, he couldn't stop thinking of Natalie. Caleb noticed Trever and Damon were not Woodland students, for he never saw them around campus. One thing didn't go unnoticed: Natalie had a boyfriend, and it wasn't him. He decided he would not give up on Natalie so easily. One advantage Caleb had going for him was that he and Natalie attended the same school, and with Trever out of the way, he could make Natalie his girl. Caleb decided not to keep his feelings hidden from her anymore. He had to act fast because Natalie was a tribute in the games. Leaving him with little time to win over Natalie, Caleb thought long and hard about what he would do next to win Natalie's heart before the games started.

# Chapter Fifteen

# The Games

The trumpets sounded at six o'clock a.m. around campus for five minutes. Natalie didn't mind the wake-up call because she was already awake. She took a deep breath, exhaled, and said, "Today the games begin," while the trumpets thundered away.

Across from her bed, she heard Sam awakening. Stretching her arms apart, Sam yawned and sat up on the bed.

"Are you awake, Sam?"

"Who could sleep with those blasted trumpets going?"

Natalie smiled at her friend and gazed out the castle's window.

"How long have you been awake?" asked Sam.

"Not knowing what awaits us in the arena has kept me awake all night." Natalie walked over to Sam's bed and sat next to her. "No matter what we face in the games, we will face it as a team. There's one team that's going to win the games, and it's going to be seventh grade; besides, all's fair in war and competition."

Both girls fist-bumped in their PJs and said, "Seventh-grade strong by choice."

"Why don't we try to get some more shut-eye before the games begin, huh?"

Natalie agreed. She snuggled under her blankets and drifted off to sleep.

They set the games to start at 9:00 a.m. Sam woke Natalie up and said, "We'd best get ready; Natalie, it's eight o'clock."

Natalie nodded, got out of bed, and opened her trunk. She retrieved the one-piece spandex uniform. Woodland Academy was written across the uniform's top in block format, and underneath it was the number three stitched in. On the back of the garment was her last name, Evergreen.

Sixth and seventh grades had different odd numbers, while the eighth and ninth grades received various even numbers. Each tribute wore black spandex shoes in the games.

Natalie's team headed to the games with the other teams.

Woodland students deemed it a tremendous honor to win the games. The winning team would receive eternal glory, recognition, praise, and the Quarter Annual Cup. The games were the school's Elders' grandest events; this is where tributes are chosen to attend classes not offered to the rest of the student body. Tributes selected by the Elders were taught secret mysteries of the school and concealed courses no one could mention. No one ever knew what students were learning and mastering, but the tributes themselves, who kept that knowledge of the school under embargo. Frequently, non-tributes from the previous year would ask tributes out of morbid curiosity about what they were learning and doing, but no tribute would tell, for the elders forbade them. Throughout the history of the games, tributes' names, feats, and accomplishments were recorded in the history of the games. Students wanted to win because they would go on to greatness, securing their legacy in the Hall of Fame, a tradition dating back centuries.

The packed stadium was filled with students who had been anticipating the games since the first day of school. The wait was over. Students wore their vibrant hall-colored hats, shawls, boots, coats, and gloves to the games. The band played while students cheered with enthusiasm over the sounds of cannons.

After the firing of the cannons, it was time to start the games. The Headmistress brought the games to order. The faculty listened in the stands as she opened the games with an inviting welcome. Then followed the announcements of the team's captains. Students cheered for their favorite team captains in their halls.

The Headmistress explained the aim and purpose of the games. "The rules are simple. Each team must complete its games before time runs out. Each team will receive instructions and aid in the games. You must figure out how to exit the games quickly before the opposing teams. The team that leaves the game first wins first place, second place, and so forth."

In her gray caped gown, Headmistress Lois stood on a large platform stage on the field and turned her attention to the tributes and spoke. "Tributes, please join me on stage." She gestured for them to come forward on the platform. There were four sizable glass elevators on the platform. Teams took steps onto the platform in a single-file line by grade level. Four glass elevators were on stage, with each grade level number written above its doors. "Tributes, you may enter the elevators. Know this: if any team wishes to leave the games, that team must leave the games together, and instantly, you will exit the games and be given a forfeit. If you remain in the game and time runs out, your hall will lose ten points and be placed fourth in the competition.

Teams that complete their games will be awarded up to fifty points. The first-place hall receives forty points, the second-place hall receives thirty points, and the remaining twenty points. Good luck! Let the games begin!" Quickly, she exited the stage, and the glass doors closed.

Above the platform, in mid-air, golden numbers began a countdown. "Ten, nine, eight, seven, six, five, four, three, two, one," counted the crowd.

A shot clock buzzed, and tributes dropped below ground in the blink of an eye. Butterflies filled their abdomens as they fell into underground chambers. Bloodcurdling screams inside the elevators roared as the chamber lights flickered off and on, and the elevator continued to drop for what seemed like a thousand hours. The elevators came to a halt, and the doors opened at the same time. The tributes entered their arenas in awe and amazement because they were on a football field just a few seconds ago; here, they are in a vast, strange land they knew nothing about.

In the stadium, four enormous separate holograms appeared before the school's body from the field, allowing everyone to view what was happening in the games.

Natalie's team walked into a wintry white forest while the sixth-grade's door opened to a lush rainforest. The eighth-grade door opened to a white sandy beach with glowing, clear peacock blue ocean water. Meanwhile, the ninth-grade door opened to a sweltering desert with dunes.

Tributes walked into their arenas, and instantly their uniforms changed. Natalie's team, also known as Team B, was snuggly warm in their puffy crème hooded coats, scarves, mittens, pants, crème beige beanie hats, and snow boots.

Sam didn't care that their uniforms changed; she was happy she wouldn't freeze to death. Sam hated cold weather; her mind raced back to when she was eight years old. One frigid winter, snow fell ten inches, blanketing the city. Her family thought it would be fun to go out and build a snowman. Her hands had gotten so cold inside her gloves, forming the snowman's head until her hands burned as if they were on fire. The throbbing pain was like tiny needles piercing her skin repeatedly. Her hands and fingers throbbed, and they hurt more as she warmed them by the fire. Never did she ever forget she couldn't move her fingers, and if her parents had not told her otherwise, she swore her fingers had gotten frostbitten. From that day on, she hated cold weather with a passion.

As the teams began getting a better look at their surroundings, they found a brown burlap bag tied with white rope next to the elevator's door. A few feet away, they saw a pair of glowing blue eyes floating toward them without a body.

"Whoa, what's that?" cried Dexter. His heart skipped two beats, and his knees started shaking as the pair of eyes drew closer.

They stood, unable to move, as they couldn't believe their eyes. This ghostly figure materialized into a fluffy white fox that came near them and sat on its hind legs. "Hello! Tributes, my name is Shadow Faxx. I am here to aid and escort you midway through the game."

Charlotte thought her mind was playing tricks on her. No matter how sly foxes are, they don't talk. But here, this adorable fox, who looks like a stuffed animal you win at a carnival, is speaking intelligently to them, which was staggering. "You're here to help us?" asked Charlotte.

"That's correct, and you are?"

Charlotte whispered to Dexter, "Pinch me, please. I can't tell if this is real or if I am dreaming."

"I hate to burst your bubble, but he's as real as the nose on your face."

"Great, just great," said Charlotte.

Natalie interrupted, "Please forgive us, Shadow Faxx. We've never seen a talking fox before."

"It's alright; I know this must come as a shock to you, but you need not fear me, for I am on your side; little tributes."

Natalie was a natural; she talked to Shadow Faxx as if she spoke to animals all her life. "I am Natalie Evergreen, the team's captain, and this is Dexter Greene."

Dexter smiled at him.

"And this is Samantha Harper," to whom she pointed.

"Good day, mate," said Sam.

Shadow Faxx acknowledged with a regal nod.

"This is Dave Kissinger, Lyle Boggs, Mary Tolls, Eddie Piper, and you've met Charlotte Simpson."

Charlotte waved, but it was clear the lights were on, but no one was home behind her eyes.

Dexter waited to hear what Shadow Faxx would tell them next. "Tributes, you have little time. The clock started the moment you entered the arena. Check your wrist and say, "Time left."

Natalie pulled back her coat sleeve and saw a sleek black watch on her wrist. She did as Shadow Faxx commanded. Holding her watch up to her lips, she asked, "Time left?"

Fifty-five minutes displayed in 3-D before her; five minutes passed; *Shadow Faxx was right. We've got to get moving,* she thought to herself.

"Look inside the bag and read the card," prompted Shadow Faxx.

Natalie opened the bag, found the card, and read it to the rest. "Tributes, you are in the Wintry Forrest. Shadow Faxx will be your temporary guide. You must rely on each other. Use your wits to figure out the clues in the poem to exit the game. Use supplies from the bag when needed to help you along the way. Do remember the Elders are watching; best of luck, Headmistress Lois Stein Howell." Natalie flipped the card over and read the poem.

*Move down the path.*
*Observe your surroundings; the square root of nine is the math.*
*Unusual surprises around the bend; use what's in your midst.*
*Never let your guard down, use your wits,*
*Take refuge over the river; see the thing shapely formed.*
*Add the initial sound of the poem.*
*Initiate, initiate, initiate.*
*Nerves are your friend.*
*Start from where you began.*

"The first clue means we have to find the right path and continue on it until it's time to solve the next clue from the poem," said Charlotte.

"Very good!" said Shadow Faxx.

"Which direction do we take to find the right path?" asked Eddie Piper, who looked around the forest.

"Everyone, spread out and walk," said Natalie.

Lyle Boggs said, "We should walk north."

"What makes you so sure?" asked Eddie.

"My father and I go camping every summer. He told me if I ever got lost in the woods to walk north and listen for water." He took two steps north, and the snow turned into a crystal glass road. The clouds rolled back, revealing a clear sunny blue sky. In the backdrop, three huge, rugged mountains with snow-peaked caps.

"Follow the road tributes, before it disappears, hurry!" said Shadow Faxx.

"Good thinking, Lyle," said Natalie.

"It was nothing," Lyle replied as he grabbed the bag of supplies from the snow. "Move out, everyone!" Natalie commanded.

Everyone hurried down the road together with Shadow Faxx at their side.

# Chapter Sixteen

# Arenas

Sixth grade, also known as Team A, walked into a tropical, lush rain forest arena in their rugged terrain safari gear. Team A moved into the area as if they had been there before, the team in black T-shirts, rain hats, khaki knee-high shorts, and pants. Around their waist, members had access to black utility belts. Inside, its secret compartments on the belts housed insect repellants and other survival tools to help them in the arena.

They blazed the trail through the marshlands in waterproof boots. Team A wasted no time figuring out clues from the metal cage hanging from a bamboo tree. Keev`oo, their guide, was perched inside the cage with more supplies such as a water bottle, a long, sharp knife, rope, and a map. Keev`oo was over twenty-five centimeters long, black with a golden-orange yellow crown mantle. His wings were black-tipped, and his feet black. His iris and bill were yellow. He was the most beautiful Regent Bowerbird Dale

Lester, the team captain, had ever seen. He read the card and located their positions on the map provided. Dale looked at his watch and said to his team. "We have to head west quickly if we want to secure first place."

"You've answered well," Keev`oo said to Dale as he perched himself on his shoulder. With his teammates behind him, he led them through the jungle.

***

Team C, eighth graders, were clothed in a Boyle shorty long sleeve one-piece navy blue, turquoise, and red front zip wetsuit. The doors opened to a sandy beach arena. Large flax leaves hung from several trees on the island. The mist from the ocean created a prism in the wind as the rippling waves washed up on the shore. The ocean water was a peacock blue. The mist of the ocean tickled their faces gently. On the beach, a black net chock full of supplies.

Simone Redd found the net's instructions and read them to the group. "We have to leave the island to get to the next clue, according to the card," said Simone.

"How on earth do we get off this island? I don't exactly see any boats or rafts around here?" Tim Meeks noted that he couldn't swim a toll.

Simone looked at the net again and noticed a large shell tangled in it that hadn't been there before, with a note inside. The note instructed her to blow into it three times. Simone placed her lips on the tubular shell and blew three times. Nothing happened, and after a few seconds, Tim said, "Look, guys. Something is moving in the water, and it's approaching fast!"

Everyone stood watching when two dolphins swam to the shore. "Which of you called?" asked one dolphin.

"I did," said Simone.

"Are you the team captain?"

"I am."

"Greetings! My name is Silver, and this is Blue. Blue cannot speak, but he is one of the fastest swimmers in the ocean."

Blue nodded his head back and forth, splashing water onto the tributes. The tributes laughed at the playful dolphin.

"Have you read the card?"

"Yes, but I don't see how we can get off the island to get to the next clue."

"I don't think we have to wonder where we have to go next," said James Gaudy, pushing his bifocal glasses onto his face.

"What makes you say that?" asked Simone.

"Don't you see the cay ahead?" He was pointing to it in the water.

"What cay?"

"It's about twelve miles out," cried James.

Simone saw nothing; she looked through a pair of binoculars from the net supplies. The cay was there, as James said. When she removed the binoculars, the island was gone. She looked through the binoculars again. The cay was there.

"It's obvious we need glasses to see the cay to get to it. How are we going to get to the cay? I am probably the only one here who can't swim," cried Tim, terrified of the water.

"I didn't know you couldn't swim, Tim. For Heaven's sake, we're roommates," replied James. "I told no one; I kept it to myself until now."

"Tim cannot swim, and we don't have an inflatable raft to help us get to the island. What are we going to do?" James asked Simone.

"We have to get across somehow; the time is ticking," Tim said, looking at his watch.

"We can help you get across," Silver said. He made several dolphin distress noises, and a group of dolphins swam to shore instantly. "Simone, you can command them," said Silver.

"Tributes, we're going to ride the dolphins to get to the cay."

The team used flippers, rope, goggles, and pocketknives from the supplies. Simone devised a plan to get her teammates off the island to the cay. "Everyone, place the rope into your dolphin's mouths and tie the rest around your waist nice and tight. Use the rest of the rope as reins to balance your weight as you ride the dolphins with your feet planted firmly on your dolphin's back," Simone commanded.

"It's like riding surfboards, except the boards are dolphins," James said to Tim as he took a position to ride his dolphin.

Twenty minutes passed as they looked at their watches. Facing the cay, Simone told Tim he would ride Blue and one of his kin. "Hold on tight to the rope, Tim, and you will be fine. Silver and I will surf beside you the entire way." She kneeled and whispered to Blue, "Please, Blue, keep him safe and don't lose him."

Blue let Simone know innately as he looked her in her eyes; he would take care of Tim. The team had suited up and was ready to go. Leading the way, Simone commanded the dolphins, "To the cay as fast as light." With Simone on Silver's back and his kin, they shot through the water like a bullet, leaving a Colt 45 barrel. The team continued onward to find the next clue.

***

In the last group, Team D's arena was a desert with massive dunes. The ninth graders were Arabian nomads in the game. The sun beamed down on their heads, but the boys' turbans and the girls' sheer, lightweight Tuareg scarves kept their heads cool from the Sahara Desert heat. They wore white robes and loose drawstring cotton pants to keep them cool in the desert heat. Stratus clouds smeared across the sky. The dunes were as tall as giant anthills and great for sand gliding.

The team figured out the clues and met their guide, Midnight, an Egyptian Siamese. His ebony coat turned bluish when the sunlight warmed it. Midnight's neck collar had Egyptian hieroglyphics engraved into the golden collar. In the center of the collar hung a milky pearl opal, underneath it a single gold tassel. His green eyes changed to gray if danger was near and yellow whenever his mood changed.

Shannon Flemings, the team's leader, led them through the desert using clues on the card found in an empty water pot. The teams searched for the next clue through the sand as the parchment card instructed when they unwarily walked into the sinking sand. They had sunk slowly to the bottom of the sands, which didn't help their time on the clock. Finally, the sand gave way to an underground tunnel. Everyone dropped to the bottom, and Shannon asked, "Is everybody alright?"

Kevin Strong looked over the team as they shook the sand off themselves. He replied, "Yes! We're fine."

Mike Simmons asked, "Where are we?"

"I don't know, but we have got to find a way out of here," Shannon said, encouraging the team to keep going.

The team quickly regrouped and continued to look for a way out. Thomas Lynch, the rotund, inquisitive member of the team, helped figure out most of the game's clues and knew the journey would not be comfortable, but he agreed with Shannon that they had to keep going, even though they didn't know where the tunnel was leading them.

# Chapter Seventeen

# Getting Out

Team B was deep into the winter forest, and they heard not a sound as they continued onward. "Is it me? Or is this part of the forest creepier than ever? I feel we're being watched," said Charlotte.

"We are," replied Shadow Faxx promptly.

"How do you know?" asked Sam as she kneeled next to him.

He leaned back and sniffed the air with his coal nose. "I picked up a familiar scent as we had been walking for the last five minutes. We're being hunted. Keep your ears open and your eyes peeled," Shadow Faxx said cautiously.

"Everyone, stay together and keep moving," commanded Natalie.

Soon, the path came to a clearing in the forest with three massive mountains in front of them, with less than forty-five minutes left on the clock to go.

"Where do we go now?" Lyle asked.

Natalie reached into her pocket, retrieved the card, and read the poem aloud once more.

*Move down the path.*
*Observe your surroundings; the square root of nine is the math.*
*Unusual surprises around the bend; use what's in your midst.*
*Never let your guard down, use your wits.*
*Take refuge over the river; see the thing shapely formed.*
*Add the initial sound of the poem.*
*Initiate, initiate, initiate,*
*Nerves will be your friend.*
*Start from where you began.*

Lyle considered the first letter of the poem and said, "That's it! The poem spells out MOUNTAINS!" Lyle had done it again and solved another clue.

"Brilliant, Lyle!" said Charlotte.

"Which of the mountains do we take?" asked Dexter.

"Remember the poem said the square root of nine is the math; the square root of nine is three," replied Charlotte.

"Does that mean we have to climb the mountain?" asked Sam, who didn't take too kindly to heights.

Natalie thought long and hard about the last clue. "I'm not sure, Sam," said Natalie. "The last clue said, the end will lead you where you began. I think we have to get to the third mountain and look for another clue, and that will tell us what to do next."

"Wait a minute, that makes perfect sense," said Charlotte to Natalie. "We won't have to climb the mountain but enter inside, and that will lead us to where we began."

"Excellent little tributes!" said Shadow Faxx.

Natalie's team had figured out how to exit the games, and she couldn't have been prouder of her team. Now she was ready to lead her team to victory. "We have to get across the river to get to the mountains."

"Newsflash, you guys, none of us have a boat or a canoe to get across," said Dexter to his team, bewildered at the thought of crossing a river without a floatation device.

"The poem answered that as well; we have to use what's in our midst," said Charlotte.

"What are we waiting for?" said Mary.

"Nothing!" replied Dave.

"Congratulations, tributes, you have solved the game! Follow me," said Shadow Faxx.

They followed the trotting fox down the path toward the mountains. Shadow Faxx stopped in his tracks abruptly, as if he had been caught in a trap.

"What's wrong?" asked Natalie, wondering why Shadow Faxx halted.

His nose pointed in the air, and his ears were pointing straight up; danger was near. "Stay close; we are not alone anymore!" Shadow Faxx demanded.

"Tributes form a circle," said Natalie. Natalie saw red eyes and the breath of a wild animal lurking behind the black bar trees in the thicket of the woods. Slowly, five black wolves with fangs exposed came forward. They growled and snarled at Shadow Faxx and the tributes.

With their backs against each other, Eddie sarcastically replied, "Unusual surprises around the bend."

"We've got to do something, or else we're toast," cried Eddie Piper.

"Head for the oak tree, climb as fast as you can!" said Natalie, in hopes the hungry pack of wolves would not devour her and her team.

"We can't leave the trail now when we're this close to the mountains," screamed Dave Kissinger, who had spoken little since he entered the games.

"Oh, now he speaks!" cried Sam.

Natalie's forehead wrinkled, and her cheeks were apples when she looked at Dave and said, “Do you have a better idea? We've got to, or none of us will make it out of here alive.” Natalie stared at the wolves and continued, “Everyone run on three. ONE, TWO, RUN!” yelled Natalie.

The wolves pursued the tributes as they ran to an oak tree. A leap became a gigantic stride. There was something magical that gave them the power to fly. They landed safely, including Shadow Faxx, onto a sturdy, large middle branch in the tree.

Dave, trailing behind, was last in line to get to the tree.

“Hurry!” Everyone cried from the middle of the tree. The more he ran, the more the wolves were gaining on him. Two seconds away from the oak, Dave took a considerable leap while mid-air, as one wolf sliced Dave's hind right leg. His wound was severe. Four bright red clawed stripes shone through his ripped pants.

Back at the stadium, students gasped when Dave's leg was viciously attacked.

Dave whaled in anguish as the warm, bright red blood streamed down his leg. Charlotte took her scarf and bound it around his leg to stop the bleeding. He never felt pain like that ever in his life. Dave thought any longer on the ground; he would have been a goner. He was glad he was still alive.

“We can't stay here forever; we have to defeat them and get back to the trail!” said Dave as he felt his wounded leg.

Eddie looked down at the salivating wolves circling the tree.

“But how do we do that? Not to mention, get across the river and enter the third mountain before our time runs out?” Mary Tolls asked.

The wolves patiently waited for their prey above them. Natalie knew Dave's leg needed medical attention;

prolonging their escape increases Dave's risk of infection. Out of ideas, she knew every move she thought could cost their lives.

"Let's leave the game; there's nothing we can do," Charlotte said with moist eyes for her team.

The look on their faces told Natalie they were ready to give up. "Do you all feel the same way?"

No one said a word.

Natalie took a deep breath and snapped off two branches above her head from the tree, leaving a sharp point on the ends. She broke a smaller piece of wood from the tree and threw it.

The wolves followed the sound with their heads, and without a thought, she dropped from the tree while the noise distracted the wolves. The wolves quickly turned their attention back to Natalie, and one attacked her in midair. It weighed three times Natalie's weight, knocking her to the ground. There came a wailing cry from the wolf as he lay on top of Natalie in the snow.

The team watched in horror from the tree while the hungry wolves waited to gobble Natalie up.

"Is she dead?" Sam asked, fearing the worst.

Both lay lifeless on the ground in the snow. Slowly, the tributes saw slight movements. Natalie pushed the wolf off her; the wolf landed on the branch's point, puncturing him in the heart.

Lyle and Dexter broke branches and came to her aid, killing two wolves in the fight. Recognizing their defeat, the two wolves remaining gave up and scurried cowardly back into the woods.

Eddie, Lyle, and Dexter helped Dave from the tree while Shadow Faxx and the girls followed behind. "Three cheers for Natalie, our brave captain. Hip, hip, hooray hip, hip, hooray hip, hip, hooray!" cried her team, lifting her onto their shoulders.

"Tributes, we've got to get to the river, now!"

They stopped celebrating and followed the white fox to the river.

The tributes made it to the riverbank, where chunks of ice cracked across the river. "Let's hitch a ride on the ice to get across to the mountains on the other side."

"Of course! Use what is in our midst said the poem," Charlotte exclaimed.

The water current floated the ice toward the tributes, and they floated on top of the water on the ice across the river and made it safely to the other side.

"This is where I leave you tributes, good luck, and from this moment on, use your wits. Natalie, you have shown tremendous bravery. I know you will lead your team to victory. Now go, little tributes," said Shadow Faxx, and with a blink of an eye, he vanished.

The tributes made it across the river and hurried to the third mountain. There was a cave at the base of the mountain. Above its entrance, written in black letters, "Congratulations tributes! You have found the key to exit the game. Beware! Once you enter, you will have twenty minutes to find the exit before the air runs out of the cave. Do not enter the cave until ready; time will not start over."

Judging by the cave's size, Natalie knew the cave was too small for all of them to enter together. "There are eight of us. How do we make it through the cave in time before the air runs out, and how can we know how far off the exit doors are?" asked Dexter.

"Why can't they just say here is the way out? Instead, they give us another test from hell!" said Lyle.

His teammates looked awkwardly at him, for he was coming apart at the seams.

"Shadow Faxx reminded us of what the poem told us; we must use our wits here. For this feat, we must find the solution. We have thirty minutes left to leave the games, and we have twenty minutes to exit the cave before the oxygen runs out, right?" asked Natalie.

"Okay, this is what we're going to do. One of us will enter and determine how far the exit door is from the entrance and report back. We will quickly devise a plan to get out before time runs out; since I am the fastest and lightest, I should go first."

Everyone agreed to the plan.

"It's settled. I will go in and come back as quickly as I can," cried Natalie.

The cave door opened as soon as Natalie stepped in front of the entrance. She entered the dim, damp, musty cave, but she kept walking, fearing nothing. Natalie found the end of the chamber in thirty seconds. At the end of the chamber, she saw the light; a few feet away was the exit. Inside, the elevator burned a glowing light. Relieved she found it, she returned to her teammates, knowing exactly how she would lead her team. She returned within the one-minute total. "The way out is two feet away, and we have eighteen minutes left. The cave is small, but four of us can fit in if we walk behind each other. Tie your scarves together and onto the back of my belt so we don't get separated in the chamber."

Natalie successfully guided four of her teammates to the exit. She led three more out and returned one last time to Dave. Luckily, Dave, small in stature like Natalie, made it easy for her to help him through the chamber. She put her head under his arm as he leaned on her like a crutch.

The cave's door opened and closed behind them once they were inside. Within three minutes, they joined their teammates in the glass elevator. The elevator had one button. "Press it, Sam," Natalie said as she continued to hold Dave up.

The elevator started going up, and everyone in the stands stood by, ready for their arrival on stage. The doors opened, and Natalie's team walked out of the elevator back in their original game uniforms.

They saw an older woman dressed in a hunter-green, striped, round collar dress, and over it, a long white apron that reached her ankles. A white armband with a green cross was on her arm, and her sleeves were long with round white cuffs. She had a white kerchief cap with a small, tiny hunter green bow upon her head that hid her silver hair underneath it. She looked at Dave's leg. "There, there; we're going to fix you right up. You're going to be all right." She signaled several men in white to come and lift him on the stretcher. The orderlies carried Dave off the field to the hospital wing.

"Miss Simpleton, the school's nurse, will take good care of him, don't worry, Natalie. He will be okay." Said Sam, comforting her friend.

Natalie was relieved that her team completed their challenge.

Headmistress Lois took to the platform and announced to the crowd, speaking directly into the microphone, "We now have our first-place winner's seventh grade."

Natalie's team was celebrating their victory on the field as shouts rang out from the stands. "Way to go, team Natalie! Way to go!"

Natalie and Sam smiled as they watched the school cheer for them from the field. Afterward, the headmistress prompted the first-place winners to take their seats in the first-place reserved seats as they waited for the rest of the teams to complete the games.

***

Meanwhile, the dolphins brought Team C to the cay safely and swam away. Upon their arrival, Simone found the next clue. "You guys come and have a look at this," she summoned them to walk over to the edge of the woods. There was a thin piece of wood in the ground, the size of a yardstick, surrounded by black fishnet with shells and a starfish tapered inside of it. The sign nailed to the wooden post read in black letters.

*Tributes, you're not done.*
*The fun has begun. It's time to set sail.*
*Your mission: get to the second boat, go.*
*Below deck. Get to the boat in time. Or*
*you will be up to your necks in tides.*

"Just great, another riddle to figure out! And where are these boats? I don't see a boat anywhere!" said Tim. He plopped down onto the warm sand with his hands buried in his face.

A strange blast of wind from the east blew upon the shores. Out on the water appeared in the distance, something shiny. Standing at the shore's edge, Simone pointed to the water's objects with her feet in the cool water. Seeing what was going on, her teammates gathered around her to see the massive structures heading their way. What could it be? They wondered.

Rapidly moving was a three fifty-footer Beneteau 50 upon the water heading in their direction. The sails were tall and massive, clapping in the wind. The yachts were eye-catching and unique in style; one was white, another black, and the third was navy blue with open steps in the back of the boats. There was no captain on board, and the boats navigated themselves, resting midway between the cay.

"There are the boats. We have to get to them fast!" said Derrick.

Beep, beep, their watches showed a countdown from ten minutes.

"Our watches have begun the count. We must get to the boat's pronto before those ten minutes expire," said Connie Edmunds, who was eager to get on with the next challenge with flying colors.

Simone, knowing they needed the dolphins again, realized she had left the shell behind. Glancing down at the sand was the shell on the sand. The shell had not been there before. She blinked twice, for she knew the shell was not there a second ago. The shell came to her when she needed it to. She picked up the shell, blew into it, and the dolphins returned. "This is it, everyone. If we can get to the boats, we will have completed the game. Ride hard and hold on tight," said Simone as she mounted Blue.

The tributes rode their companions to the boats. James and Derrick had a blast riding the waves down a wall of water. They had gotten the hang of riding the dolphins.

Blood rushed from Tim's face as he clung to Simone for dear life as they zoomed across the sea to get to the boats. The victory was near. Each could taste it. Their smiles turned upside down when they saw several great white sharks heavily guarding the boats.

The sharks wasted no time attacking the dolphins, keeping them from the boats each time they attempted to get near one. Time was not on their side, for they had to get to the boats within ten minutes, and every minute wasted spelled trouble for the team.

Simone knew they had to develop a plan, so she gathered her team together and asked Silver what to do.

"We have to go under them to defeat them," said Silver.

"You mean we have to go underwater; that means we will have to hold our breath underwater. I don't think I can do it," cried Tim.

"You can do it, Tim! Fill your lungs with air."

"But how do I do that?" he asked.

"Just take a deep breath and close your eyes," said Sarah, who was a champion swimmer.

"How long will we be underwater?" Sarah asked Silver.

"Don't worry, air breather; We will not submerge you for longer than thirty seconds. We will get you safely to the boat, trust me, and hang on."

The water started swirling like eddies in a tub, heading down the water drain.

"We have run out of time; remember what the clue said? We would be up to our necks in tides. The water is turning against us!" said Derrick, looking at his watch.

"We have nine minutes left!"

The swirling tides pulled Simone's team into the sinking hole. Silver shouted to his kin, "Up and out!"

The dolphins found strength and power and emerged from the eddy with thrust and super speed. The sharks were ready for their prey as the dolphins swam toward them with the tributes on their backs.

"Tributes take a deep breath," Shouted Simone, as she commanded the dolphins to go under the sharks, taking a few of her teammates to the boat.

The dolphins swam like a fired torpedo under the water, outswimming the sharks.

"They made it!" shouted Simone. "Okay! Tim, hold on tight, and when I say **NOW**, take a deep breath and hold it as long as you can and never let go of me." Tim shook his head.

"Let's get this over with," he said in his bravest voice.

Simone commanded Blue, who returned with his kin to take the second half of the team to the boat. It was time to get the rest to safety. "Get Ready, Tim?" The dolphins swam with their target in sight.

"**NOW**," Simone shouted as they submerged underwater.

The sharks, not wanting to lose their prey, went underwater to attack. Two sharks took a bite of Blue's tail from both sides, and crimson red rose to the top of the water. Throwing Simone and Tim off Blue, after the aggressive attack, Simone swam and rescued unconscious Tim. The sharks returned, swimming full speed toward them to finish them. With nowhere to go, they were sitting ducks in a pond.

Their bodies turned sideways with teeth exposed for the kill when six dolphins, swimming full throttle, attacked the sharks from their blind sides, causing such a blow that the sharks gave up their pursuit.

Silver swam under Tim and Simone with a rope in his mouth. Simone grabbed the rope, tied it around her and Tim. She lay Tim across Silver as she sat behind him on Silver's back. Silver shot from underwater over the sharks to the back of the boat. The team was happy; they made it.

Derrick and James helped Tim onto the boat.

Sarah began CPR on Tim right away. “Come on, Tim. Come on,” she continued CPR, and Tim started expelling water from his lungs. “He's going to be okay,” said Sarah. “Tim, can you stand up?”

He whispered, “I think so.”

“Derrick helped Tim to his feet. We have to go,” said Simone. Before leaving, she looked over her shoulder and asked Silver, “Did Blue make it?”

Silver shook his beak back and forth.

“I am so sorry… Silver, I will never forget him or you. We owe you everything; you saved our lives, and we will be forever grateful to you.” Simone said with tears flowing down her cheeks.

Derrick looked at his watch and said, “Simone, we have to go; we have only minutes left to leave the game!” He removed his left hand from her shoulder as she kneeled to say goodbye.

Watching from the stands, Woodland was sad when Simone waved goodbye to Silver, their friendly guide, as he and his kin swam away.

Simone pulled herself together and said to the team, “It's time to get out! Follow me.” She led them to a door of glass etched windows. Without delay, Simone opened the door and entered below deck. There was only one room, and it belonged to the missing captain. Victorian-aged furniture filled the room with exquisite, priceless Victorian art portraits that interacted with the team when they walked into the room.

"This boat is incredible. It's not physically possible, according to the size of the boat, for this room to be this massive, but this room could easily hold over two hundred people," said Sarah.

"Would you get a load of this? Straight ahead, twelve o'clock is the elevator that will take us back to the stadium," said Tim.

James and Simone entered last, after the team. "Press Level One, James," said Simone, and in a flash, they were back in the cheering stadium once again.

***

Team A continued to look for the waterfall as the map suggested, as they blazed through the jungle. They were deep in the jungle when their watches chimed for twenty minutes. They had to find their exit before time ran out.

"Guys, we must get to the waterfall as the map said. We can do this. According to the map, we should come to it now," said Dale as he pointed to the waterfall on the map. Mosquitoes were buzzing around Shelton Summers. Unfortunately, his insect repellent wasn't highly effective against those small blood suckers because his face and legs were covered in red bumps.

Dale pointed to the waterfall on the map. "Do you hear that?" he asked with an enormous grin on his face.

"It sounds like water!" said Carrie Hemphill.

The jungle opened to the sounds of a calming, relaxing shore of water with gray rocks protruding through the water.

"The waterfall!" said Commodore, second in line behind Dale.

"X marks the spot. When do we get out of here? I could go for a juicy hamburger with fries right about now," said Jack.

"Is that all you can think about is your stomach right now?" asked Carrie.

"Aw yeah, not everyone can eat light like you, Carrie." Jack sneered at the girl who dreamed of becoming a food cop one day.

Keev'oo, their guide, said, "You must go under the waterfall tributes to exit the game. I will show you, and then I must leave you. Soon, you will be back for lunch in no time, Jack."

"Can't you stay with us until the end of the game?" asked Glen.

Keev'oo, their winged companion, had become part of the team. "I'm sorry, master Glen, but those are the rules. You will no longer need me. There is a secret opening under the fall; enter and keep going to exit the game."

"This keeps getting better and better. We must enter a dark, scary lair. What if killer vampire bats are in there waiting to suck every drop of blood out of us?" cried Shelton.

"I think someone's scared of the dark," exclaimed Commodore. Commodore wasn't afraid of anything; he seemed to embrace his fears and smile in the face of danger. "What if Bigfoot is in there?"

"Don't be ridiculous, Shelton. There's no such thing as Bigfoot. "You've been watching too much television," said Nandi.

"Everybody knows those Bigfoot sightings are completely false," said Commodore.

"Believe as you like, but I think Bigfoot is real."

"Man, whatever."

"Enough, you guys! You heard Keev'oo; it's our way out. I'm sure there is no reason to panic; we are going into the cave, and that's final," snapped Carrie.

A rainbow appeared in the sky as they continued to the cave. The waterfall was high up, cascading foaming suds at the end of the fall. Birds flew high above in the sky. "Here is the entrance tribute; good luck until we meet again," said Keev'oo.

The tributes said their goodbyes before Keev'oo flew back into the jungle. Suddenly, tributes were swept off their feet as the water from the fall poured inside, creating separate super water slides. They slid up and down, round and round, as the water carried them down a narrow one-drop pool of water where they emerged together.

"That was so cool! Can we do it again?" asked Commodore.

"Are you kidding me? We're lucky to be alive. Who knew where these treacherous slides were taking us?" said Carrie crossly.

Jacked fired back, "Where is your sense of adventure?"

"I left it behind during that horrible drop," said Carrie.

"Can anyone tell us where we are right now? This was not on the map," said Nandi Harris.

Dale, the team captain, couldn't answer Nandi's question, but he knew he had to give his team hope. "I will look for a way out. Everyone, stay put; if I am not back in one minute, send someone after me."

"If there is a way out, good luck searching," said Matt.

"There is always a way out." He took a deep breath before he sank underwater to search for a way out.

A beaming light shone in the water above him. He followed it to the surface and discovered it was an alluring cenote. Dale took another deep breath and swam back to his teammates when his foot got caught in seaweed. He struggled and couldn't get free; he needed help. Carrie cut the seaweed with a pocketknife, freeing him from his snare. They swam back to the team. "Thanks, Carrie!"

"You saved my life." He leaned forward and caressed her hands gently. "It was nothing." She blushed as she laid her hands on top of his. Dale explained what he found and led his team to the surface of the underground pond. They swam to a ladder attached to a wooden pier and climbed it to the wooden wharf. The elevator was waiting at the end of the pier for them to exit the games. They raced to get inside; Dale pressed button one, and immediately, Team A was back safely in the stadium. Woodland applauded as the sixth grade had come in third place in the game.

Team D was far away, down the long, creepy tunnel. "You heard of the tunnel of love, but this is the tunnel of someone's nightmare."

Shane said to his team members, and judging from their silence, he would get no arguments from them about his critical assessment of the tunnel. Shane wasn't comfortable with dark, damp, musty tunnels with creepy sounds echoing throughout the tunnel. Randy flashed his pocket flashlight around the tunnel. "Hey, we're in luck! There are some lamps in the corners," said Randy.

Mike retrieved a box of matches he kept from the supplies and lit the handheld black lanterns. They continued onward and came to a fork at the end of the tunnel.

"Do we take the tunnel to the left or the right?" asked Seth.

"We are to take the right tunnel," replied Midnight.

"I don't know what we would have done, Midnight, if you were not here with us," said Shannon.

"Don't thank me yet until you're out of the game safely," said Midnight to his trusty companions. The left tunnel differed from the previous tunnel because it was covered in ancient Egyptian hieroglyphics. Shannon looked at the symbols and began reading one aloud. "Here lies the next clue," he continued, reading as his teammates gathered behind him.

"What is it?" the team sounded.

"We must enter the next room; however, we must pass one more test before we can exit the game. We have to keep going; it's not far now."

"How did you learn to read Egyptian?"

"My mother taught me, Seth; she's an archeologist, an expert in Egyptian antiquity, culture, and languages."

"So, your mother is an explorer, huh? What was that like growing up with a mother for an explorer?"

"Cool, Mom used to take me on some of her digs; unfortunately, she couldn't take me everywhere with her because it was too dangerous, but she always Skyped and sent birthday cards and gifts home a week early before my birthdays and holidays whenever she couldn't be home."

"That must have been tough on you and your dad."

"It was in the beginning, but my dad and I are close. We take care of each other while Mom's away."

The boys realized they were near the entrance when a startling light blazed ahead of them. The light was coming from the next room.

Midnight walked into the room first, and the team followed behind him. The room was filled with ancient scrolls tucked neatly into open shelves along the walls. Twelve breath-taking columns reaching fifteen feet toward the ceiling were among the many focal points in the room. The room was as big as Grand Central Station. Along the room, quaint Greek tables, benches, and several busts of ancient keepers of the antiquities were stationed throughout the hall. There were large openings above the wall, allowing sunlight to pour into the grand hall from outside. There were thousands of scrolls properly categorized with their books placed under the following subjects: Medicine, Law, Arithmetic, Astronomy, Comedy, Poetry, and Drama, to name a few.

"What is this place?" asked Thomas Lynch. Midnight knew but didn't answer; he wanted them to take it all in before revealing their whereabouts. On the wall hung a huge painting of a man of nobility.

"Who is he?" asked Kevin Strong.

Midnight jumped onto a table in front of the group and said, "Gather around, for I have little time. It was over two thousand years ago; a great military genius had conquered many lands. His name was Alexander the Great, and he was a former student of Aristotle, the philosopher. Aristotle instilled in the lad a love for books, education, wisdom, and knowledge. According to Aristotle, he believed the fate of empires depended on the education of youth. Therefore, he lived by this principle and later became a military warrior who conquered many lands and empires while crushing the Persian rule. Alexander valued knowledge as a tool for power. In the fall, 332 B.C., this Greek warrior set his eyes upon a city one hundred and thirty miles northwest of Cairo, Egypt. Alexander saw that the harbor was good for a naval base; it was the Island of the Pharaohs. Egypt was under Persian rule, and this Greek warrior named Alexander crossed into the city. Egypt hailed him as a liberator from Persian oppression. They welcomed him as a ruler and crowned him pharaoh of Egypt. He named the city Alexandria, which became the Empire of Knowledge."

"Midnight, is this The Library of Alexandria? And the mural of the ceremonial pharaoh, is it Alexander the Great?" Shane Miller asked curiously.

"Yes, and yes," said Midnight. Knowing this, the library took on a new meaning to the tributes, for no one knew where the lost Library of Alexandria was located. They devoured the room with their eyes in every detail of the hall. They placed a large replica of the ancient sphere of Earth in the center of the room, with circumference measurements going around it.

"You should know the knowledge of the world was collected and stored here. Agents of the library seized books from ships that docked in Alexandria. The library agent copied books by hand and returned the copied version later by ship to their owners. It was Alexander's idea to build the library, but he died before construction began. His successor, Ptolemy 1, executed Alexander's plans for a museum and library. In the royal city inside the Serapeum, a lecture hall, classrooms, dormitories, and a botanical garden were housed. The books grew and grew, attracting the greatest Greek minds to the library. Here they studied and made discoveries of the brightness of the stars, size of the world, the steam engine, and geometry, also, medical discoveries; here doctors operated on animals, then later medical exams on humans after death," said Midnight. Shannon asked, "How is it possible the library survived when millions of scrolls were destroyed by a catastrophic fire by the Romans?"

"Daughter Serapeum was created, and copies of the scrolls were made from different locations. The library guardian collected the works and moved the books back to their original home," said Midnight.

"Midnight, your eyes are gray!" said Randy.

"This means danger is near. Something is coming!" Midnight didn't know what dangers, but he knew they were no longer alone or safe. Midnight arched his back and hissed.

The team stood still when a gust of wind encircled the hall. Four tall, mysterious figures in black cloaks materialized before them. One figure in the middle spoke to them. "You've entered this domain at your own risk. You may not leave until you have proven your worth," said one figure. At no time could they see their faces, but only hear their voices.

Shannon intrepidly asked. "Who are you, and what do you want?"

"Who we are isn't important, but what is central is the time you have left. To leave, you must answer a riddle, and if you answer correctly, you may leave," said the dark hooded figure while another figure was pointing to an open entrance showing the exit. The fourth figure spoke, his voice husky, and said, “If you cannot answer correctly, you will repeat your actions until your time runs out.” One of the mysterious figures stood in front of the threshold, blocking the entrance so they could not escape. Shannon looked at Midnight and said, “You guys, we got this. We are some of the greatest minds to enter Woodland Academy, and we can solve their riddle.” His team was on board with accepting the challenge.

“Ask your riddle,” said Shannon.

“Tell which of these categories above the scrolls the riddle pertains to, and you must explain the meaning of it. You will find the categories behind you. Listed above the scroll’s cubicles, written in English: Law, Medicine, Physics, Astronomy, Poetry, and Mathematics.” Shannon and his team read them and asked, “State your riddle.”

“Very well! I provide no heat, and I follow you everywhere you go. My eyes are watching you day and night; you can see me only if the conditions are right. What am I?” Shannon turned to his teammates to collaborate.

“We all know we can rule out law, medicine, poetry, and mathematics,” said Randy.

“What makes you so sure?” asked Shannon.

“Because this object comes out in the day and the night, but whatever it is, it's not the sun because it can't be seen at night and it provides heat,” said Randy.

“He's right. That leaves only two categories: Astronomy and Physics,” said Shane.

“I bet you the riddle stems from astronomy. I'll bet my mother's church hats on it,” exclaimed Kevin.

“Okay! That's great, but what is it?” asked Thomas.

“I got it!” said Seth. “It's a star!”

“Are you sure?” asked Shannon apprehensively.

“Yes, I am sure?” Seth replied, smiling from ear to ear.

Shannon faced his tormentors, and he opened his mouth to answer when they heard, “No! That is not the answer,” said the voice.

“Did you hear that?” asked Shannon. He knew it was a woman's voice who spoke in their midst. Her voice was soft and enduring, like a mother comforting her child after scraping his knee on a payment.

“Who said that?” everyone asked.

A lovely siren appeared before the tributes in a long red and purple tunic; her curly, brown hair was pinned up with beads and pearls woven through a single, long braid that was around her head. The siren said, “Tributes, only you can see and hear me for now. I am Hypatia, the guardian of the Serapeum.” The figures saw the tributes speaking with someone in the room whom they couldn't see.

“If you're the guardian, then who are they?” asked Shannon.

“They are the infamous threat to knowledge, science, and philosophy, and when these men were alive in 415 C.E., they accused scholars of being pagans. They mauled scholars and carried out vicious hate crimes against Jewish populations. You cannot trust them. My life was taken from me by their hands,” said Hypatia calmly.

“They cannot see you, but we can.”

“Yes, little one, and I am here to help you like Midnight.”

BEEP, BEEP sounded their watches.

“Guys, we're running out of time. We need an answer,” said Shane.

“First, you were right; it is an astronomy question, but the object of the riddle isn't a star,” Hypatia said solely.

“But it said it follows you, and it comes out during the day and night. Stars do, and because it's far away, it can watch us, but we can't touch it,” Countered Seth.

“No one can.”

"The answer is not a star, but you were right to consider the cosmos. But what else besides stars are in the galaxy?"

"Why didn't I think of that before?" asked Shannon. Shannon thanked Hypatia and said, "I know the answer! We have the answer to your riddle," Shannon said to the figures as he pulled out a scroll from the astronomy's cubby.

"You have chosen wisely," said the second figure. "But what is the answer to the riddle?"

Shannon repeated the riddle one last time and answered, "There are a couple of answers it could be, but there is one answer that fits the description. This object provides no heat or warmth; therefore, it's not the sun; it provides light, and because this object is 238,900 miles away, we can see it during the day and night. Modern space mechanisms can touch it."

The dark figure grew impatient with the team's leader and shouted, "Tell us the answer!"

"The answer is the moon. Its surface reflects light from the sun, which makes the moon glow. The moon reflects between three and twelve percent of the sunlight that hits it. This effect happens under the following condition when the moon is in orbit around the planet, which determines the moon's brightness from Earth."

Shannon unrolled the papyrus scroll in his hands, taken from its category. The scroll was blank, but words appeared in black ink, "You solved the riddle." Shannon showed his teammates the scroll.

"We did it!" They cheered, and Shannon placed the scroll back where it belonged and smiled at his team and Hypatia. Furious, the tributes figured out their riddle and its meaning; they refused to let them leave the library. The evil tormentors scowled in rage, swarmed the air, and charged toward the tributes.

"I'll hold them off. Get to the garden!" said Hypatia. She raised her hands, causing a cataclysm of burning ash to disintegrate two of the evil tormentors.

Shannon's team rushed to the garden. With only four minutes left on the game clock, Midnight followed them into the garden. "This is where we say goodbye," said Midnight.

"We shall miss you, Midnight!" Shannon shouted as his team waved goodbye and ran into the garden.

"It was an honor to serve you. Now hurry, go!" said Midnight. Midnight returned to help Hypatia fight. He vaulted to the face of one of the dark figures. Midnight began relentlessly scratching his eyes, sending the figure into a hysterical frenzy. The tormentor gave up, leaving one tormentor behind.

Hypatia was no match for the last tormentor; he held her off with a clever, strong electromagnetic wave from his hands, pushing her back, revealing her identity. To his surprise, she was back; his counter disabled her, but not for long; he followed the tributes to the garden.

Straight ahead, the glass elevator was a few feet away from the entry. The tributes were close to victory; now, everyone entered the elevator except Thomas, who was taken unexpectedly by the tormentor. He threw Thomas into a water lily pool.

"Thomas!" they cried in horror, and the tributes rushed to Thomas's aide, who survived his brush with death in the pool.

Hypatia and Midnight, in full pursuit of the tormentor, rushed into the garden to save the tributes. Hypatia manipulated the water in the pond to rise, trapping the tormentor inside a water bubble, propelling him a thousand miles away. The team helped drenched Thomas back to the elevator and pressed the button, and as the doors slowly closed, they waved goodbye to Midnight, who cradled himself in Hypatia's arms as she waved farewell to the tributes.

Ninth grade finished last. Lois was glad to see them and relieved that they made it out of the games in one piece. Woodland cheered for them as they joined the rest of the tributes on the field.

# Chapter Eighteen

# The Tournament

Team B and C were first to compete in a round of head-to-head combat with each other. Afterward, Team A and D would compete to determine who would advance to the last tournament. Each team knew where and how they would compete in the next segment of the tournament; however, the Elders kept what they were planning for their tributes top secret. Later that Wednesday afternoon, students were summoned west of the campus to the tennis court. Upon arrival, to their amazement, the tennis court had transformed into an indoor gladiator arena.

Simone and Natalie's teams waited inside the tribute's striped, colored tent for the school's administrators outside the arena. On top of the tent, the Woodland Academy's flag. Coach Sax parted the velvet curtains. Inside, tributes were mingling in small circular groups. He cleared his throat to get their attention. "Tributes gather around now!" Hating the mere interruption, the groups quieted and gathered around to listen to Coach Sax because the tournament was about to begin. "Team captains, you're to choose one member from your team to go out and compete in today's event."

Natalie wondered why the team's captains were excluded from competing for the event. After all, she was their best athlete on the team. Natalie didn't contest and did as she was told. She and Sam were so close to discovering the secrets Woodland concealed from its students. Her team needed to advance to the finals; if not, her and Sam's plans and winnings would have been for nothing. The question was, which teammate would she select to bring the seventh grade to another victory?

Natalie considered each of her teammates, but it was clear who she would choose. She chose Lyle Boggs because he was smart, fast, and had a strong heart. Simone from Team C chose Derrick, and for good reasons; he was taller and muscular. His long bangs covered his left eye while the rest of his hair was short, tapered to his neck. Derrick was sure he could take Lyle down in a matter of minutes. Natalie didn't care about Derrick's smug grin. He flashed her; in fact, it made her blood boil lava. There he was, gloating over the moon as if he and his team had won already. If he thought for a second, his delusion of grandeur intimidated her; he was sadly mistaken.

Headmistress Lois, in her long black robe, entered the tent. She wore a jumbo red and black plaid beret attached to the hat's right side, a green holly of clustered red berries. Her face was shining; her bright lips red as her rosy cheeks quickly spoke, "Have you been told your instruction?"

"We have," replied Simone fervently.

"Good, let's begin!" She chortled a bit and began talking to Coach Sax.

Natalie pulled Lyle over to her to give him one last pep talk, as any good coach would do. She encouraged Lyle not to focus on his size but to focus on the task at hand.

"Trust your instincts, Lyle, and bring this one home. You can do it."

"I'm not afraid, Natalie." She smiled and patted his shoulder for good luck. Natalie motioned Dexter, Sam, Charlotte, and the rest of the team to put their hands on top of Lyles. "B team! On three," said Natalie.

Headmistress Lois walked over to Natalie's team after finishing speaking with Coach Sax. "Very well, the rest of you not taking part may return to your seats in the box among your peers in the stands."

Before leaving, Natalie looked back, giving Lyle two thumbs up in the air. She found it hard to leave him; everything was riding on Lyle's victory over Derrick.

"Miss Evergreen, if you please," Headmistress Lois gestured it was time to leave the tent.

Suddenly, her feet were cemented to the floor. She found it hard to leave her teammate behind. If she had it her way, she would face Derrick in Lyle's place if she could. She put one foot in front of the other in a snail-paced motion and exited the open slit curtains.

Headmistress Lois followed behind her.

Coach Sax was left alone with the remaining tributes to fill them in on the games' details. "Boys in the trunks over to my right, you will find everything you need to enter the event. In a few seconds, I will announce you. Once you hear your name, enter the arena ready to compete." Afterward, he bid them good luck and left them alone to get ready for the game.

The boys opened the trunks inside; they retrieved a helmet, a mouth guard, sports gloves, sports shoes, socks, arm, knee pads, and gladiator attire.

Over in the corner were room dividers. Lyle and Derrick changed and met in the middle of the tent. "What do you think they have planned for us?" Derrick asked curiously.

"I don't know. I'd expect we're about to find out," the boy said with wide brown eyes, dark brown hair on the sides with a short blonde tip.

Derrick extended his hand toward Lyle's hand. "Good luck, and may the best man win."

Lyle shook his hand in the name of good sportsmanship. In the middle of shaking hands, their names were announced loudly. Lyle was nervous, but he hid it well as the music played, while the crowd applauded as they entered the arena with their helmets in their hands.

"Attention, attention!" said Professor Lois.

Instantly, the crowd became quiet. Headmistress Lois continued, "Today, Team B and C will compete in today's event. Since Team B placed first from the beginning of the competition, Lyle Boggs will be the captain, and Derrick Kingsley will be the challenger in today's sporting event because his team placed second." More applause followed from the crowd.

Officials padded the arena with plush cushion mats. Up high were too tall, slender platforms facing each other. It looked like a thin, tall spool of thread up top. Each had a round, flat platform with an outer ring flashing red in the center of the platform. Students could feel the excitement in the air while placing their bets on their winning and losing candidates. Many bets were placed against Lyle losing to Derrick within three minutes of combat. Approaching the boys, two seniors handed them each a pugil stick. The sticks were long and padded with horizontal white circles wrapped around their navy cylinder cushions at each end of the stick.

"Jousting?" Derrick said as he turned to Lyle.

"Well, that explains the helmets," said Lyle.

"Tributes will have thirty seconds to overthrow his opponent from his platform if he can do it within the time limit, without falling off, wins. If both fall, the game and time will start over and continue until there is a winner." There was a small, open half-gate elevator at the base of the round platforms. "Tributes, please step onto the platform," said Professor Lois.

Instantly, the small platform rose to the top of the circular stand as the flashing light burned red underneath their feet. The scoreboard in the background displayed 30 seconds on the time clock. Both boys stood in t-shirts, jerseys, and shorts. Except for Lyle, uniform colors were navy and hunter green, and Derrick's uniform was black and hunter green.

"Place your helmets on now. When you see your opponent's light turn green, attack," said Professor Lois.

With their jousting sticks in their hands and feet planted firmly, they waited after the countdown of three. A foghorn sounded, and the lights turned green.

Derrick struck first with a quick thrust, and Lyle answered back with a thud of his own to Derrick's collarbone. Derrick hit Lyle's face mask, moving him closer to the edge. Natalie gripped Sam's hand as Derrick nearly defeated Lyle. After Lyle's dizziness subsided, he shook it off and kept going. Lyle countered with an incredible blow to Derrick's forehead. Derrick's eyes crossed from the impact; he wavered back and forth as if he were in a drunken stupor. Not letting up, Lyle swept Derrick off his feet with a martial arts Kung Fu move. Derrick tried to recover before losing his balance, swinging his stick one last time at Lyle, but missed him entirely. Lyle defeated Derrick, knocking him off his platform with thirteen seconds left on the clock. Derrick dropped his head in defeat the moment it was over.

"He did it!" shouted Sam to Natalie. They stood applauding and cheering, as did the school. Lyle's genius countermove secured his team a spot in the finals.

Matt Foster from Team A and Brock Myers from Team D competed next. Matt lost to Brock in the second attempt during the match. After twenty-six seconds left on the clock, Matt lost the match. Team D advanced to the finals. Back at school, everyone returned, still buzzing about the match. No one believed Lyle could win but Natalie. She was thrilled when Lyle won the match. *Tomorrow, Woodland will have its final winner of the Annual Academy Games*, thought Natalie. In the meantime, she celebrated their team's victory with her friends that evening back at school.

# Chapter Nineteen

# The Maze: End of Games

Tournament on Thursday was cold. The tournament began at high noon, a few acres away from the academy. The school spared no expense selecting the last arena, and it would be nothing like what the school had seen before. School prefects led their grade to the grand Antediluvian Coliseum. This structure was pure marble; columns of white quartz made the Colosseum a beautiful work of art. The arena could generate heat from the floor to the benches. It was perfect for watching the games unfold because it was built on a high elevation, making it easy for Woodland's students to capture every moment of the game. Tributes were to compete inside a maze of icy walls that shimmered in the sunlight. Not only was it a maze, but also a world inside a maze, with an enchanted forest of lit snowy trees and elements of surprise behind the divided rows.

Perhaps the entrance to the maze was most intriguing. There were two sculpted nine-foot snowmen for each team. Each was vibrantly designed; the first one had a red beanie with a white ball on top of its head, while peppermint fur swirled around its forehead and ears. Around its neck, a peppermint scarf with red and white tassels was tied in a loose knot on its right side. Two black sticks for arms with red mittens and white at the mittens' opening protruded from the body's middle part. Two eyes of black coal and a black button for the nose. Five coals for a mouth, and lodged between his mouth was a wooden smoking pipe. Three shiny red glittery snowflakes lined the snowman's belly; below it was an oval's entrance like a funhouse. Team D's snowman was the same height but had a light blue and white winter scarf, mittens, and a cap. It had a nine-foot broom in its left hand that moved up and down. Instead of coal for eyes, there were black buttons, and for the nose, a vibrant orange carrot, and a shaped smile of twigs created his mouth. The maze featured not only snowmen, but also friendly winter animals.

However, in the game, they placed a nasty varmint to challenge both teams. The mole was a foe, and they needed to stay clear of the mean critter if they wanted to win.

Natalie and Shannon's team made their arrival at the coliseum. Beforehand, both teams were given stabilizing weapons capable of immobilizing their opponents in the game. The officials of the game called it the neutral air blaster. The air blaster worked like a taser, immobilizing team members in the game. Half of the members on the team received neutral blaster guns. They strapped their weapons to a Velcro belt that snapped in place across the chest. The belt could be worn in front of the uniform or at the back of it. The neutral blaster showed the level of power and rounds left to fire through a small window on the gun. This toy-like gun resembled the Nerf Super Soaker. It was sleek and easy to grip.

Natalie, Lyle, Mary, and Eddie were given neutral blasters, and the rest of Natalie's team was taken to a remote part of the maze. Shannon, Seth, Keith, and Thomas got neutralizers while Shane, Brock, Mike, and Randy were taken to a remote part of the maze by Natalie's team. Inside the coliseum, Lois spoke from the stands with the tributes standing in front of giant snowman sculptures.

"The tributes are about to enter the snow fort. They must get to the wooded maze to find their team members. Opposing teams can be slowed; tributes can use the neutral blaster. Get to your team as quickly as you can before the other opposing team does. Both teams are to beware of the brown, pesky mole who moves through the maze-like Sonic the Hedgehog. If the mole touches a tribute, it will freeze him or her solid. Tributes must avoid the mole at all costs." Speaking directly to the tributes, she continued, "It doesn't matter how many of you find the remaining tributes; if one of you does will count. There are things in the maze that will amaze you, but stay focused. You will be happy to note that there will be no time restrictions in the maze. Do not waste time because whoever gets to his team first has the advantage of winning the tournament," said Lois. Natalie noticed when Lois spoke; she pressed her crystal brooch pinned onto her shoulder, and her voice projected as if she were speaking into a microphone. She stood where everyone could see her as she made the pronouncements *interesting*, thought Natalie as she prepared to enter the snow fort.

"Woodland, please join me as we send our brave tributes who are about to make history into the games. Let's give them a proper sendoff, shall we?" Woodland students clapped, waved, and shouted for each team like never before. Lois placed earplugs into her ears to silence the noise from the arena.

"Tributes take your places," commanded Lois. A door slid open at the base of the snowmen for entry into the snowy fort. Each team entered wearing the same uniform when they first entered the glass elevators to the arena.

"Tributes you may enter when you see an orange spark in the air." Immediately, an orange flare shot into the air, and the tributes entered the game. After they came out the other end of the snowman, waiting for Natalie's team was a medium-sized primary-colored car with a sign that read DRIVE ME outside the car's door.

"Do you think it's safe to get in?" asked Mary Toll, who was hoping it wasn't a trap.

"I think it's harmless; let's get in," said Natalie, and she jumped in the driver's seat.

"This car is cool," said Eddie, wanting to know how fast she could go, but there were no gear shifts or indication of how fast it could go. It came with custom beige bucket seats and two silver pedals: one for stopping and one for going. It had a big red steering wheel inside the car. Eddie glided his hand down the hood of the car and thought This car is amazing. Starting the engine required no key but the push of a button.

With their neutral blasters strapped to their backs, off they went deep into the arena. Mary and Natalie rode in front, Eddie and Lyle rode in the back, ready for an adventure. Nothing could prepare them for what was about to happen next. At first, the ride started slowly, and during the ride, snow leopards, polar bears, and snow owls came out for the children to enjoy as they passed by them. Suddenly, something unusual happened: a lap bar emerged automatically from the car's seat, locked over the Tribute's chest, keeping them protected inside the car. Then, the car gained momentum from a normal car ride to a snowmobile ride in one. The wheels were raised and replaced with long skis from the front to the back of the car. They glided over the snow smoothly and then onto swishing down hilly slopes and winding turns and to unforgettable G-force double loops. It was like riding a roller coaster at a theme park.

It was the most remarkable, fun, thrilling ride the tributes have ever ridden. Without warning, the car came to an abrupt stop in front of the snow fort. The lap bars retracted, and each got out of the car. The car, now four wheels again… drove away, leaving them to the maze's snow fort forest.

The snow walls were tall and shimmered with icy crystals in the light, and two inches of snow covered the fort's ground.

"We need to devise a plan to rescue the others." Said Natalie.

"What do you suggest, Natalie?" asked Eddie.

"I am suggesting we split up. This maze goes on for miles and miles, and we'll have better luck finding them if we split up. If we run into any trouble, use your neutral blasters. Remember, we have eight shots, so make every shot count. Keep your eyes peeled and watch out for the mole; he will be wickedly fast and impossible to see. However, Professor Lois didn't say the neutral blaster would not affect it; if you see it, give it a good blast. As soon as one of us finds our team members, the sooner the game will be over, and we'll be Woodland Champions. Let's get after it," Natalie said to her companions.

Lyle thought Natalie's plan was a good one and that it could work. Natalie entered the fort first, and the rest followed in pursuit. The maze separated Natalie from her group; she was determined more than ever to find her teammates and a way out of the fort. The fort's walls shrank in size, and the mole was loose and approaching Mary quickly, for he had caught her scent as she maneuvered through the fort maze. Breathing heavily, with her neutral blaster pointed straight ahead and her finger on the trigger, ready to shoot anything moving. She came to a dead-end, and when she turned around, everything went black, and she was frozen solid. It happened fast; poor Mary didn't stand a chance against the clever mole. The mole had done its job. He left her frozen icicle body behind to find his next prey. Eddie made progress through the snow fort successfully until Thomas Lynch, who had hidden on top of the fort's wall to take on his opponent, zapped him. The wall was minimized in size as Thomas jumped down, pleased; he'd gotten the best of Eddie, and continued through the fort.

Shannon's team was four members to Natalie's two, including herself, who was in the lead. Lyle stopped in his tracks when he saw a leopard. He would not have spotted it if she hadn't stopped to take a drink of the tiny, trickling, bubbling brook. A second later, he heard footsteps crunching through the snow. Someone was coming; he hid quietly behind a snowy willow pine tree. It was Kevin; he noticed the leopard and tried to leave without disturbing her. He walked a few paces backward slowly. Luckily for Lyle, he had Kevin smack in the middle of his scope. Leading his target, Lyle shot Kevin with his neutral blaster, immobilizing him on the spot. Hearing the commotion, the animal pranced back into the forest. Lyle whispered, "Got you." Leaving Kevin there, he continued searching for his friends.

Shannon found the maze challenging to defeat. He wandered around aimlessly for minutes, not knowing how to get out. Every turn led to a dead end while he repeated the same directions. He began perspiring as beads of sweat ran down his forehead. Terrified, he felt he might never find his way out in time before Natalie's team. He hated knowing this was not his best event, but never would he admit that aloud, but pushed through the aggravation and kept wandering forward. One of Shannon's members was down, making the score three to two. Yet, no team knew of its progress or plights because they were separated. Natalie ran into Shannon. He quickly fired a shot and missed her. She ran as fast as her legs could carry her, leaving Shannon alone again. Natalie's heart was beating like a drum. She came close to being immobilized. She stopped momentarily to catch her breath.

In his teammates' range, Seth came to a clearing near the fort; to his surprise, he saw both teams locked away behind two short stone turrets up top. His team members were shouting, "HELP! HELP! UP HERE!"

Immediately, he ran to help his friends, but from nowhere, the mole struck him from his blind side and froze him solid. Shane, Brock, Mike, and Randy saw the attack, and in an instant, their hopes of one of their team members rescuing them seemed impossible. Yet, they still hoped someone from their team would free them from their prison. Natalie was only a few feet away from both teams. Natalie, Lyle, Thomas, and Shannon were all left to finish the game. Thomas was the best in the maze, but a large net had trapped him in the maze. He walked into a booby trap designed to stop a player from rescuing his teammates. The more Thomas struggled to get out, the more he could not free himself from his snare. He prayed someone would come along and free him, but no one came.

Natalie was having a bit of trouble while maze-running; she tripped over a mound of snow. She rose and wiped the powdery substance from her face and eyes. Once she regained vision, the mole had frozen her solid. The last thought of her was that *it's over*. Unable to move, Shannon was getting nearer and nearer to his team. Behind Natalie's frozen body, a small figure appeared. Why, it was Dave Kissinger; he found Natalie frozen stiff. If he had only gotten there sooner, maybe he could have helped her. Still, he didn't know how he could help her. A man came toward him, dressed in bright colors of royalty. He looked like a wooden nutcracker soldier. In his hand, a sword he carried to ward off any dangerous threat in the forest. The soldier, named Captain Kohlford, marched toward him and the frozen statue.

"Oh, my, she's frozen solid," he said compassionately. "Swacka has been busy."

"You know who has done this?"

"I do! It was Swacka, the pesky, mesky mole in the maze whose only joy is to stop anyone from achieving their purpose or destiny."

"That's awful," said Dave.

"I can help you. I am the captain of the guards of the fort."

"I am Dave Kissinger." He pointed to Natalie.

"She is Natalie Evergreen, my team captain."

"Is there anything you can do to help her?"

"I can't do a thing, but you can."

"Anything! What must I do?" Captain Kohlford went on, "You must tag her."

"How do I do that?"

"You must touch her." Dave looked into Natalie's eyes, but she was unresponsive. He laid his hand on her hand. At first, nothing happened; Captain Kohlford watched to see what would happen next. The icy blast melted away, and Natalie was mobile again. His heart was overjoyed because Dave had saved her.

"Dave, what are you doing here? How did you unfreeze me? How is your leg?" Natalie asked.

"Sam got word to me in the infirmary. We made it to the last tournament, and I thought I'd come and help. Abaeze, our hall's prefect, led me here. I followed behind you, and here I am. By the way, my leg is doing fine; thanks to the salve Nurse Simpleton applied now, it's good as new."

"Boy! I've never been happier to see you. Thanks for rescuing me."

"Don't thank me. Thank Captain Kohlford. Without his help, you would still be a fudge popsicle stick. He told me how to undo Swacka's doom."

"How was it possible?" Natalie asked Captain Kohlford.

"There's a power that exists within your fingers. It is more powerful than any magic, spell, or curse, and its love. In Dave's inner heart, he wanted you to be free; he believed within his heart and mind, releasing that power through his finger," said Captain Kohlford cordially.

"Of course, that's why Professor Lois called the tournament Tag-O-Lit," Natalie said cheerfully. "But didn't

Professor Lois mention the games would end and the winner of Tag-O-Lit would win the games?" "Yes, she did. Clearly, the school had other plans; we must continue competing until—"

"Until what?" He asked, not sure if he really wanted to know the answer. She thought for a moment and said, "Until we get to the grand finale." Ready to move on, Natalie and Dave thanked the nutcracker soldier for his help and explained they had to find their friends.

They said goodbye, and off they continued through the maze. Shannon hit another snag and came to two dead ends again, giving Natalie and Dave the time they needed to catch up. Shannon eventually found his way out, as did Natalie and Dave. Each of them came to a small clearing. In front of them were their friends held locked away on top of the stone turrets. Miraculously, the mole was no longer a threat. Now it was up to them to free their friends from their compound. To do that, Natalie, Dave, and Shannon realized they had to put a ball through a golden hoop suspended nine feet in the air.

The golden hoop was attached to a long pole to the hoop from the ground. It had a backboard and no net. There, on the wooden maple tree stump in the center of the aged rings, lay the golden round ball, still waiting to be removed to play the game.

Whichever member gets his ball through his team's hoop wins the game. Scoring a shot through the hoops suspended in the air was not an impossible mission, but challenging because each member had to avoid being hit by their neutral blasters. Shannon fired a blast at Dave, missing him by half an inch. After firing, he went for the ball, shooting a three-pointer from downtown.

Dave fired two rounds at Shannon; both attempts failed to keep him from shooting. The ball left his fingers in rotation in the air. "**Nooo**!!!" Natalie screamed. The ball hit the backboard and bounced off the rim, and then hit the ground. Shannon, disappointed he had failed, ran to retrieve the ball, as did Dave. Dave got to the stump before Shannon and picked up the ball from the ground. Natalie, watching the turn of events a few feet away, ran full speed toward Dave, jumped on the magical glowing stump, and yelled, “BALL!” to Dave.

The stump acted as a springboard, enabling Natalie to leap high in the air. Shannon fired a shot at Natalie in motion, but Dave was quicker, zapping Shannon in the leg seconds before Natalie scored the winning dunk. She landed on the ground, scraping her knee.

It was over. The bars opened, releasing Charlotte, Sam, and Dexter to run down the compound’s stairwell out the opening, hugging Natalie and Dave as they celebrated their victory. “You've done it, Natalie. That shot was out of sight, just EXCEPTIONAL,” said Dexter.

Natalie and her team did it. They won the Woodland Academy Games, the Quarter Annual Cup, the school's house points, and bragging rights; they joined with raised hands to the audience. Woodland Academy's confetti covered the students in the coliseum and Natalie's team. Sadly, Shannon's team lost but were good sports about it.

The Elders made their selections and were ready to announce their chosen picks early next Thursday, and began planning the victor's ceremony. The game had ended. Professor Lois officially declared the winners of Woodland Academy games: Samantha Harper, Eddie Piper, Mary Tolls, Dave Kissinger, Charlotte Simpson, Dexter Greene, Lyle Boggs, and the best captain Woodland has seen in these two hundred years, Natalie Evergreen.

Winning the games was one of Natalie's most significant accomplishments because she did it with her friends. After the tournament was over, Professor Lois had the tributes spring from the game to join their houses. They were all fine, going about their day as they always did.

Natalie, back in her quarters with her fellow victors, continued celebrating but broke ranks to be alone to reflect. "I thought I'd find you here. Everyone's asking about you downstairs." She found Natalie watching the lake from the school's balcony close to her room.

Natalie confided in her best friend. "Sam, we won, and soon we will know the truth about the school. Part of me is thinking, what if I don't like what I find out?"

Sam listened instinctively. "Natalie, we did it, and I'm sure there is nothing to worry about. We've been through a lot worse. Let's enjoy the moment for now, and whatever arises, we cross that bridge later," said Sam, hoping Natalie would cheer up. Before leaving, she hugged her and left Natalie to her thoughts.

The sun was setting in the west. Woodland was beautiful at this time of the hour. Natalie felt Sam was right; maybe there was nothing to fear; after all, the worst was over; little did she know her world was about to be turned upside down.

# Chapter Twenty

# Chosen Victors

The snow melted within a week after the games, but what a time it had been. Students from several grades wore Team B Hall colors; they wore seventh-grade hall shirt buttons with Natalie's team faces transitioning to motion replay of their time in the games. Natalie's winning dunk and heroic acts were featured on the hologram throughout the school. Doves flying in the sky spelled Natalie's name during the week as she walked to and from her classes. Looking at the doves, she whispered aloud, "I love Woodland Academy." She loved the school's beauty, charm, elegance, wonder, and its students and professors. Woodland was as magical as it was mysterious; honestly, it was like no other school she'd gone to before.

Natalie was almost finished reading *Is God Real?* Assigned by her reading teacher. She felt the read was intriguing, but she wasn't totally on board with this whole

God thing. Natalie pondered while walking to Miss Sherman's class. Suddenly, she felt a gentle touch on her shoulder from behind. She turned to see who had touched her. "Caleb," her face aglow with happiness. "It's good to see you again!"

He enjoys hearing that. It made him feel his absence from her made her heart grow fonder of him. He beamed.

"Do you know? I don't know your last name." Said Natalie as she twirled a strand of her long, curly hair around her index finger.

"It's Grey, and congratulations on winning the games. I thought you were really brave."

"Thank you! I'm glad we won." He looked sincerely into her eyes and replied. "You're quite famous around here, Natalie. Every girl in this school envies you or wants to be you."

"I can't take credit alone. I had a great team."

"See. That's what I like about you; you're very humble. Most would hog all the glory, but not you, Natalie Evergreen. You're one of a kind." *Was he flirting with me*? If so, Natalie didn't mind it at all; in fact, it was endearing. A subtle smile followed her soft, rosy face. He took a deep breath and asked, "Natalie, would you like to go out with me sometimes?" He snapped back to reality when Natalie said, "Caleb, Caleb, are you all right. I lost you for a second there."

"Oh, I'm fine!"

"Did you hear? The entire castle is talking about it; the Elders are going to announce the victors tomorrow."

"I know without a doubt, Natalie, they will choose you."

*How exciting*, thought Caleb. It would delight him to see Natalie chosen and her teammates. "During the third period, the ceremony will take place," she happily retorted.

"I'd better get to class; Miss Sherman doesn't like it when her students are late. See you later, Caleb Grey." He waved goodbye as he headed to class. Natalie walked into the classroom and sat behind Sam.

"Damon called last night, and he said you haven't talked to Trever in weeks," Sam said, concerned. "He's been worried about you."

"I haven't called because all I can focus on is the restricted area of the castle and Miss Sherman's reading assignment."

"I thought you were crazy about Trever."

"I am, but it's complicated, and there's Caleb." Sam sat straight up in her seat after hearing her mention Caleb's name. "Oh, you mean that cute little quarterback you were telling me about before the games?"

"Yes, he walked me to class seconds ago."

"And?"

"And what?"

"Did he ask you out?"

"No, and we're just friends."

"Besides, Trever is my boyfriend, and I care a lot about him."

"Then you'd better call him at once."

"Yes, ma'am!" Natalie replied like a good little soldier in the Army. The girls laughed, and the bell rang.

Miss Sherman entered the room. Everyone had taken their seats quietly and waited for Miss Sherman to start class.

"Natalie, you and your team did well in the games, and I couldn't be happier that it was you who won, not to mention Lyle, Sam, Dexter, Eddie, Mary, Charlotte, and Dave. I am proud of each of you. The school has been celebrating your team's victory for a week and was so gracious in postponing classes until the games ended. The games are over; therefore, we can get back to our regular schedules and the reading assignment, which brings me to your next writing assignment. In the book, God refers to Jesus as the Lamb of God. I would like you to draft a full essay on why He's called the Lamb of God and why it is important to Christians. You must use scriptures to back your claim. Next, explain what literary device best fits the Lamb of God. Last, you must take a stand on whether you agree that Christ is the Lamb of God, why or why not? Your paper will be due within two weeks. Happy writing, everyone. As for today, I would like to discuss figurative language; please open your textbooks to chapter nine."

At last, Thursday morning arrived sunny and clear, a perfect day for crowning Woodland's chosen victors. Sam didn't overthink the ceremony but was glad the games were behind them; she and Natalie could get back to where they left off with Damon and Trever. In the back of Sam's mind, she worried Natalie was letting the school mysteries consume her. Sam knew once Natalie made up her mind about things, nothing could stop her. Although Natalie adored Trever, she had bigger fish to fry, learning all there is to know about her enchanting school. Natalie concluded that dating Trever would have to wait until she had accomplished her goals.

Classes were interrupted at ten o'clock a.m. "Students report to the football field immediately." Said Headmistress Lois through the intercom. Every team that took part in the games was there waiting for his name to be called. The student body was in place now, and the school's choir sang the national anthem a cappella. What followed next was the voice of Professor Lois, but no one saw her. An extended hunter green platform stretched across the field with two small steps behind it on the field. Next to it were five men dressed in black suits and white gloves standing next to each other in a single line. To the left was Coach Sax, the presenter of the awards. "Faculty and students of Woodland Academy. We have gathered here to announce this year's chosen tributes. Foremost, every tribute fought well together and as a team in the arenas," said Lois. The crowd applauded. "You made the school proud and be extremely proud of yourselves, for you were a valiant group of brave girls and boys. If it were up to me, I would choose all of you to represent the school as long as you shall live." More applause followed. "Unfortunately, this is not my decision to make; it is the Elders who choose, and they have done so for over two hundred years." In his black suit, Coach Sax stood proudly at ease with his white gloves placed behind his back. Lois continued, "Before I announce the names, I would like each person to stand and come to the platform and face the audience. Each of you will receive three different medals. Now, without further ado, your 2023 chosen ELDER ELITES are:" Lois read the list below in order.

| Names | Grade |
|---|---|
| 1. Dexter Greene | 7th |
| 2. Eddie Piper | 7th |
| 3. Thomas Lynch | 9th |
| 4. Charlotte Simpson | 7th |
| 5. Dave Kissinger | 7th |
| 6. Simone Redd | 8th |
| 7. Shannon Fleming | 9th |
| 8. Samantha Harper | 7th |
| 9. Lyle Boggs | 7th |
| 10. Tim Meeks | 8th |
| 11. Carrie Hemphill | 6th |
| 12. Seth Misters | 9th |
| 13. Natalie Evergreen | 7th |

Six women escorted each victor in shifts to the platform in their hooded hunter green long dresses. The last person to step onto the platform was Natalie. Soon afterward, each victor in hunter green windbreakers and jackets with the school crest featured on the top right side waited to be crowned. Coach Sax walked over to the men in black suits and retrieved medals from their trays. There were three medals of honor: bronze, silver, and gold. After their names were called, Coach Sax placed bronze medals tied to hunter green ribbon around Seth Misters' and Carrie Hemphill's necks and received a bunch of red clovers and purple tulips; also, a silver pair of bird wings were fastened to the top right corner of their jackets. Those receiving silver medals, flowers, and silver wings are Tim Meeks, Charlotte Simpson, Thomas Lynch, Shannon Fleming, Samantha Harper, Lyle Boggs, Simone Redd, Dexter Greene, Eddie Piper, and Dave Kissinger. The final gold medal and wings went to Natalie, who took her place on top of the platform's higher step. Because Natalie had won the game, she received gold, the highest honor. Natalie shook Coach Sax's hands while smiling after she bit her gold medal, pretending it was chocolate, and happily waved to the student body.

# Chapter Twenty-One

# Hall of Doors

TThe ceremony ended, and the victors were taken at once to the forbidden part of the castle. A tall man greeted them. He had long, snow-white hair that hung down his back. Natalie and the other tributes did not know who he was, for they had never seen him on campus; it was their first introduction. He stepped forward slowly with his hands hidden inside his cloak. He removed his white cloak hood from his head and had a gold headpiece of leaves designed on his head. He said in an elderly voice, "Welcome, elites, to Majestic Abbey! I am Jeremial, but you may call me Jerry; please follow me."

The elites followed him into the structure building. They came to a wooden door with seven letters scrambled at the top of it. He touched each letter with his right index finger as if it meant something important. Charlotte, seeing what he was doing, realized he spelled New Eden. When he touched each letter, they burned like golden embers from a fireplace. The door opened, and to their amazement, they saw a long corridor of doors.

"What is this place?" asked Sam.

"We call it the Hall of Doors," said Jerry. They continued walking and came to the seventh door on the right. "This is your classroom. You will receive grades and be assessed on what you learn here," said Jerry to the group.

"Natalie, you will get the answers you seek, and you will excel." *How does he know my name?* She asked herself.

"Natalie, I've known you since you were a baby. I've been watching over you your whole life." He was speaking to her in her mind. Only she could hear him talk to her. "You were always meant to be here; much awaits you."

"How do you know I'll excel? I don't know if I will. I've just arrived?"

"Do not fear, Natalie, because He is with you."

"He? Who's he?"

"Don't doubt anymore, but only believe," Jerry said to her softly.

The classroom was spacious, with a portable old-fashioned black and white chalkboard resting in front of their seating area. There was a teacher's desk with jars, an apothecary, books, and other random objects placed on top of it. Inside the jars were scrolls, herbs, and maps.

"Your teacher will be here soon; please take your seats."

Natalie, Sam, and Charlotte sat next to each other while the rest took their seats. A tinkling bell sounded three times, and in plain sight, a body appeared before them.

"Don't be afraid. I am Raziel, and I am your instructor."

"Can you tell me how you do that?" asked Natalie, who realized her teacher was no ordinary one.

"Certainly, I am an angel of God."

"Prove it," said Dexter.

Raziel's crème cloak became whiter than white and brighter than the sun. Dexter's eyes got bigger than two full moons in the sky. He put his hands to his eyes because of the brightness of the light. He was afraid to look upon him in his glorious state, but he knew he was an angel. At once, his garment had returned as it was before. Everyone was amazed at what they had witnessed in the room.

"Do not be afraid. I am here to help prepare you for what's coming. Here in this part of the castle, we exist outside of time, but when you return to your regular classes, it will be as if time never stopped."

"Unbelievably cool," said Simone as the rest nodded in agreement.

"I am known as the Keeper of Secrets. You've met Jeremial, the Mercy of God. I will assist you with prophetic visions in this class; this is a skill you must possess as intercessors for the outside world. We will not have you blind but will equip you before you are sent to the multitude. You are never to use your gifts in vain or for money, and you are never to abuse the fruits of the spirit for selfish gains or acts. Never should you enforce anything on your fellow man; he must ask for help and accept faith of his own free will, no EXCEPTIONS, or you will be banned from being an elite. You are to use your gifts without exposing the order of the school. Do you understand?"

Everyone in the room nodded. Raziel walked over to his desk and continued with his hands placed behind his back.

"I'd like you to look at these objects on my desk."

There was a pocket watch with its hands missing, an old wooden violin, and a long peacoat naval jacket with ten gold buttons sewn in twos across the jacket's front. Two medals were pinned to the jacket's right, and four round rings were stitched on the jacket's wrist. He placed the pocket watch in front of Lyle Boggs, the violin in front of Tim Meeks, and the naval jacket in front of Seth Misters.

"Pick it up, tell me what you feel and sense from each object."

Lyle touched the watch, and he sensed an icy chill come over his body; his breath was icy in the room. The class gasped; it was Tim's turn. He strummed the violin, and he saw a vision of a short man in a black jacket, white shirt, and a short black tie holding the violin in front of a small orchestra at a glitzy event.

"I saw a musician well-skilled along with his bandmates, and surrounding the band was a party of grand people having dinner on a ship. This musician enjoyed entertaining a large dinner party," said Tim. He couldn't explain why he could see what he saw without good reason.

Seth sensed the jacket belonged to a captain of some sort.

Razz asked them to concentrate harder and snapped his fingers once, when a magical, warm tingling sensation fell over the three boys.

"Sir, these things belong to the crew who set sail aboard an ocean liner in the year of nineteen twelve."

"Is it the Titanic?" squealed Charlotte. "The ship they claimed was unsinkable."

"Yes," said Razz, "And the violin belongs to Roger Marie Bricoux," Tim said, holding the instrument in his hands. "The pocket watch belonged to Sinai Kantor, a wealthy passenger aboard the ship," Replied Lyle. "The jacket belongs to none other than Captain Edward John Smith, who went down with the ship." Said Seth.

Everyone was impressed with Tim, Seth, and Lyle's words of knowledge.

"Outstanding lads," said Razz. Although none of his pupils were clairvoyant, being an elite came with its unique gifts and privileges. "I will train you how to use your special abilities to help humanity when called upon. In time, you will meet the Elders; however, only when you have grown more. This school has existed for over two hundred years because it is a private order successfully hidden in plain sight, protected by a code of conduct established by God, which also keeps the ministry safe from the outside world. Angels of God have been here for centuries, ministering, serving, and protecting man as God commands. Woodland is a gateway between two worlds: Heaven and Earth. Our mission is to train you to work alongside angels until you graduate from Woodland. Know this: many are called, but few are chosen to be where you are. If you choose to stay, it's your choice, but your knowledge of what you have seen and heard today will be obliterated if you choose to leave. You will have twenty-four hours to think it over. We will resume here tomorrow at seven o'clock, don't be late. You may return to your other classes," commanded Razz.

The elites raced happily to their next class. Natalie didn't know what to think and said, "Sam, I didn't know this school would be like this."

"Are you going to stay, or are you going to leave?" Natalie asked her galvanized bestie.

"I'm staying; my parents will be thrilled about it. I plan on telling them as soon as school is over today."

"That's wonderful, Sam. I'd like to tell my parents, but they won't be happy about it. I really don't think they'd believe me if I told them."

"What are you going to do?"

"I don't know. I must think about it more. I'm sure I don't want to hurt my family."

"Natalie, I'm sorry you have to bear this decision on your own. You'll make the best choice, and whatever you decide upon, I'll support you one hundred percent." Natalie's eyes turned misty.

"I wish I'd never entered the games. Oh, Sam, what am I going to do?" Natalie asked respectfully.

"Nat, I can't answer that for you, but what do you want?"

"I know how much you love it here, and I know you would never want to leave," said Sam, and she was right.

Natalie could never leave her beloved Woodland behind. With a heavy heart, Sam told her, "I think you should decide on what makes you happy." Natalie listened to her friend but didn't say more. Sam went on, "If all else fails, my mother always told me, 'When in doubt, pray.'" Then they headed to Miss Sherman's class.

Natalie and Sam got ready for bed for the night. Natalie mentioned nothing more about the Hall of Doors, her decision, or the archangel Razz to Sam. She thought and thought, but couldn't decide what her next move would be. Natalie overheard Sam telling her parents about her decision over the phone, and like Sam, they were thrilled about it. If only her parents were like Sam's, things might be easier for her, but they weren't. Not wanting to think about it anymore, she fell off to sleep. While in a deep sleep, Natalie had a night vision.

> *She saw an enormous pair of hands extended from a white robe, and gold shimmered, dust showered over her while she lay on the bed. "NATALIE, NATALIE!" She heard and answered, "I am here," said Natalie. "YOU NO LONGER NEED TO DOUBT ANY MORE. I AM REAL AND I AM WITH YOU. I HAVE GREAT PLANS FOR YOU AND YOUR FAMILY." She could see a huge throne and an alluring light that covered the man's face and chest, leaving his feet exposed. A hue of bright colors of a rainbow shone behind him, creating a beautiful edifice. The voice said, "I WILL SHOW YOU THE MYSTERIES OF HEAVEN. I HAVE CHOSEN YOU TO WORK MY PURPOSE. HAVE FAITH AND BELIEVE." She woke with tears streaming down her face, and she knew what she must do.*

# Chapter Twenty-Two

# The Seer

The next day, Natalie went to Miss Sherman's office to talk to her about her dream. Natalie found Miss Sherman's door partially open when she arrived. She tapped on the door three times.

"Come in," Miss Sherman said kindly.

Inside, nicely lined shelves of seventeenth-nineteenth-century hardcover volumes of intellectual inspiration, nooks on the opposite side of the room drew Natalie further into the room. There, behind her desk, a black and white rectangle street sign read ENGLISH DR in block lettering, adding a nice accent to the red brick herringbone backsplash wall. A four-pane oval window rested in the center at the top of the wall, overlooking the green, spacious grounds outdoors.

On her desk, Natalie looked at an old vintage photo of Woodland Academy. The school looked different today than it did in the photo. The school had undergone several modern designs over the years. Soft yellow light from the floor lamps cast ample lighting in the room. A black vintage typewriter with a wooden cube of the date, day, month, and year rested on her distressed 1900s-style oak desk. Underneath it lay a Persian rug, and in front of her desk, two antique library desk chairs.

In the middle of searching the shelves for a book, she stopped to learn why Natalie came to see her. "Well, to what do I owe the pleasure, Miss Evergreen?" she said, sitting in her imported executive chair.

Natalie came closer to her desk.

"Please have a seat," said Miss Sherman. A trio of tall English books, with two lovely sterling silver doves' bookends, helped ease the tension of why she was there early in the morning. Natalie bit down on her lip softly and spoke.

"Good morning, Miss Sherman; I am sorry to trouble you at this hour."

"It's no trouble at all, Natalie; I always have time for Woodland's students, especially its Champions."

Natalie sat in the comfortable chair and said, "Miss Sherman, I was led to come to you, for I knew you were the only person who would understand."

"Yes, go on."

"God spoke to me last night."

"What?"

"I know it sounds crazy, but I never believed in God until now, and I'm sure it was Him who spoke to me."

"How did He speak to you?"

"Through a dream. God told me not to doubt but to believe."

"Did He say anything else?"

"He said He had plans for my parents and me. He said He was going to reveal to me the Mysteries of Heaven. Then I saw the throne room. I couldn't look upon His face, but only the throne and the lower part of His body. In His presence, I heard angelic music and singing. I remembered being saturated with…" Her retelling of the experience stirred her emotionally.

"Saturated in what?" Miss Sherman asked, mystified.

"Liquid love; it rested on me long after I awoke from the dream."

"It appears, Natalie, your dream was not just a dream but an open vision of Heaven."

"I don't understand."

"Natalie, there are several types of visions. The most common are dreams, but not limited to dreams only, but also panoramic vision, visuals, divine vision, and even out-of-body experiences, to name a few. Panoramic vision appears as multiple moving pictures in your mind's eye. In short, you're watching a short movie through your eyes in your head. Now, pictorial visions are images flashing in your mind like a snapshot. The picture is a visual to help you understand what God is telling you. When one sees something unexplainable in the physical world, filling them with awe, it is called divine vision. And then, there's a near-death experience. This means a person's spirit can leave his body and interact in the spiritual realm. This vision can also occur in deep prayer. However, it occurs… It's important to know, God is protecting that person's soul the whole time."

"You mention an open vision of Heaven; what is it?" asked Natalie, internalizing every word Miss Sherman spoke to her.

Miss Sherman continued, explaining, "An open vision of Heaven is a channel between the natural to the spiritual realm. You're not just Natalie Evergreen, but Natalie the SEER."

"I am a seer. God has chosen me to be a seer?"

"Yes, I believe He has."

"Why me?"

"I don't know, but if what you tell me is true, you will come to know His purpose and fulfill His plan if you will trust Him. It's also important that you understand what kind of Seer God has called you to either a prophetic or an intercessor. One thing is for sure: you're going to need the power to endure if you choose to accept Him. If you decide to walk with the Lord, you will embark upon a new journey, and it will not be easy; it will be tedious but fulfilling. Natalie, you will need to be strong." Miss Sherman encouraged her and continued, "But be of good courage for the LORD OF HOST will be with you."

"This power? How do I receive it?" asked Natalie.
"Are you willing to trust Him completely?"

"I am."

"I would like to pray the Prayer of Salvation with you, and afterward, you will be endowed with power from on high," said Miss Sherman with a heart of joy.

Natalie received the Lord gladly in her heart and became a Christian. After the prayer, Natalie asked, "What do I do now?"

"You wait and pray."

"What if I fail?"

"You won't because you're in excellent hands."

"Miss Sherman, how long have you been a servant of God?"

"Quite a while."

The sand in the hourglass on her shelf was quickly emptying, and the hour was getting late. It would be time for Natalie to go to the Hall of Doors. Natalie embraced Miss Sherman because she gave her life to God.

"Remember, Natalie, all things are possible with God when you believe."

Natalie smiled and said, "See you later in class, Miss Sherman."

"Very well, off you go!"

Natalie left Miss Sherman to find Sam to tell her about her faith before Razz's class began.

None of the elites wished to discontinue their class sessions and vowed to remain the chosen elites. When Razz ended class, Natalie told him about her dream and Miss Sherman. He was pleased and told her continually to seek Him daily. It was final; Natalie accepted her call to become a Seer of God.

Natalie's guide continued to visit her nightly. A token no student at Woodland. During one visit, her guide came to her and asked her to go with him. They zapped instantly to the front entrance of Woodland Academy. She, in her PJs, walked with him away from the school's entrance to the dove statue in the yard. The dove came to life and flew high into the air. They watched him as he flew higher into the puffy white clouds with their backs turned away from the school. "The Elders thought it was time you saw Woodland in her authentic form," said her guide.

Natalie slowly turned to look at the school, and what she saw nearly took her breath away. Woodland, in all her bright glory, looked like a heavenly city fit for his royal citizens. The pearl-made structure was its grand oyster. In front of the building were two large gold thirty-foot angel statues, sounding slender trumpets, standing apart from each other. Sweet musical tunes bellowed from the swaying green grass as gentle breezes blew across the grounds. White daisies planted across the lawn made the luster of the grass glisten. Sidewalks were paved in gold, and the lamp poles were black onyx, and the lamps were in a glass emerald case. Its splendor and beauty mesmerized Natalie.

He explained that the school's most significant treasure wasn't the school, but the unveiling of wisdom taught at Woodland Academy. "God has the answers, and

He uses revelations, prophets, and the Holy Ghost to reveal His mysteries during the fullness of time," said her guide as they walked the grounds.

Finally, her guide revealed something Natalie would never forget. He whispered, "Our Father built Woodland Academy from the heavens."

Then she was back in her body, resting soundly in her bed again.

By March, Natalie was up to her restricted third class. After being taught visions, the third eye realm, the elites learned how to minister to hurt and broken souls around the world in seconds under the angels' supervision in their second class.

In the third class, they taught the elites the acts of defense; Natalie learned to fight not against flesh and blood, but against principalities, against powers, against the rulers of this world's darkness, against spiritual wickedness in high places. To defeat these evils, she and the elites learn how to possess the armor of God.

The helmet helps guard their minds against Satan's lies, traps, and confusion. This defense taught the elites how to renew their minds, casting down imaginations, and the chief thing that exalted itself against the knowledge of God, bringing into captivity every thought to the obedience of Christ. With the helmet of salvation, elites can believe what appears to be impossible. Satan counts on God's elites not to protect their minds because this is where he launches his attacks. Salvation is not a one-time act but an ongoing, eternal state for daily protection and deliverance from the sin nature and Satan's wicked tools and devices.

Soldiers wore a breastplate in a battle to protect their vital organs, such as their lungs and heart. Christ's death accounted for righteousness, offering a covering of righteousness to block Satan's attacks on our hearts and souls. This armor is known as the breastplate of righteousness.

Around a soldier's waist, the belt of truth. The belt keeps the breastplate in place, and it guards against the elites not being fooled by every wind of doctrine of trickery and deceitful scheming by men.

Roman soldiers wore special footwear, like sandals or boots, when temperatures turned cooler. God's elites go into battle with their feet shod with the preparation of the gospel of peace. This helps them take and share the gospel wherever they go.

A sword is a weapon used to cut and protect. The sword represents the Word of God, and it is alive and active. It penetrates even to dividing souls and spirit, joints, and marrow; it judges the heart's thoughts and attitudes, making it cut like a knife. Interpreting the word with understanding can penetrate the most stubborn hearts, changing lives entirely.

Finally, a soldier took to battle with a scutum, also known as a shield. This shield was like a large door, and it covered the warrior entirely, which helped protect against arrows launched from high above. Many times, the enemy attempts to plague us with doubt. The shield of faith recognizes the deceptiveness of his tactics and instantly quenches, extinguishing fiery darts and arrows.

Before they could fight the forces of evil, each had to exhibit each virtue whole heartily; without the armor of protection, no elite could win spiritual battles without the weapons of God. Until they were ready, they remained in training under the tutelage of the "Worker Bee" angels who receive their orders from archangels Jehudiel and Sealtiel.

The third week of March brought in boisterous winds perfect for flying kites and budding blossoms around the campus, and inside Woodland's doors, students began packing to go home for spring break. Roberto picked Natalie up from school. While at home, she finished the book and began working on the book's presentation.

# Chapter Twenty-Three

# Sparks Fly

Lucy heard the car pull in; she'd opened the front door and waited for her Little Nina to come inside. As soon as Roberto opened Natalie's car door, she rushed into Lucy's arms inside the house. Lucy hugged her and said, "*¡Bienvenido a casa! ¡Te extrañé muchísimo,* Little Nina!"

She answered, "I missed you too, and I have much to tell you." Natalie looked around the foyer for her parents and asked, "Where are Mom and Dad?"

"They called and said they were on their way home five minutes ago. Your father's car has been in the shop for a week; the brakes needed repairing. The dealership called and said the car was ready, so they went to pick it up a little while ago. Mrs. Evergreen took your father in her car to retrieve it," said Lucy, as Roberto brought Natalie's luggage inside the house. "Wow! How you've grown since we last saw you." Roberto said, entering the kitchen. Lucy agreed with Roberto as she inspected her and sensed something was different about her after Roberto joked about her growth spurt.

"Um, I can't put my finger on it, but there's something different about you," cried Lucy.

"I'm the same as I always was," said Natalie.

Roberto interjected, "Señorita, Lucy has a surprise for you. Do you still love oatmeal walnut raisin cookies?"

"You bet I do!" Her mouth watered for the homemade treat. "I know there are a dozen of them waiting for you in the cookie jar."

"I'd love two."

"Help yourself!" said Lucy. Natalie opened the red and black chef cookie jar and bit into the warm, delicious oatmeal treat. "Lucy, these are the best cookies ever," said Natalie. Lucy smiled and asked her how things were going at school.

"I'm learning a great deal, and I've made new friends." Suddenly, they heard keys opening the front door.

"Mom, Dad, you're home!" exclaimed Natalie.

"Pumpkin nose!" said Lloyd, walking through the door. Natalie's parents hugged their daughter in the middle of the parlor.

"Now that you're home, we can catch up. Lloyd and I have been planning your return daily," said Melissa.

"I can't wait," said Natalie. "First things first, what do you say, gang, to movie night, an old Evergreen's tradition?" asked Lloyd, holding up *Harriet* in one hand and *Artemis Fowl* in the other.

"Sounds great," said Natalie.

"And for tomorrow night," said Melissa. "I thought we would go see *Hamilton* on Broadway."

"I heard it's a fantastic musical," said Natalie.

Later that night, Natalie watched a movie with her family but fell asleep during the film. Lucy covered her with a light pink plush blanket. "It's not like her to fall asleep during movie night," said Lloyd.

"Honey, she's been busy with extra-curricular activities, winning games at the school, while maintaining over a point four GPA; no wonder the poor child is exhausted," whispered Melissa. "We're raising one amazing daughter, aren't we?"

"Yes, we are, and I have never been prouder of her than I am right now," said Melissa.

Lloyd kissed his wife tenderly on her soft lips and finished watching *Harriet* on their 72-inch flat-screen TV.

The next day, Natalie faced-timed Trever and told him about winning the tournament, and he told her all he'd been doing. After talking for two hours, Natalie and Trever were going stronger than ever again. Natalie's cell rang after she hung up with Trever. "Natalie, have you finished reading the book?"

"Yes, I have."

"Have you thought about your presentation?"

Before she could answer, she heard her mother calling for her. "Sam, I must go. I'll call you back later."

"Okay, bye!" said Sam.

Her mother said, "Knock, knock," as she walked into her room.

"Sweetheart, the play starts at seven tonight, and our plane leaves at three o'clock this afternoon. Therefore, we will leave at one this afternoon. When we get to New York, we will check into the hotel, rent a limo, and the driver will take us to the Broadway Theater. Make sure you pack right away."

"Yes, Mother. How long will we stay in New York?"
"Long enough to do some sightseeing and shopping! We will return by the middle of the week."

"Outstanding," said Natalie as she went into her closet to get her pink and white polka-dot suitcase. Her mother left her to pack, and she went to her office to send a fax.

By Wednesday, the family had returned from New York. Natalie enjoyed the play, shopping at Saks and Tiffany's. Thursday, she rested, and Sunday, she finished the book report for the presentation. Satisfied, she placed the book onto her bookshelf as she did before and her report into her book satchel. Spring break was over, and Natalie returned to Woodland. Lloyd and Melissa saw their daughter off as Roberto drove her back to school.

A few days passed, and the Evergreens' house was quiet again. Lloyd missed his daughter and went up to her room to be close to her. The room was nice and tidy. He sat on the bed for a few seconds, taking an interest in her love for books; he walked over to her bookshelf. He ran his fingers across the spines of the books. Lloyd noticed a book turned with the leaves facing him. Thinking nothing of it, he placed it back correctly on the shelf. He picked it up, and to his detriment, he read the cover: *Is God Real?* His eyes raised, and his jaws tightened as he thumbed through the text. Inside, he saw post-it notes found inside the pages.

The book made a thud sound as he plopped it down on top of his wife's office desk. Melissa, on the phone, looked at her husband and said, "Dr. Mannford, I will have to call you back; something just came to my attention." She hung up.

"Babe, what's wrong?"

He lashed out, "This is what's wrong?" He pointed to the book on her desk.

Melissa read the cover. "Where did you get this?"

"I found this in our daughter's room."

"You were snooping?"

"No, of course not. I went to Natalie's room because I miss her. I was sitting on the bed, then I walked over to her bookshelf and discovered one of her books was out of place on the shelf. I took the book, placed it correctly onto the shelf, and found it."

"Maybe it doesn't belong to her; it could be Sam's book."

"Unlikely, I found notes written in her hand inside." Melissa looked through the book while pacing the floor. Melissa read some post-its and a few chapter headings and asked her husband. "You don't think Natalie believes in all of this, do you?"

Lloyd could not say no too convincingly. "Melissa, she's been keeping this from us. She never told us she was reading this. Natalie knows we don't believe in God; we have taught her better than to believe in an unseen God who fills people's heads with flights of rubbish used to control people's lives and their destinies. I have taught her there is no God, just people in a world filled with crime, sickness, and violence," said Lloyd to his wife as his jaws tightened.

"Lloyd, I think you should calm down and hear her side of the story," said Melissa peacefully.

"If she's been hiding this from us, I wonder what else she has been keeping from us that we don't know about?"

"Lloyd, you've got to keep calm and keep an open mind. I know Natalie wouldn't do anything irrational," said Melissa.

"I think it's time we take a drive up to Woodland and have a talk with our daughter immediately."

Lucy, overhearing the couple talking, feared for Natalie.

The Evergreens drove to Woodland the next morning, as Lloyd said they would. Back at school, Natalie realized she had left the book for Miss Sherman's reading assignment at home. She needed to get it back before her parents could discover it. Fortunately, she realized her parents had left her room off-limits when she was away, but she had to admit having the book with her would put her mind at ease.

Lloyd and Melissa arrived at the school early, and they didn't tell Natalie they were coming to see her. The Evergreens walked into the immaculate school. In the center of the hall was the school's atrium. The Quarter Annual Cup with Natalie's team's names written along with her team's grade level and year was placed inside its glass case. Melissa asked a student walking down the hall to point them to the school's office.

Miss Sugarman was busy typing a letter for Professor Howell, who was out of the office for the day. The Evergreens stood in front of her desk, waiting for her to acknowledge their presence. "May I help you?" she asked, looking up from her typewriter under her cat frame glasses attached to a flashy chain.

Lloyd read her nameplate on her desk and said, "Miss Sugarman, I am Dr. Lloyd Evergreen, and this is Dr. Melissa Evergreen, my wife, and we would like to speak to our daughter, Natalie Evergreen, at once!"

"Well, welcome to Woodland Academy!" said Miss Sugarman. Her long red nails began pecking at the computer to locate Natalie's schedule. She found Natalie's student record. When she discovered her record, she said, "Perfect timing; she's at lunch, but it will take a few seconds," said Miss Sugarman, sending a school prefect to fetch her from the canteen.

"Is there somewhere we can wait?" asked Lloyd.

"You can wait in the conference room, right through the doors to the left." They walked past her desk to wait for their daughter in the conference room.

Within five minutes, Natalie walked through the doors. "Mom, Dad, what are you doing here? I was about to call you. I left one of my reading books."

Before she could finish, "You mean this?" asked her father.

Natalie felt her heart drop to the floor. There he was, holding the book she had been keeping from them. The thing she feared the most had come upon her. “Dad, how did you find that?” Natalie asked.

Her father fired back. “Never mind how I found it. The question is, what was this book doing in your room?”

“Dad, I know how this looks, but I can explain.”

“What do you have to say for yourself?”

“I wanted to tell you and Mom. Honestly, I did.”

“How long have you been reading it? No, scratch that; why didn’t you tell us about it?” Lloyd’s voice rose, and Melissa rested her hand upon his shoulder to calm him as she leaned in to hear what Natalie had to say.

“I am sorry you found out this way. I was waiting for the right time to tell you.”

“How about now?” Lloyd snarled.

“Lloyd, I think we owe it to ourselves to hear Natalie out about why she kept the book a secret,” said Melissa.

Natalie continued, “Miss Sherman asked the class to read it and do a book report on it and present it to the class at the end of the school year. The book report will count one-half of the class grade, and I’ve been reading the book since the beginning of school. Miss Sherman also asked us to take a stand about the book,” said Natalie.

“So, it was your teacher who put you up to this, huh?”

“Dad, none of this is Miss Sherman’s fault. I wanted to read about God to learn if he is real or a myth, and I didn’t tell you because I knew you would react this way and not let me read the book.”

“You were right to assume. There was no way I was going to let you read this because it’s not real.”

“You're wrong about it; God, He is real.”

“This book is dangerous. Already it's changed you, and that's why I didn't want you to read it. I've always told you the truth.”

"You have, but I know God is real. He has revealed Himself to me in the spirit. Dad, you only know what you think based on what you study through science and how you perceive the world through your eyes. You're having trouble believing, which makes it hard for you to believe God is real in your heart."

"What is that supposed to mean?"

"It means if you can't see it, touch it, then it doesn't exist, but because you can't see God, it doesn't mean He doesn't exist; after all, we can't see the wind, but we know it exists."

"I can feel the wind; therefore, it exists and is real."

"Likewise, we can't see God, but we can feel him, which makes Him real like the wind," said Natalie.

"I've heard enough, and I am going to have a word with your teacher, Miss Sherman, and Headmistress Howell of the school, and demand that Miss Sherman stop teaching this book. If Miss Sherman doesn't, I will withdraw you from Woodland Academy," said Lloyd.

"Dad, you can't do that. I love it here, and God is real; why don't you believe me?" Tears rolled down her face as she turned to her mother and said, "Mom, please don't let Dad take me away from Woodland, my teacher, my friends, and Sam." Her mother listened but didn't want to say anything.

"Who does this teacher think she is, giving her students this book to read without asking us first?"

"It is not about the book, but this school is a magical place," said Natalie.

"First, the book, now the school's magical," Lloyd said sarcastically. Natalie didn't want to tell her father about the supernatural things about Woodland Academy, fearing he would not believe her, but she did in hopes her father would believe her.

"This is no ordinary school. At first, I didn't believe it either. But after I won the tournament and became an elite, that's when I learned the truth about the Mysteries of Woodland Academy. My spiritual guide, who was assigned to me, explained why supernatural occurrences happen here, and it is because the school was built by —" Lloyd interrupted before she could finish.

"That is the most ridiculous thing I have ever heard of; it's a school, nothing more. Besides, I see nothing out of the ordinary happening here."

"You haven't been here long enough to notice," said Natalie. She took a significant risk revealing Woodland to her father, but if there was a chance, he believed her she'd take the gamble. Lloyd shook his head; he didn't know how much more he could listen to it.

Natalie continued, "This is not only an institute for learning, but they use it for far more. The school's Elders chose specially selected groups to represent and go into the world to change it for the better, to do good, provide peace on Earth and goodwill toward man," said Natalie to her father passionately.

"Sweetheart, I'm all for you changing the world, but I do not want religion forced upon you by a religious antic; none of this is your fault but Miss Sherman. I can't wait to give her half of my mind. Because of this book, Miss Sherman has been reading to you; it has you believing the school is a magical institution of learning, a bunch of hogwash." Lloyd tried to convince his daughter that the school was just a school, and the book was clouding her judgment in discerning fact from fiction.

Natalie knew her father was having a hard time believing the truth. It was easier to blame someone for his daughter's new idealism than to accept that his daughter was losing her mind.

Miss Sherman came into the office to check her mailbox. Miss Sugarman greeted her. Miss Sherman heard a heated discussion coming from the conference room about her reading assignment. Miss Sherman walked into the conference room and said, "Excuse me, I'm Miss Sherman, Natalie's Language Arts teacher, and I couldn't help but overhear that there is a problem with the reading assignment I assigned."

"So, you're Miss Sherman; we're the Evergreens, Natalie's parents, and we are outraged you have been teaching Natalie this absurdity," he said harshly, waving the book in front of her face.

"Excuse me; I don't understand why you're upset when you signed the form agreeing Natalie could take part in the reading assignment."

"What consent form?" asked Melissa.

"I'm talking about the consent form with your signatures I have from you inside my desk," said Miss Sherman.

"Dear lady, I do not know what you're talking about, and I can assure you we never signed a consent form from you." Said Lloyd, not understanding any of it.

Miss Sherman turned her attention to her student. "Natalie, did you sign the form?" asked Miss Sherman softly.

Natalie confessed she forged her parents' signature and had given it to Miss Sherman.

"Natalie, I can't believe you did this. You're grounded." He pointed his finger at her. "We'll talk about it more when we get home."

Lloyd apologized to Miss Sherman for Natalie's behavior. He stormed out of the room to see Miss Sugarman for withdrawal forms. The curly-haired blonde secretary gave him everything he needed to start the withdrawal process.

"Before the withdrawal can be complete, you'll have to meet with Professor Howell, the headmistress. Before you can officially withdraw your daughter from Woodland, Professor Howell must sign off on the forms; however, she is out today, but she will return tomorrow morning. I will let you know when she can meet with you as soon as she returns. Shall I pencil you in?"

"Yes!" said Lloyd, handing her his card.

The blonde secretary with red lipstick on her front teeth gave Lloyd the forms he requested and checked his daughter out for the day. While Lloyd was busy signing Natalie out of school, in the conference room, Natalie asked Miss Sherman to forgive her for deceiving her and apologized to her mother. Melissa's heart melted because she knew Natalie was genuinely sorry for the things she had done.

"Natalie, what you did was wrong, but we will discuss it later," said her mother.

Miss Sherman forgave Natalie, and Lloyd entered the room again with the forms and said, "We are leaving now!" He gave Miss Sherman her last ultimatum. "Either you stop the reading assignment, or I am withdrawing Natalie from Woodland Academy, permanently."

"I am sorry, Dr. Evergreen, but I cannot do that."

"I am sorry too." He looked her deep in the eye and walked out with his family.

Melissa didn't take too kindly to Lloyd's decision. "Don't you think you're overreacting? Natalie has two months of school left. Surely, you won't do this before she can complete her final grade?" asked Melissa. Lloyd ignored his wife's comment in the car and drove his family home. When he didn't answer, she knew there was no talking to him any further.

# Chapter Twenty-Four

# Home Sweet Home

*The ride home was long, silent, and awkward*, thought Natalie. The tension in the car was thick as pea soup, and Natalie couldn't believe how fast things had gone from bad to worse so quickly. All she could feel was bad. What will she say to Sam? What about the elites? Why would God choose her only to let her leave Woodland before His plans were complete? Natalie didn't know what to think anymore, but she never wanted to hurt or embarrass her parents. Never did she feel so lost.

In her despair, she remembered what Miss Sherman had spoken to her in her office. "Be strong and of good courage during your trials."

It was clear her heart and faith were being attacked; it was a test. Through it all, Natalie refused to believe God had abandoned her. Suddenly, God opened her eyes into the spirit realm. A bright light opened before her in the car's backseat; it was another open Heavenly vision.

> *Rays from bright light cast a golden Roman helmet on her head as she looked at her reflection in her father's rear-view mirror. A golden breastplate replaced her school uniform, and next to her on the black leather seat, a hand-held shield and sword. "BE NOT DISMAYED I AM WITH YOU," said the voice from the Heavens.*

Natalie knew whose voice it was. It was the voice of God. The light dimmed, and Natalie gazed back at her reflection: she was back in her school uniform, and the armor disappeared.

Natalie's parents didn't hear the voice speaking to their daughter in the car; only Natalie could listen to the voice. Torn between faith and family, she continued to humble herself before them.

The tension between Natalie and her parents was so thick they could cut it with a knife. Finally, they made it home; Natalie went straight up to her room when she left the car.

"We're not done talking about this," said her father.

Natalie went upstairs, called Sam, and told her everything that happened. Sam was heartbroken.

Her father went inside and poured himself a drink from the wet bar. He poured a bottle of bourbon over two ice cubes into his short glass. Loosening his striped navy tie, he sat comfortably in front of the bar in his pressed navy slacks. There, he tried to make sense of everything that happened that day.

In walked Melissa, "Lloyd, I know you're angry about today, but pulling our daughter out of school and her friends at the end of the year doesn't seem like the right thing to do," said Melissa, standing next to him at the bar.

Lloyd, squeezing his forehead gently with his fingers, closed his eyes briefly and said, "Melissa, you heard the things she was saying about the school. Now, she hears voices; God's voice?" He breathed a deep sigh, "That's crazy, Melissa!"

She was about to reply, but stopped when she saw Natalie standing in the doorway. Natalie confessed she was a Christian to her parents. Her father walked over to one window and pretended as if he wasn't listening to her. Lloyd had turned his back on his daughter with a heavy heart.

Natalie dropped her head and said softly, "I thought you should know." Then she returned to her room and sobbed.

"I thought I knew our daughter. I can't stand to look at her anymore. She's not who I thought she was," said Lloyd as his muscles tightened.

"Lloyd, you can't be angry forever; she's still our daughter, and nothing can change that."

"Melissa, please, I need you on my side."

"I am on your side, but I don't want to lose our daughter because of this. Yes, she shouldn't have lied to us or forged our signatures. But she did it because she knew we wouldn't let her read the book. Lloyd, she was curious. After all, we never talk about religion in this house. She read it to make up her mind about God. We have always taught our daughter to follow her heart and dreams. But you wanted her to change the world your way through science and medicine; you wanted her to be like you."

"That's not fair, Melissa."

"You haven't been the same since your Grandpa Joe died. I know you had a hard time letting go."

"That has nothing to do with this."

"Are you sure?"

"Yes!" Lloyd said, powerless.

"The point is, she believes God is real. Whether He is or not, I have never seen her like this before," said Melissa.

"Natalie has been hoodwinked by that brainless teacher of hers."

"And what kind of school is Professor Howell running at Woodland Academy?" asked Lloyd sarcastically.

"How do you suggest we handle this?" asked Melissa.

"We have to separate the lock from the key."

"Meaning?"

"We will have to remove Natalie from Miss Sherman's classroom and get her to the best doctors money can buy," said Lloyd.

Annoyed, she replied, "We are not putting our daughter away. I can't believe you suggested that. Not after we grounded her for three months, which is the longest we ever punished our daughter."

"It's until she gets better."

"Absolutely not, Lloyd," Melissa said, putting her foot down. "There has to be another way that doesn't lead to putting our daughter in a mental institute. I will talk to her, but there's no way we're sending our daughter off to some loony bin," said Melissa, leaving the room.

Upstairs behind locked doors, Natalie prayed to God for help; in the middle of her prayer, she heard two knocks at the door. She finished and opened the door. It was Lucy at the door.

Lucy said reluctantly, "Your father has asked me to retrieve your cell phone, laptop, and Apple watch."

"I understand," said Natalie, and handed over her effects from her side table.

"I heard what happened today."

Natalie shrugged her shoulders. There was nothing anyone could do to help her or get her father to forgive her. Seeing how down she was, she said,

"Natalie, it takes a special person to stand up to your parents and a bigger one to stand up for what he or she believes. You have a heart of a fearless lion, which is why you were born July twenty-sixth, Little Nina."

"But my father is furious; he refuses to speak to me, and he thinks I'm touched. Mother doesn't know what to make of this. I'm afraid we may never get past this," said Natalie.

"Give it time; things have a way of turning around when you least expect them. Your father loves you, Natalie, and he will come around," said Lucy. She hugged her and went downstairs to give her father the requested items.

And so the word made it to the elites. Natalie was leaving Woodland Academy. Charlotte, Dexter, Sam, Lyle, and Dave knew they had to do something, but what could they do when the outcome would remain the same? During their study period, the elites put their heads together to stop Natalie's parents from withdrawing her from Woodland.

Hours later, Lloyd called Miss Sugarman and requested a hearing with Professor Howell, demanding that Miss Sherman stop teaching religion in her classroom. If she didn't conform, he'd withdraw Natalie from Woodland permanently. Miss Sugarman made a note of it, and she told him she'd call him back tomorrow.

Lois Howell returned to campus the next day. Miss Sugarman filled her in on the details of Natalie's parents and Miss Sherman's dilemma. Professor Lois considered the request and said, "Tell Dr. Evergreen he has a board meeting, and we will meet in the conference room on Thursday, March 23, at nine a.m. sharp."

Miss Sugarman jotted the information down on her notepad with her pencil. "I'll let him know right away." She picked up the phone and informed Dr. Evergreen about the upcoming meeting. Lloyd agreed to attend the meeting on Thursday.

In the meantime, Professor Lois met with Miss Sherman privately. Miss Sherman told her what Natalie had done regarding her parents' signatures. "Did you know she forged her parents' signature?" Lois asked.

"No. I didn't," said Miss Sherman.

"This could get out of hand, and we will do everything in our power to make sure it doesn't. We don't want any negative press concerning the school. We're going to do this by the books and resolve the matter with wit and precision," said Lois.

Lloyd thought about *Memphis; home sweet home* is where they will return if the board continues to let Miss Sherman teach God in her classroom. He believed that if he moved Natalie away from Woodland, perhaps she would forget about God and the school in time.

Melissa decided she'd talk to Natalie. Her last-ditch effort to get her to denounce Christianity and the hearing voices. If Natalie agrees to it, she could easily be removed from Miss Sherman's class and stay at Woodland Academy. Melissa went to her room and knocked.

Natalie replied, "It's open!" Natalie thought how pretty her mother looked in her string of white pearls and black and white polka dot short-sleeved knee-length dress. Everything Melissa wore fit her petite frame well.

Melissa said to her daughter, "Honey, I'm here to talk to you about the voices you hear in your head. Sweetheart, isn't it possible you have been working so hard you thought you heard voices because you were overworked?"

"Mom, I know you think I am crazy, but I am not mad."

"Natalie, I am really trying to understand. But what you're telling me is hard to believe," said Melissa.

"God talks to me, and I was having open visions of Heaven and of the school. I think my visions have something to do with you and Dad somehow because God told me He has plans for my family and me."

"What plans?" Her mother asked, intrigued.

"I don't know," said Natalie. "Natalie, your father is having a tough time accepting your faith. He means well, and he loves you very much; all you have to do is deny God, and things can go back to the way they were."

"Mom, I can't do that. I will not denounce God because He is real, and if Miss Sherman had never asked me to read the book, I wouldn't have gotten to know God or how wonderful He is. I'm glad I read the book, and I have never been happier about being a Christian. Before I became a Christian, my life was grand, but something was missing; it was unfulfilling. Although I have not been a Christian long, Christianity has changed my life, and I can not live without faith anymore. Mom, I love you and Dad, but I cannot do what you're asking me," said Natalie.

"Tomorrow, we have a meeting with the board, and Professor Lois and your father will demand that Miss Sherman stop teaching religion in her classroom. If they do not carry out his petition, he will withdraw you from Woodland, sell the house, and we'll move back to Memphis. You should know I am not happy about removing you from school, but I doubt I can stop it after tomorrow."

Natalie listened to her mother, but she didn't agree to anything. "Whatever happens after the board meeting, I will accept no matter the consequences," said Natalie.

Melissa realized she could not change her daughter's mind, but agreed they would have to let things unfold and focus on the outcome later. Melissa left the room, and Natalie got down on her knees to pray for divine help.

# Chapter Twenty-Five

# The Hearing

The sun rose high in the sky early Thursday morning. Although it was a bright sunny day, there was a chill in the air, and Lloyd thought to dress warmly, and from his walk-in closet of rows of shoes, watches, and Ray-Ban sunglasses, he chose a wool brown jacket along with an ivory button-down shirt, a multi-colored burnt orange, crimson striped silk box tie. His pressed light tan dress pants looked tailored-made on his body. He was satisfied with the shape of his goatee, his barber had given him, and his smile was white as the first fallen snowflake of Christmas. Last, he dabbed a little Versace Man After Shave behind his ears and below his neck in front of the mirror. Lloyd's smooth brown skin complemented his shaven head. Afterwards, he put on his watch, chocolate brown wool socks, and brown dress shoes, and waited for his wife and daughter to finish dressing. Melissa came downstairs in a red dress and a black blazer with a gold pin attached to the upper right side of her jacket. It was a gift from her mentor from medical school. Around her neck, she wore a string of black pearls, and around her left wrist, two gold bangles. Her red-bottom black heels gave her a sophisticated, polished look appropriate for this morning's hearing. She put her hair into a French roll, and her makeup looked soft and natural. Soon, the family was on their way to the meeting.

Natalie and her father were still not speaking to each other. She wondered how long he'd continue the silent treatment, probably a million years. They made it to the school thirty minutes early. Lloyd parked the car, and Natalie wasted no time getting out of the vehicle. She stepped out of the sedan wearing a short black mod A-line dress. Around her neck, she wore a sweet white lace beaded collar choker. The lace was lovely, with tiny rhinestones circling the pearl that lay over the lace in front of the choker. Over her dress, she wore a warm, long, black cashmere sleeve sweater. Instead of tights, she wore white hosiers and black Mary Janes.

Lloyd got out of the sky-blue sedan, opened his wife's door, and helped her out of the car. Closing the door behind her, he pressed the remote attached to his car keys; the car lights flashed twice and beeped.

Natalie walked ahead of them into the building, where the elites were waiting for her in the hall. Sam, Eddie, Charlotte, Lyle, Dexter, and Dave gathered around her and told her how they missed her in class. She was glad to see each of them, but their reunion had to wait; it was time for the meeting to start. Natalie's parents entered the conference room.

"Good luck today, Natalie," said Sam.

"Thanks, I am going to need it," Natalie replied, and went inside with her parents.

Because of the hearing, the elites were excused from classes to support Natalie. They waited outside in the hall until the meeting was over.

Lloyd, Melissa, and Natalie entered an altered conference room from the previous visit. On the oblong table were board members' nameplates facing the audience with long, slender microphones for the speaking panel. The room resembled similar features to a courtroom. The Evergreens sat in the audience chairs until Board members walked into the room. Ten Board members in black robes entered and sat in their respective places at the table. Each member brought their laptops, pencils, pens, and legal pads to place in front of their name tags. There was a pitcher of ice water and short glasses on a long silver platter, which sat on the table for board members to drink. They conversed with one another as they waited for the hearing to get underway.

Professor Lois, already in the room, tapped her dark cherry wood gavel once and said in a stern voice, "Good morning, everyone, if I could have your attention, please!" The room got quiet. "I'd like to welcome you all to today's private hearing, and if everyone would take their seats, we can begin. I am Professor Lois Stein Howell, Headmistress of Woodland Academy, and acting Chair of the Board. First, we will open with the school's mission."

The group stood and recited, "Our mission is to accept the glorious knowledge of our highest order to receive the gift of illumination to empower and lift the total man, to be a light, do good toward men as we hold these truths to be the core of our foundation of education."

Afterward, everyone pledged allegiance to the United States flag.

The Chair continued, "The meeting aims to hear and rule if Miss Sherman, a faculty member of Woodland Academy, should or should not continue teaching from her lesson plans; a book regarding religious content." Holding the book up for everyone to see, Lois continued, "The record states the book was chosen as a resource to complete for a book report in a Language Arts classroom. The Board will rule whether it should allow Miss Sherman to teach regardless of whether *God Real* or not. The Board will hear discussions concerning this petition brought forth by the concerned parent, Dr. Lloyd Evergreen. He is the father of Natalie Evergreen. But first, the chair calls Miss Sugarman, secretary, to introduce members of the board."

The curly blonde-haired woman spoke softly and gleefully into the microphone. "Good morning."

Everyone replied, "Good morning."

"Madam chair; Professor Lois Stein Howell, Secretary; Miss Sugarman, Vice-President; Mrs. Julie Collins, Treasury; Don Shaffer; Standing Committee; Oliver Lawson, Belinda Jackson, and Mr. Oscar Little, Special Committee: Mr. John Strassberg, Silas Vascow, and Thatcher Lovell," said Miss Sugarman as she passed the school's bylaws and charter to each board member.

"We will hear from parents, teachers, and students during the hearing regarding the subject at hand. There will be eight people who will approach the podium for discussion. Please keep comments respectful to the Board and direct all comments to the chair. You will have three minutes to speak. I urge you to focus on your major points. You want to be heard within the time limit. If your time expires, please conclude, take your seat, and yield the floor to the Chair. Also, do not speak without the Chair's recognition first. Before discussions begin, I would like to add that five school Elders will observe the meeting virtually. They will not take part in the meeting, only observe to assist the Board in future hearings better. First, up for discussion is Mrs. Simpson."

Truthfully, the Elders were not watching virtually, but from Heaven. The Elders were always watching over school affairs entrusted to them for centuries.

Mrs. Simpson's husband came with her but left the speaking to his wife because he was terrified of public speaking. Sam told Charlotte what happened to Natalie, and

Charlotte asked her parents to speak on Miss Sherman's behalf as a character witness at the hearing.

"Thank you, Madam Chair. I want to state Miss Sherman is an excellent teacher whose had a positive impact on my daughter's learning since Charlotte entered Miss Sherman's classroom. She's more excited about learning than ever. Often, she comes home raving about the exciting things Miss Sherman taught her. I have no problem with Miss Sherman's book report because we've always believed in God and couldn't be happier with Woodland's curriculum and its teachers. Miss Sherman is gifted and talented; she inspires and motivates student learning. Vote **NO** to stop Miss Sherman from teaching engaging topics and using resources that my child loves. Thank you, and I yield to the Chair."

Miss Simpson took her seat next to her sleepy-eyed husband. Miss Simpson was a mature Bostonian woman with green eyes and red hair. She straightened her blue and white checkered skating long dress with red wool tweed stitched around the color and down the dress's front. Miss Simpson properly straightened her blue and white checkered long-sleeved skating dress before sitting down. Charlotte, her daughter, was also a redhead, but dyed it champagne blonde when she started Woodland. Charlotte's father sat with a scrubby little beard, a woolen man's cap on his head, and a warm, cozy light sweater and brown trousers. The chair called Mr. Boggs, and he spoke in favor of Miss Sherman, as did Mrs. Kissinger and Mrs. Piper.

Now it was time for Dr. Lloyd to speak; he approached the podium. "Good morning, Madam Chair. Today, I am here to urge you to vote against Miss Sherman teaching God in the classroom, using a reading assignment to push her religious views and antics upon my child. First, let me say I don't believe in God, nor do I want my daughter taught such notions in her classroom. We did not know our daughter was being taught religious content behind our backs. We don't condone this reading assignment, and we weren't told about the assignment by her teacher. Miss Sherman chose this book while imposing it on her students to read instead of letting her students choose a book of their own. Later, my wife and I learned Miss Sherman sent permission slips home for parents to sign regarding this ghastly assignment; however, we never saw them. My daughter, Natalie, signed the form without us knowing about it. We reprimanded our daughter, and I can assure you she will not do this again at any other school she attends. The book contradicts everything we have taught her psychologically. Since reading the book, she thinks there is a God, and the school is magical. I do not want my daughter's education squandered on chutes and ladders fairytales. We do not want anyone encouraging Natalie to believe in a God that does not exist. To be clear, I believe in science and what I can see, touch, smell, and hear. If I cannot see, touch, smell, or hear it, it does not exist, and that's my Psalms 23. And if the Board doesn't reach a unanimous vote and censor Miss Sherman's classroom autonomy, I will indefinitely withdraw Natalie from Woodland Academy. I thank you for listening, and I yield the floor."

The next speaker was Coach Sax, who favored Lloyd's discussion on the Evergreens' grounds, not knowing their daughter was being taught religious content without her parents' consent, and they didn't have the same choice as other parents did. He pleaded with the Board to stand with Lloyd, banning Miss Sherman from teaching a controversial subject in her classroom. Stopping her alone would stop her from exposing Woodland to negative press when the school has avoided indecent exposure for over two hundred years.

After Coach Sax's engaging discussion, the Chair called Miss Sherman to the podium to speak.

"Thank you, Madam Chair, and I will begin by addressing what I do in my classroom. I create an environment conducive to learning by engaging my students with thought-provoking assignments that challenge them to think critically while introducing new concepts to their prior knowledge. As a teacher, I must put a fresh spin on learning styles and frameworks. This is what we're known for here at Woodland Academy: going beyond the norm, allowing our students to become partners with the teacher, the curriculum, grading, and their learning process. Also, this dynamic applies to parental involvement with the school and their child's educational plan. I want to state that I have in no way done anything wrong but chosen a book. I thought my students would question and provoke conversation about the world and how God sees the world, and how He will make it better for His creation. Last, I ask my students to express their thoughts about the book's content and take a stand on whether they believe in God, and justify their answers based on their perspective of the book. I do not seek to impose any religion upon my students, but I support them if they choose to give their lives to God. I am an advocate of free choice. My Lord does not impose His will on anyone, nor will I. My students have responded to the book positively and are learning countless reading skills while breaking down the plot's structure, fundamental ideas, and the author's ultimate purpose. My students love discussing the book with their classmates and me. While it is true, I did not speak to the Evergreens about the book; I sent home permission slips, asking parents if they would let their child take part in the reading assignment. I didn't know Natalie's parents never saw the permission slip, and for that, I apologize; however, I didn't know Natalie signed the form, but I know the book has had a profound effect on her because she accepted Christ in my office. As for the book, according to the school's charter, I reserve the right to teach the ancient text, and the book I chose is based on the Bible. My students love the book and are flourishing in the lessons, and I am receiving positive feedback from my students' writing assessments and pop quizzes on the book. Please do not stop my students from reading and completing their final grade presentation; they logged the hours, and it would be utterly unfair. If you censor my autonomy, you will alter the light that ignites students' love of learning in my classroom. **Vote No** against this attack on me and my classroom today. Thank you, I yield to the Chair," said Miss Sherman proudly. She left the podium and sat down with the rest of the attendees.

Applause arose after Miss Sherman finished. Madam chair banged her gavel three times to restore order. "There will be no clapping; please remain quiet as the hearing continues; the chair calls Natalie Evergreen, who will be the last speaker," said Madam Chair. Natalie rose to speak to the board.

"Good morning, and I'm happy to speak today. First, let me state how much I love Woodland Academy. My parents enrolled me here because of my best friend, Sam, who became a student here before me, not wanting to end our friendship; I applied because I didn't want to lose my best friend. When I arrived, I thought this school was like all other schools, but I found the school to be exceptional, above any school I've ever attended, and I thank my parents for allowing me to study here. I am aware of the chaos I've caused, and if I could do it all over again, I wouldn't change a thing. My classes are tough, and my teachers challenge me for the better; the annual games made me aware of how great Woodland Academy is; the games made me strong. However, we are here to question what Miss Sherman has been teaching me in reading class. I know my parents say the book is controversial, but I thought it was an interesting literary piece. When I learned the book's title, I couldn't explain it, but I felt compelled to read the book. So, I lied and hid the book from my parents, and worst, I deceived my teacher, forging my parents' signature permitting me to read the book, and for that, I apologize not only to Miss Sherman but also to my parents, classmates, and now the Board. I wanted to tell my parents the truth, but I knew they would disapprove of the book in my heart. None of this is Miss Sherman's fault, nor my parents.' Disobeying my parents wasn't what I wanted to do, but I read the book because I wanted to learn for myself if God is real. After all, we never talk about God at home. In the end, my life has changed since I gave Him my heart." Natalie knew her father would disapprove of what she said, but she could not take it back. "I take responsibility for my actions and ask you to forgive what I have done and absolve Miss Sherman because of my mistakes. She is a wonderful teacher, probably the best teacher I've ever had. Miss Sherman cares for her students, and she's a brilliant human being. **Vote No** against the motion and stand with Miss Sherman's teaching methods, strategies, and practices implemented in her classroom. I yield to the Chair." Natalie turned and took her seat slowly.

"The Board has heard the discussion, and now I will remind you once again that the item of business is why we are here. Dr. Lloyd Evergreen asked for this meeting, petitioning the Board to stop Miss Sherman, an instructor of Woodland, from teaching a book that teaches religion in her classroom. Dr. Evergreen's reason is that it goes against what he believes… knowing that his daughter was not being taught religious content. Before we go any further, one of our Board members would like to have a word. Therefore, the Chair yields to John Strassberg." Said Professor Lois.

The eldest Jewish man spoke, "In compliance with the school charter and bylaws, teachers can teach religious text or sacred texts that are not limited to the Bible but to Latin, Dead Sea Scrolls that are canonized or not, for educational purposes. This school was founded upon Biblical principles and will always defend and uphold the Holy Bible because it is a private school created for believers and unbelievers worldwide. I yield to the Chair," said Mr. Strassberg as he closed the school's official policy book.

"I move the ban on censorship of Miss Sherman's autonomy is stricken from the record. She may continue to teach from whatever resources serve in her students' best interest, regardless of religion, in her classroom," said Oliver Lawson, the distinguished black man with salt and pepper hair and beard on the panel.

"I second," said Silas Vascow, who was of Italian descent.

"It has been moved and seconded that the ban on censorship of Miss Sherman's autonomy in the classroom should be stricken from the record, and she can continue to teach from whatever resources serve in her students' best interest, regardless of religion, in her classroom at Woodland Academy. All oppose?"

"Nay!" said two Board members on the panel.

"All in favor?"

"Aye!" said the seven members.

"The ayes have it; the motion has carried the ban of censorship of Miss Sherman's autonomy in the classroom be stricken from the record, and she can continue to teach from whatever resources serve in her students' best interest, regardless of the religion in her classroom at Woodland Academy. That covers the first item on the agenda. Next item of business, student's withdrawal from Woodland."

After hearing the Board's decision, Coach Sax's face burned. He pursed his lips, shook his head, and left the room before the hearing was over. Seeing his reaction, the Board members continued.

"I move that Dr. Lloyd Evergreen may withdraw his daughter whenever he or his wife chooses to. He or his wife can enroll their daughter back into the academy whenever they like. Natalie Evergreen to return to Woodland Academy. The school will gladly welcome her back," said Belinda Jackson.

"I second," said Thatcher Lovell.

"It has been moved, and we have a second, that Dr. Lloyd Evergreen may withdraw his daughter, and if he or his wife chooses, can enroll their daughter back into the academy when they would like her to return. Woodland Academy will gladly welcome her back. All oppose?"

The members were silent.

"All in favor?"

"Aye."

"The ayes have it. Dr. Lloyd Evergreen may withdraw his daughter if he or his wife chooses, and can enroll their daughter back into the academy when they would like her to return. Woodland Academy will gladly welcome her back. Before we close, I would like to state that the school will miss Natalie Evergreen; she was a rising star, and we know she will be successful anywhere she goes, as she was here. We are sure we have not heard the last from Miss Evergreen."

After the Madam Chair summarized the agenda and stated actions taken concerning the item of business, she said, "That's all for today's meeting. I want to thank our Elders for viewing the meeting by virtual experience, and I thank everyone for attending." Then, she signed the withdrawal papers and said, "We are adjourned." She rapped the gavel once, and the hearing was over.

Lloyd clenched his fist and signed the last official form concerning the outcome of the meeting; then, before leaving, Lloyd was confronted by Charlotte and Eddie in the hall. They asked, "Why are you taking Natalie away?"

"Natalie saved us in the games. She's an exceptional student and is a good friend. You are making a huge mistake? Natalie belongs here with us," said Charlotte.

The elites began shouting and protesting, and demanding that her parents leave Natalie at Woodland. Melissa listened to Natalie's schoolmates but didn't respond to the student body as they made their voices heard. Natalie's father was too angry for rebuttal and stormed out the school's front door with his family to the car. Tears streamed down Natalie's face as she looked back through the back window at Sam and her friends who followed behind them, still protesting. Natalie waved goodbye to her friends as they sped away from the school.

# Chapter Twenty-Six

# Deadman's Curve

The Evergreens were twenty minutes away from Woodland Academy, traveling on Route 16. Lloyd gripped the steering wheel tightly, and his foot pressed down harder on the accelerator concerned Melissa. Although Melissa couldn't change the Board's decision, she could do something about how fast her husband was driving. "Lloyd, they don't call this road Snake Mountain for nothing; it's full of deadly twists and winding curves. Can you please slow down?" She looked frightened. So, he heeded his wife and eased his foot off the gas pedal. If Melissa had control of the car like a driver's education teacher, she would slow the car down for him.

Natalie was glad her mother cautioned her father to slow down. Her heart rate started beating at a normal pace.

Lloyd finally broke his silence. "Can you believe those kids and those spineless Board members back there who handed down that humdrum decision?" Lloyd cynically asked Melissa.

She sighed, rolled her eyes; she did not want to relive the whole thing again.

Lloyd continued, "I did not know the student body would show up shouting and ranting, let Natalie STAY! The nerve of them with their picket signs causing a scene as if we're the villains here; I never." It made Lloyd angry every time he thought about what happened. The more heated he got, the further the speedometer's needle moved on the dashboard.

"I cannot believe how clueless we were about how famous she is at Woodland Academy. Natalie means a lot to the school and the students there," said Melissa, astonished at the level of support her daughter received from the school. "After all, she was the queen of the annual games."

"Natalie will never see that school again. We are moving back to Memphis, pronto," Lloyd said emphatically to Melissa.

She turned and looked into Natalie's moist eyes. It was innate. Natalie knew her mother disagreed with her father; her eyes revealed she was heartsick. Melissa didn't want her daughter to be unhappy.

Natalie responded to her father's remark, "Dad, I don't want to return to Memphis; I want you to please reconsider?"

"The answer is NO! I know what's best for you," said Lloyd.

"But Dad."

"But Dad, nothing; we have given you everything and supported you in all matters, but this time I cannot let you attend that school any longer."

"Dad, I know Woodland is where I'm supposed to be."

"The answer is STILL NO! THIS DEBATE IS OVER AND DO NOT ASK ME ABOUT IT AGAIN."

Natalie loved her father, and no matter how she disagreed with him, she would remain in her obeisance. She would respect her father's decision, even if it meant she'd never return to her beloved Woodland Academy.

Melissa eyed her husband.

"I know that look, Melissa; my mind is made up," said Lloyd.

They approached a curve on the road. Lloyd braked before going into the sharp curve afterward, then returned to his speed; he wanted to get home quickly, reserve a U-Haul, call his former boss, and get his old job back in the bio lab. Unwarily, Lloyd forgot about the Dead Man's curve, which was the road's deadliest curve, and they were approaching it fast. Seeing the curve, he went for his brakes, but nothing was happening; he didn't want to panic. He tried the brakes again; the car was moving too fast in the curve. On the other side of the curve's rail, a fifty-foot drop cliff of large rocks is below in the ravine. Beads of water formed on his forehead, and he knew he wasn't in control of the car. "Lloyd, SLOW DOWN NOW!"

"I CAN'T!" he shrieked.

"Whatcha mean YOU CAN'T? IF WE DON'T, WE'RE GOING TO SMASH INTO THE RAILING!" she screamed.

Luckily, Melissa and Natalie remembered their seat belts when they got in the car. Melissa's heart dropped as Lloyd kept slamming on the brakes. It was terrifying, and Natalie felt they would die, so she began praying fervently aloud. The car smashed into the railing, leaving half of the car hanging over the cliff. On impact, Melissa hit her head hard against the dashboard, and Lloyd hit his head against the steering wheel before the airbags burst forward. The brakes had malfunctioned, and the rails kept the car from going into the ravine. Natalie, with no injuries, had miraculously survived the crash. She called to her unconscious mother; her head was severely bruised, while blood trickled down from her mouth and nose.

"Mom! Mom! Can you hear me?" She didn't respond. "Mom, wake up, wake up!" Then she thought, *Where's my dad*?

He was not in the car, and a pool of blood dripped off the steering wheel and from the hole in the windshield. She knew he had been ejected from the car, and the bloody, shattered windshield confirmed her fears.

First, she had to help her mother, and then her father. Melissa, unresponsive, sat with her head tilted downward. She silently prayed again and nudged her mother between the openings of the seats. "Mom! Mom! You can't die; wake up, please." Sobbing, she dropped her head, then, slowly, her mother started gaining consciousness while her head was down. She heard her mother coming too.

"Mom, you are awake!"

"Yes, honey, I am," Melissa said between short breaths; her body was racked with pain.

"Are you hurt?"

"No, Mom, I am okay."

"Thank goodness!"

"Can you walk, Mom?"

"I don't think so." Her mother gasped. "My left leg's pretty banged up." Melissa looked at the steering wheel and the windshield; it didn't take her long; she knew Lloyd had gotten the worst of the accident. The glare of the sun hurt her eyes, and her forehead ached; Natalie helped her mother to safety a few feet away from the car. It was a slow walk; Melissa couldn't put any pressure on her leg. Natalie used her body as a crutch to help her mother away from the crash site.

"You will be okay here; I'm going to find Dad."

Natalie returned to the damaged, broken car. She crawled over to the driver's side; she looked out the car door window, which was broken. Half the car was hanging over the cliff; then she heard a squeal a foot below; it was her father; he was alive and hanging on for dear life to a long branch piercing through the soil. The branch was the only thing that kept him from falling to his death. The branch punctured a hole through his jacket. He grabbed hold and hung on to it for dear life. His body weight caused the branch to loosen from the soil. The branch would not be enough to save him from plunging to his death; it was coming apart at the seams.

Inside the car, Natalie felt the car shifting forward. She had no way of getting to her father. It horrified Natalie; the car was slipping, and it would crush him underneath it; her father had little time to be rescued.

A stranger pulled his car over to the other side of the road, got out to find Natalie in the front seat, and asked, "Excuse me, miss, may I be of help?"

"Yes, please help us; my father is down there and can't make it to the top."

"You're going to have to leave this vehicle; it's not safe."

Seeing the car was about to go over, he came in just in the nick of time. He was an answer to her prayers. The dark-haired man had blue eyes and a kind smile. His red and black lumberjack sweater and blue jeans made him look like Brawny from the paper towel. He wasted no time getting to his car's trunk to retrieve a harness and a hundred-foot rope. Next, he tied one end of the rope to the strongest part of the rail and plummeted down the cliff to rescue Lloyd.

"Give me your hand?" said the man.

Lloyd extended his hand toward the gentleman and grabbed him before the branch fell to the bottom of the gully. Both men clung to the rope, and the car gave way toward them. With a quick thrust of the Samaritan's legs, they swirled out of harm's way; the car hit bottom and crashed, causing a loud explosion. Fire and smoke rose from the explosion like a mushroom cloud. Black smoke rose to the top. Before long, they made it to the top; Lloyd was seriously injured. The muscular stranger carried Lloyd to his family and laid him next to his wife.

"We owe you everything; thank you for saving my husband and daughter. How can we ever repay you?" asked Melissa. "What is your name?"

"My name is not important, and you don't owe me anything. I was in the area and saw you folks needed help. I did what any compassionate person would have done." With that, he returned to his car.

"Wait, your name… please." Melissa implored with every ounce of strength she had left.

He smiled and said, "My friends call me Ralph." Then he put his equipment in the car and called 911 emergency and stayed with them until help arrived.

Hearing the sirens of the police and ambulances approaching, he walked over to his car and waved goodbye, and when he did, his raiment turned sparkling white. His massive, feathered wings expanded apart, hiding the body of the car behind them. Nothing but space was left after his departure.

Lloyd, Melissa, and Natalie witnessed his transfiguration right before their eyes. As soon as he revealed his identity, Lloyd blacked out.

When help arrived, Natalie told the authorities what happened, but omitted how an angel saved her father from instant death. She told the police that a man showed up and helped save her father.

"Did you get his name?" asked the officer on duty.

"No," said Natalie. "He remained anonymous?"

"That's too bad; the guy is a hero," said the officer. The officer gathered all he needed from Natalie's testimony for his police report.

Paramedics tended to the Evergreen's injuries. Soon, a chopper touched down, airlifting Natalie and her parents to the nearest hospital.

# Chapter Twenty-Seven

# The Aftermath

Natalie called Lucy and Roberto from the hospital's phone and told them about the accident and her parents' conditions. Roberto and Lucy arrived at St. Luke's Hospital; they found Natalie waiting in the lobby.

"*La Nina*!" said Lucy as she embraced Natalie with a warm hug.

Natalie poured into her arms and wept onto her shoulders.

"There, there now, it's going to be alright, Little Nina," said Lucy as she slowly rubbed her upper back. "Has there been any change?"

"No, they have taken both Mom and Dad to surgery; the doctors said they will let me know more as soon as they can."

"Are you hungry?"

"No. Believe it or not, I can't eat a thing." Natalie sat down on the padded couch. Lucy sat next to her while Roberto stood beside the door with his chauffeur hat in his hands. "The paramedics said Dad had a concussion when he arrived at the hospital. The doctors performed an MRI and found brain trauma. Afterwards, he slipped into a coma."

After two hours, the door opened, and two doctors walked into the room in their scrubs and white coats. "Hi, I am Dr. Charles Stanford, Chief Physician, and this is Dr. Pamela Mannford, Specialist in Neurology."

"Dr. Lloyd Evergreen came through surgery fine, but he suffered internal bleeding in the head and a light stroke and slipped into a coma. The good news is I stopped the bleeding, but we don't know how long he will be in a coma. We are hopeful it's temporary; if he awakes from his coma, we think he may make a full recovery, but only time will tell. He is stable, and you can see him whenever you like," said Dr. Mannford.

Dr. Mannford was an attractive doctor. She pulled her hair into a ponytail, and her nails weren't polished but manicured. Her deep walnut skin was smooth, and her makeup looked soft and natural. Then she told them they were going to do everything they could for him.

"Now, about your mother, Dr. Stanford will tell you more, but before he does. I would like you to know, Natalie, your mother and I went to medical school together, and Dr. Stanford will be her primary doctor. He is one of the best doctors in the country. Your mother is in excellent hands." Said Dr. Mannford.

"Dr. Evergreen's left leg suffered a displaced fracture. The bone fragments on each side of the break needed to be aligned. I aligned the bones and will cast when the swelling has subsided. Also, she suffered a minor head injury; I closed the wound with a few stitches. It's going to take some time, but your mother is going to be fine. We have moved her to another room. She's on the third floor, Room three hundred and six," said the clean-shaven, young doctor. Natalie could tell by looking at Dr. Stanford that he skipped a couple of grades in school and finished early. "And your father is in Intensive Care on the fourth floor, Room four twenty, and you can see him." Said Dr. Mannford.

Natalie and Lucy thanked the doctors.

"I want to see my mom first," said Natalie.

"We can go together. We can take an elevator," said Dr. Mannford.

Off they went to see Melissa. The elevator doors opened, and the nursing station was busy with nurses answering calls and people's questions in front of their desks. People were getting in and out of the elevators, reading the signs above their heads to find their rooms.

Dr. Mannford said, "It's right this way."

They got out and took a right. Melissa's room was four rooms down on the left side of the hall.

"Here we are," said Dr. Mannford. She tapped on the door once and entered; Melissa was awake.

Natalie stood on the right side of her mother's bed. Dr. Mannford stood at the base, and Lucy and Roberto stood on the left side of the bed. "How are you?" asked Pamela.

"I've been better," she said with humor, her head bandaged, and her leg elevated in a sling with metal devices holding her leg in place.

"Are you in any pain, Melissa?"

"Right now, no."

"If you need something for pain, buzz the nurses, and they will bring you something." Said Dr. Mannford. Melissa nodded.

"You and your family are lucky to be alive. There must have been an angel on your shoulders."

Melissa smiled, remembering that if Ralph, their archangel, hadn't shown up, her husband and daughter probably would be dead. "Yes, the Man upstairs was surely looking out for us."

Natalie looked at her mother, startled. *Did she say she believes in God*?

After giving God credit, she grabbed her daughter's hand and looked into her eyes, and a single tear rolled down her cheek.

Natalie, overjoyed, smiled as she too, cried tears of joy. "I am happy you survived, my friend," replied Dr. Mannford.

"So am I," said Melissa.

"Dr. Stanford is your doctor, and he's great. He will be up in a few minutes to explain your injuries and treatment. I'm your husband's physician, and there is more concern regarding your husband's condition. Would you rather I speak to you alone?" asked Dr. Mannford.

"Pamela, go ahead. Lucy and Roberto are like family, and whatever you have to say to me, you can say in front of them," said Melissa, concerned.

"Your head injury wasn't as severe as your husband's. Lloyd was bleeding internally from the brain and suffered a stroke. The good news, I was able to stop the bleeding, but he slipped into a coma afterward."

"Oh no," cried Melissa.

"Melissa, you're a neurologist, and you know what I am about to tell you."

"I do."

"He may never wake up and suffer memory loss permanently," said Dr. Mannford. "However, there's a chance he will wake up, but now it's up to him. We won't know more until he wakes up. We're going to keep him comfortable and keep a watchful eye on him. There is nothing more we can do but wait," said Dr. Mannford.

Then, she listened to her heart with her stethoscope and shined a light onto her eyes, and said, "Try not to worry. Once the swelling goes down, I'll be able to determine more.

I'll let you know if anything changes. If you need anything, let us know. Feel better, hon," said Dr. Mannford, leaving to check on her other patients.

"Mom, do you think Dad will lose his memory for good?" asked Natalie, who couldn't bear the thought of her father not knowing who she was or her mother, not to mention Lucy and Roberto.

Melissa answered, "No, baby. I know your father, and he's going to beat this."

"Is there anything you need?" asked Lucy.

"Yes, take Natalie home and give her back her cell phone. Please call my hospital and let my superiors know I have been in a terrible car accident and am in the hospital, and please call Lloyd's job, too. Use the Rolodex on our desks to make the call; Natalie will help you. Also, can you bring me a couple of nightgowns, housecoats, and slippers during my stay? Please pack Lloyd a light suitcase as well. Roberto, will you be a dear and bring them back on Natalie's next visit to the hospital?"

"Sí! Mrs. Evergreen," said Roberto.

"Thank you so much, and Natalie, can you go see your father for me?" asked Melissa.

"Yes, mother, I'll be back as soon as I can."

Lucy and Roberto went with her to the ICU floor.

Leaving the elevator on the fourth floor, they found her father's room. There he was, this strong-minded man, lying in bed with a tube in his mouth providing air to his lungs. *He can't be hurt like this,* thought Natalie. She always looked up to her father; seeing him like this made her sad. Natalie kneeled in front of the small sofa and prayed. Lucy and Roberto bowed their heads as she prayed.

"Dear God, my father is in a coma, and he needs you. He is a good father, and he loves my mother. My dad is a doctor who works to save lives by studying diseases and creating vaccines. Please God, save him now, for he cannot pray for himself. Lucy, Roberto, and I stand in the gap for my father. Please heal my dad, and please don't let him forget who we are to him, and he is to us. And God, please give my parents a speedy recovery in Christ's name. Amen."

Natalie got up and held her father's hand. "Dad, can you hear me? It's me, your pumpkin-nose, Natalie. Come back to me because I love you. Please come back soon. I miss you." She kissed his forehead.

Lloyd, unresponsive, lay there with an IV line in his hand, pumping fluids into his veins, yet holding on.

*Mom was right; Dad is a fighter*, she thought.

"We should go now and let your father rest. Let's get you home as your mother requested," said Lucy.

Natalie nodded, and they quietly left the room. Before leaving the hospital, they returned to Melissa's room. "Any changes?" asked her mother.

Natalie shook her head, and the look in her daughter's eyes showed she was worried about him. "Remember, we have to wait until the swelling goes down; it's too early, and we must give his brain time to heal. I want you to go home, eat, and rest."

"Mom, I don't want to leave you; I want to take care of you," Melissa said with glazed eyes.

"You already did. You had a long day today; you must rest because you will be back first thing in the morning."

"Nothing could keep me away," said Natalie.

"I will call you as soon as I get home."

"You better," her mother whittling replied. Natalie blew her mother a kiss and left with Roberto and Lucy to return home for the night.

When Natalie made it home, she rang her mother's room using the house phone. Melissa's tending nurse answered her phone and informed Natalie that her mother was asleep. He politely told her to call back tomorrow, for he had not long given her something for pain.

"Please tell my mother I called." Said Natalie. "Will do and good night." Natalie hung up, then went upstairs to take a warm bath. Exhausted in her PJs, she climbed straight into bed.

Before falling asleep, her cell phone rang.
She picked it up. "Sam, thank goodness it's you."

"Natalie, are you okay? I've been calling you since you left school today." Checking her cell phone, she had seventeen missed calls from Sam. She apologized and told her about the accident after the hearing.

"I am so sorry to hear that. Are you hurt?"

"No! I wasn't hurt."

"Thank God!" Cried Sam.

"What about your parents?"

"The doctors said my mother's leg will heal in time, but my father is in a coma." "Is there anything I can do to help?" asked Sam. "No, Lucy and Roberto are taking good care of me."

"Are you sure you're going to be ALRIGHT?"

"I'll be okay, but I'm mostly worried about my parents. Thank you for calling."

"No thanks required… I'm glad you weren't hurt; my family and I are going to be praying for your parents."

"Please do. Let's talk in the morning. I'm headed to bed."

"Okay, and good night." Said Sam.

The girls hung up, and Natalie lay quietly, thinking until she drifted off to sleep.

The next day, Lucy and Roberto did all that Melissa asked them to do. Natalie tried to get a good night's rest but found it hard because the accident kept playing over and over in her mind. Her parents were almost killed yesterday. It made her realize how fragile life is and to take no one or anything for granted. She was grateful her parents survived, and with that, she gave thanks to God. Her phone rang, she picked up and said,

"Good morning, Sam."

"Morning, Natalie! I wanted to tell you that my parents and I are going to see your parents today."

"That's wonderful, Sam! I know it will lift my mother's spirit tremendously." Not long after, they hung up.

Hours later, Roberto drove Natalie back to the hospital, leaving Lucy to care for the house. When she walked into her mother's room, there were bouquets of roses, orchids, and get-well balloons sent by her colleagues and friends.

"Natalie, Doctor Stanford left my room a few seconds ago, and I have some news to share with you. First, it's going to take my leg a while before Dr. Stanford can cast it. He said he might cast it in two to three weeks."

"Don't worry. I will be okay, and I'm going to visit you every day until you're released."

"Thank you, baby."

"Have you been in a lot of pain?"

"My leg was hurting badly last night; I thought I was going to die. I buzzed my nurse, and he gave me something for the pain, and it helped." Melissa sat up in bed with the TV on mute and her leg still elevated in the sling.

"Any word on dad?"

"No, I am afraid not."

"How's the food here?"

"Bland." They both chuckled. "Oh, Sam's parents came to see me. They brought flowers and balloons."

Then she told her daughter to come sit next to her on the bed. She wanted to have a serious mother-daughter talk with her. Natalie sat next to her mother, and Melissa said, "Natalie, I want to apologize to you. I am sorry I didn't believe you when you said God was real, and if I hadn't encountered the angel with my own eyes, I might have never believed. I asked God to forgive me, and I thanked him for sparing our lives. Do you think He heard me?"

"Yes, I know He did, but do you think Dad believes God is real now?"

"I don't know if your father knew what he saw at the time of the angel's departure; he blacked out because of the concussion."

It had been thirty days, and Natalie's parents were still in the hospital. On the 24th of April, Dr. Mannford walked into Melissa's room with her hair pulled into a bun. "I have some good news and bad news to share with you about your husband's recovery." Natalie, glued to her mother's bed, grabbed her mother's hand and braced herself to hear her father's prognosis.

"Tell me the good news first," said Melissa.

"Your husband awoke from his coma this morning. He still has some swelling, but he is showing signs of remarkable recovery. We took him off the ventilators; the bad news is he has post-traumatic stress amnesia."

"What's that?" asked Natalie.

"It's when a patient can't remember the hours or the days directly following his or her injury, which is common following a car accident. It is also common that his personality will change, and experience general confusion during this period. Your father doesn't remember how he got here or the accident. However, we will continue to keep him until all the swelling is gone. He has been asking for you and your mother."

"How much can he recall now?" asked Melissa.

"I told him he was in a terrible car accident with his family."

"So, he knows who we are?" Natalie asked.

"Yes, and he's eager to see you both. I told him he could see you, Melissa, once the doctor has cast your leg. But Natalie can see him today."

"That's great!" said Natalie, smiling from ear to ear.

Dr. Stanford entered the room whistling a cheerful tune and asked, "How's the good doctor doing today?"

"I am better," replied Melissa.

"I would like to take another X-ray to be thorough, to see if your leg is ready to be cast. I am confident I will cast it today after lunch. An orderly will take you to X-ray in a few seconds." He jotted down his orders on her chart and placed it back at the foot of her bed. "I hear your husband has made a recovery. It won't be long; you good folks will be returning home soon." Turning his attention to Pamela, he asked, "Dr. Mannford, may I see you for a minute?"

"Sure, doctor."

Both doctors talked outside in the hall. Roberto walked down to the cafeteria to get a cup of Joe, leaving Melissa alone with Natalie. Melissa spoke candidly, "Your father remembers nothing about the hearing or the book, and we are going to keep it that way."

"Does that mean I can return to Woodland?"

"I don't know; I can't make any promises until I know more about your father's condition."

"Fair enough, but I am hopeful." Said Natalie, upbeat.

An orderly dressed in white came and wheeled Melissa to X-ray.

"While you're in X-ray, Mom, I'm going to see Dad. I will see you back here when you return."

Natalie paused before entering her father's room because she was about to talk to her father for the first time since the accident; she didn't know what to expect. She swallowed hard and pushed the door open.

Lloyd was watching TV when Natalie walked into the room. "Dad!"

"Sweetheart! I'm so happy to see you." Without hesitation, she flew into her father's arms.

"I'm happy to see you, too. How are you feeling today?"

"Better now that I see my little girl. How are things going at school?"

"Fine, I have a higher than a four average."

"That's my smart girl."

Natalie smiled, but deep down, she was downhearted that her father withdrew her from Woodland Academy. She missed her classmates and Miss Sherman.

In the middle of their conversation, she thought about her book presentation she would never finish.

"Natalie, did you hear me?"

"I'm sorry, Dad, were you saying something?"

"I was asking, how's your mother doing?"

"They took her down to X-ray about five minutes ago. Dr. Stanford says he may put a cast on her leg today; after that, she can see you. The bruise on her head has gotten much better." Natalie looked at his nightstand. His job sent get-well-soon cards along with a bouquet in a single vase.

"I can't wait to get out of here and go home," said her father.

"How did the accident happen?" he asked,

"The brakes malfunctioned on the car, and we crashed into the curve's rail."

"Were you hurt?"

"No, I walked away with no injuries. I was fortunate," said Natalie.

"Thank goodness, because I don't know what I'd do if something had happened to you." Lloyd was himself again. He was not angry; neither was he sulking nor snarling. Natalie had the father she knew and loved back. She didn't want the bubble to burst or the clock to strike midnight, and all the magic went away. She stayed with her father until he had fallen asleep. Natalie thought her mother should have returned from X-ray by now. She whispered to her father while he was sleeping. "I will be back soon; rest well, Dad." Natalie left a word with his nurse that she would return to see him tomorrow.

The aftermath was daunting, but things were returning to normal again. Natalie thanked God for answering her prayers.

Melissa had returned, and she couldn't wait to learn from Natalie how her father was doing. Natalie told her mother about her father and how he knew nothing about the crash, the school, the book, or Miss Sherman's class.

"He asked me how school and my grades were coming along. I told him things were fine. He was peaceful and poised; he was dad again."

Melissa listened and began hatching a nostrum plan.

"I stayed with him until he fell asleep," said Natalie.

Nurse Ivy walked into the room in purple scrubs and checked her mother's vitals. She told Melissa the doctor was casting her leg after lunch. Melissa was glad to hear it; finally, she would get to see Lloyd.

Later that afternoon, Dr. Stanford cast Melissa's leg. Satisfied with his work, he said to Melissa. "It will take three to six months for your leg to heal. Afterward, rehabilitation will begin, but I don't want you putting any pressure on that leg for now. I have been prescribed Vicodin for the pain. The total daily dosage should not exceed six tablets. Take one tablet every four to six hours as needed for pain. Do you have questions?"

"No," said Melissa.

"I'm discharging you the day after tomorrow, and we will give you a wheelchair and crutches when you leave the hospital. A nurse will have you sign your discharge papers an hour before you leave."

"Thank you, doctor."

"You're welcome, and if you need anything or have questions, call the hospital."

The next morning, Melissa prepared to go home the following day. She hired a private home health nurse to help care for her and Lloyd during their recovery. Second, Melissa called Miss Sugarman and asked her to fax over to her home office the documents needed to re-enroll Natalie in school as soon as possible. She hung up the phone, and the nurse assistant helped her get dressed. She put on a long cotton gown, a long navy-blue housecoat with a pink striped outlined collar. Then the assistant rubbed lotion on her right leg and feet. She put on her pink slippers and waited for the orderly to wheel her down to see Lloyd before being dismissed from the hospital.

Considering everything that happened, Melissa was eager to see her husband again. The orderly wheeled her to his room the next day. When she came into his room, Lloyd was sitting on the bed, flicking through the TV channels. As soon as he saw her, he dropped the remote on the bed. The orderly left them alone. She was as beautiful as the day he married her. He smiled and said, "You're still a sight for sore eyes."

"You always could make a girl feel good," said Melissa as she blushed a bit at her husband's sweet terms of endearment.

He arose from the bed and kissed her passionately. Lloyd didn't want to stop kissing her, but paused when she asked him, "How are you, my love?"

"I've been having headaches, but Dr. Mannford said they should go away in a few weeks. Dr. Mannford said I still have some swelling, and I will need to stay a few more days. Once the swelling is gone, I can start therapy to help cope with the post-traumatic amnesia, and with therapy, I shall make a full recovery."

"Honey, that's wonderful news," said Melissa.

He sighed and continued, "You and Natalie are all I have been thinking of, and based on what Dr. Mannford told me, we are lucky to be alive. How has she been holding up?"

"She seems fine, but she is strong. I guess she takes a lot after her father." Lloyd smiled at his wife. Looking deep into his brown eyes, Melissa continued, "I'm being discharged tomorrow. Natalie and I will come by and see you before we return home. We'll call you every single day until you're released."

Lloyd, in his plaid pajamas, caressed his wife's hands. They spent the next few hours talking. Melissa asked him if he remembered anything about the car accident or anything before the day of the accident.

He replied, "I remembered Natalie came home for spring break and returned once spring break ended, and the rest is a blur." To him, his family was alive, and nothing else mattered to him.

Melissa was happy she was leaving the hospital, and she looked forward to moving on with her life.

# Chapter Twenty-Eight

# The Presentation

Melissa came home to an immaculately clean, warm, and cozy home, which was the perfect welcome home present she could receive. Lucy thought of everything, including installing Stairlifts in the home. She was pleased with all Lucy had done for the house and her family. Melissa praised and thanked Lucy for her hard work and dedication. In return, she gave Lucy and Roberto a generous bonus. Afterward, she told Lucy she hired a stay-at-home health nurse.

"Nurse Adams will be here tomorrow, helping Lloyd and me recover at home for a while. Please set up the guest room downstairs from the basement."

"I will see to her comfort before she arrives tomorrow," said Lucy.

"Thank you, Lucy. I don't know what we would do without you."

"Sí! Melissa. Why don't you relax by the fire, and I will bring you a nice warm cup of Chai tea; would you like that?"

"Yes, that would be wonderful. Thank you, Lucy."

Lucy headed to the kitchen to fix her tea. Using her motorized wheelchair, Lucy ordered her to wheel herself down the hall to her home office. Lucy had left a stack of mail on top of her desk. Melissa ignored them and checked her fax machine. Miss Sugarman indeed faxed Natalie's enrollment documents. She read and signed the forms and faxed them back to Miss Sugarman right away. Immediately, her phone notification beeped in her housecoat pocket. She looked at her phone; the text was from Miss Sugarman. The text read:

> "Natalie can return to school in the third week of May. Woodland Academy understands the accident. We at Woodland wish you and Dr. Evergreen a speedy recovery. Sincerely, Miss Sugarman."

Melissa deleted the text and locked the signed enrollment forms in a manila folder inside a secret compartment in her desk for extra security to keep Lloyd from finding its contents.

Afterward, she wheeled herself back to the library and drank her hot tea with milk and sweetener. She called for Natalie to join her in the library. Natalie heard her mother calling and came downstairs and said, "Yes, Mother, you called?"

"I did. I wanted you to know how sorry I was for not being there for you when you needed me to be. Can you ever forgive me?"

"There's nothing to forgive. I love you, Mom," said Natalie softly.

"To make it up to you, I re-enrolled you back into Woodland Academy."

"You did? That's outstanding, but what about Dad?"

"He doesn't remember a thing, and he may never remember what happened. I will tell Lucy and Roberto not to mention anything about the events leading up to the accident or after the accident. I will explain to them that I don't want him to have a relapse. Don't worry about anything, Nat. We are moving forward, and we're not looking back. You stood firm in what you believed, and you didn't let anyone, including us, keep you from your faith, and you were right to fight for what you believed. I am proud of you," said Melissa.

"Roberto will drive you back to campus the third week of May. It's time you finish what you started: your presentation."

Natalie smiled at her mother.

"I know your presentation is going to knock them off their feet," said Melissa.

"I know it wasn't easy keeping your faith a secret from us, and I know now why you did it."

"Now, you said you became a Christian."

"I did."

"How did you do it?"

"It was relatively easy," she said, sitting across from her mother in a wing-back chair in front of the crackling fireplace.

"I prayed a simple prayer, and I was adopted into the Kingdom of God."

"What prayer did you pray?"

"Um… Miss Sherman called it the Prayer of Salvation. Would you like me to pray that prayer with you?"

"Yes, very much."

And so it was, Melissa became a Christian at that moment. "This will be our little secret," said Melissa with tears of joy.

Natalie embraced her mother and welcomed her into the body of Christ.

The Archangel Raguel flew down to witness Melissa's Prayer of Salvation. His quill recorded the moment mid-air on a long parchment scroll as Melissa accepted Christ as her Lord and Savior. He rejoiced and flew back to Heaven with his recordings and presented them before the Lord in Heaven.

Neither Melissa nor Natalie saw him, but a distinct sweet fruity aroma lingered in the room once he left. Natalie asked, "Do you smell it?" They asked each other as Natalie took another big whiff of the sweet aroma.

"We had a Heavenly visitation!" exclaimed Natalie after the angel left the room.

Melissa kept all these things in her heart. For now, Natalie was happy and couldn't wait to return to Woodland to be with her friends, especially Sam, who had been by her side the whole time.

Natalie had returned to school a day before her father came home, and all was back to normal. When Natalie returned, no one knew, not even Miss Sherman. When Natalie arrived on campus, she called home to check on her parents. Melissa assured her everything was fine, and her leg was getting better, and her father's memories had not returned.

School was close to ending for the summer, and with one week left, it was time for Miss Sherman's students to present their book reports to the class.

Facing the class, Sam smiled and then cleared her throat. "Ephesians 6:2-3 states, … Children, obey your parents in the Lord, for this is right. Honor your father and mother. Which is the first commandment with a promise… so that it may go well with you and that you may enjoy long life on Earth. And that's my presentation. Wait! One more important thing. Do I think God is real? Of course, I do. Why else would God make children? To drive our parents crazy!"

Everyone laughed themselves to scorn; Sam had done it; she made the gospel fun while defending her belief in God.

"Thank you, Sam, good work," said Miss Sherman.

Sam bowed and took her seat. Miss Sherman cleared her voice and said, "There is one more presentation, but unfortunately, she is not here to present because she left the school."

The class knew who she was speaking of and thought about how much they missed Natalie.

While speaking, someone knocked on her door. Miss Sherman went to the door and saw a man through the glass window. There was a man dressed as a chauffeur standing outside her door.

She opened the door and asked, "Can I help you?"

It was none other than Roberto. He moved aside, and Natalie stepped forward with her book presentation. Roberto told Miss Sherman her mother had re-enrolled her and that Natalie could present her book report to the class with her permission.

Miss Sherman, standing in the doorway, turned to her class and said, "Class, I have a surprise for you."

Natalie walked into the room.

"We will now hear from Natalie Evergreen! Natalie has had quite an interesting year with us at Woodland Academy. She defeated the odds in the games; she is a genuine hero who risked her life to save her teammates, then she helped her mother with a broken leg to safety while returning to the car to save her father, until Ralph came along. Everyone, please give a warm welcome to Natalie Evergreen!"

The class applauded with whistling and hand clapping. Charlotte, Dexter, Dave, Sam, Lyle, and the rest of the class were happy to see Natalie again.

"I thank you. I have missed you, and I am happy to be with you and present my book report before you now." Said Natalie.

Instead of a tripod-folder, to display her reading fair board, Natalie cleverly displayed the book's artwork, *Is God Real?* She used a large poster in a lenticular four-image 3-D format. The first image was the book cover, of a heavenly staircase in a blue sky with puffy white clouds and a star illuminating sun rays behind the clouds. The second image was the Earth in space with God's outstretched hands hovering over the Earth. The third was an image of the city of Heaven, and the fourth image was a shepherd holding a staff in his right hand, watching over his sheep in green pastures. The book display fits easily in the slots at the base of the image cardboard stand. Natalie placed the book in front of the reading board display at the bottom of the book cover, and read the author's name unknown. She created a PowerPoint presentation and spoke briefly on the story elements: the title, characters, setting, tone, author, conflict, solution, publication, and purpose. Now, it was time to take a position on the book, so she prepared a speech and memorized it by heart.

"At first, when Miss Sherman revealed the mystery book in her glass case at the beginning of the year, we guessed what we thought we would read about. To my amazement, I never thought she would ask us to read about God, whom I said wasn't real, but a figment of someone's imagination. I couldn't have been more wrong. God is real; He's in the wind, He's in the rainbow, and the color of the flowers; He is everything pure and lovely. He is every act of kindness. He is Love, a Healer, and a Deliverer who sent his Son, Jesus, to die on the cross to take away the sins of the world, where man could be free and live with Him eternally if we choose to accept Him. I've been told that God isn't real all my life, but God has revealed Himself to me through mind, body, and spirit since I've been here. The Comforter, the Holy One, confirmed His truth. Never will the Holy Spirit lie but testify to the truth who sent Him. In class, Miss Sherman helped me to see the sacrifices God made for his creation in the beginning. He gave us free choice to choose for ourselves if we will love Him and keep his commandments. Free will was given unto men as an act of love, not of control; if so, it wouldn't be love, and God is love. I have learned no one has the right to silence my voice or choose for me whom I may worship. Christ died for me; therefore, I do not have to apologize to anyone for my walk with God. But we have an adversary who seeks to divide us from the love of God. His name is Satan, and he seeks to get everyone to do bad things and turn away from God just as he beguiled Adam and Eve to disobey God in the Garden of Eden. Sin and death resulted, and God passed judgment, banning them from the Garden of Eden. Satan failed because he thought the Fall of Man would keep God from fellowshipping with us. Jesus redeems us back to God through His death; He became our Passover, purchasing man back with his shed blood. Satan wants to steal our worship and will never lay his life down for anyone. Satan's only aim is to be worshiped. In return, he kills, steals, and destroys, enticing men with many temptations, causing men to hurt one another and fall into depravity, leaving him in a worse state than he was before. Although faith is free, it comes with a price. In Matthew 10:34-36. Jesus told his disciples He came not to bring peace to the world, but a sword. Jesus didn't mean a literal sword to cut someone, but the sword He was speaking of was His message to Earth. Man's enemies might be those within his household. This word manifested when it happened to me; my father scorned me when he learned I had become a Christian. And then I remembered what Jesus said, 'Men should never forget they will hate you for My sake. Because those who reject Me, they will hate My followers as well.' I had to choose. Should I give up my faith to please my family or follow my heart and continue worshiping God? I embraced my faith and my love for God. Although I love my parents very much, my love for them should never take precedence over God. Do I believe God is real? Yes, I do, and I am not ashamed of the gospel, because it is the power of God that brings salvation to everyone who believes; first to the Jews, then to the Greeks as Apostle Paul stated in Romans 1:16. I know in my heart Jesus is the Son of God and is risen from the grave and sits at the right hand of God in heaven making intercession for the saints. Finally, things are better between my father and me, and I will return in the Fall full-time!"

Natalie ended her speech, and Miss Sherman stood and applauded, and more applause followed when she said she would return full-time in the fall.

"Woodland will always be my home away from home!" cried Natalie blissfully.

Everyone in the room celebrated and rejoiced together.

Headmistress Lois witnessed her speech and was happy her star pupil was back at Woodland for good.

***

School ended, and Woodland students were preparing to go home for the summer. Natalie and Sam were saying goodbye to their classmates. Dexter asked Charlotte for her email, and she gave it to him. The rest of the tributes and elites said goodbye as they got into their cars and buses to return home.

Caleb said goodbye to Natalie and Sam and got on the bus.

Sam's parents arrived, and she got in the family's car and drove off.

Natalie noticed Miss Sherman watching the students leave for home and quickly approached her to talk before getting in the car with Roberto. She said, "Thanks, Miss Sherman, for sharing the gospel; it truly changed my life."

"It was my pleasure."

"But there's one thing I want to ask you. How did you know about Ralph? My family never told a soul about him," asked Natalie. Miss Sherman smiled and walked away from her slowly.

Then, Miss Sherman stopped, turned, looked over her right shoulder, and said, "Ralph's my brother." She disappeared with a wink; a large white feather floated down right in front of her eyes.

She extended her hands outward, and it landed in her hands. Natalie smiled and thought to herself; *I love this school.*

# THE EPILOGUE

High in the school's tower, the same day students were leaving for summer break, a mysterious man with his face hidden was working at his desk with pictures of Damon's birthday party, and his guest lay on top of his desk. Who was this man, you may ask? It was the same mysterious man Natalie saw at Damon's party. Next to the pictures were several white envelopes tied with hunter green ribbon, addressed to Trever McCall, Damon Yates, Tiffany West, Denise Evans, and the Fashionistas. More invitations were addressed to Jackie, Tina, Sandy, Melody, Jade, and Pippa, none other than the Satin Dollz. How he got into the school without being noticed by faculty and students is a mystery.

Back at home, Lloyd walked into the kitchen to get a bottle of water from the refrigerator. Lucy was opening a can of biscuits, and when the biscuits popped. Lloyd heard a ringing noise in his ears; black and white images started flashing before him within half a second and stopped. He couldn't make sense of what he saw, for the images were fuzzy with white noise.

Lucy saw what was happening to him and asked, "Are you alright, *señor*?"

He replied, "Yeah!" Squinting his eyes off and on after what he saw. "I am going to take my meds and lie down for a while."

"Good idea, *señor*; rest well."

"Thank you, Lucy. I will."

Later, Lucy found Melissa in her office. "Melissa, may I talk to you?"

"Of course, please come in," said Melissa.

Lucy closed the door behind her and started whispering to Melissa.

"It's about *Señor* Lloyd. I was in the kitchen preparing dinner, and I opened a can of biscuits. The pop of the can triggered something in his head."

"How do you know?"

"He told me he saw some flashes of things he couldn't make sense of. He said he was going to take his medicine and lie down."

"I'll have Lacy look at him; thanks for letting me know. You did the right thing coming to me."

"What will you do if Lloyd's memories come back?"

"Things are going great, and I see no reason for things to change, but if you will, please excuse me; I have to make a call," said Melissa.

"*Sí*, Melissa," said Lucy, and went back to her duties in the house.

As soon as she left the room, Melissa wheeled herself to her phone on the desk. She called the pharmacy.

If there were a chance Lloyd's memories were coming back, there was nothing she could do to stop it, but she could slow it down. She would let nothing get in the way of their happiness.

*To be continued...*

## The Mysteries of Woodland Academy Part II

How far is Melissa willing to go to stop Lloyd from regaining his memories? How will Natalie and Sam respond to their former classmates from Memphis joining them this Fall? Will the Fashionistas get along with the Satin Dollz, or will chaos erupt on campus? Natalie must stay focused because new challenges are emerging.

Find out what happens next in the series.

**ACKNOWLEDGMENTS**

Publishing is no easy feat, but it's rewarding from start to finish, and I was lucky to have collaborated with a great team who worked on *Woodland Academy* to make it what it was. It came out beautifully, and without their help, I could not have crossed the finish line.

First, I would like to thank God; without Him and the call to write, none of this would have happened.

I can't thank the following individuals enough, but I hope you know how much I appreciate all you have done from the bottom of my heart.

Special thanks to my editor, Dr. Melissa Caudle. You kept me sane through the editing and development process. Honestly, I literally could not have done this alone. You are the midwife of publishing books; you help deliver my baby into the world, and I am so grateful.

Many thanks to Assistant Editor, Kathy Rabb Kittock of Absolute Author Publishing House. I am so proud to have worked with you.

Thank you, Queda Denley. Before I found my editor, you were the first to edit the book's blurb, and it turned out amazing. Thank you very much for your love and support. It truly meant the world to me.

Millions of thanks to Levente Farkas, who created the most beautiful cover design ever. You are truly gifted and attentive to details, and I appreciate how you went above and beyond to make sure I was happy with the outcome. You brought my vision to life, and for that, I say thank you for capturing the heart and soul of Woodland Academy on canvas. Thank you so much.

Special thanks to all the readers, teachers, librarians, and bookstore owners everywhere; without you, it would not be possible.

# ABOUT THE AUTHOR

K. D. Williams is a Christian author who lives in Mississippi with her family. *The Mysteries of Woodland Academy* is her young adult debut. K.D. Williams earned a Bachelor of Science in History at Mississippi Valley State University and a Master of Arts in Education, specializing in Child Development at Ashford University. In her spare time, she enjoys reading, writing, and spending time with her grandchildren.

K.D. Williams is online, and you can visit her website at https://www.kdwilliamsmgbooks.com. Feel free to contact the author on her website if you would like her to visit your school or join your podcast. Also, you can join her mailing list and comment on her blog. While you are there, kindly check out KD Williams' online store at https://kds-sacred-creations.printify.me, and finally, you can follow KD Williams on Instagram.

Instagram:
https://www.instagram.com/kdwilliams26

## AUTHOR'S NOTE

Dear Reader,

Thank you for reading my debut novel, *The Mysteries of Woodland Academy.* I want to share that Woodland Academy was created with love, diversity, and brotherhood in mind. The story aims to spread God's love through faith and storytelling. I hope that Woodland serves as a tool to share your faith and bring many hearts closer to the LORD, for He truly loves us.

If you enjoyed The Mysteries of Woodland Academy, please leave a review on Amazon or Goodreads. It will help new readers discover the Warrior Family. Lastly, more drama and suspense are coming in book two as the series continues with light and love.

K.D. Williams

www.ingramcontent.com/pod-product-compliance
Lightning Source LLC
Chambersburg PA
CBHW030357310726
48979CB00001B/343

* 9 7 9 8 2 1 8 1 5 6 0 6 0 *